the
WARSEC
Interstellar Series

the
WARSEC
Interstellar Series

4

EXPLORATION

2100-2106

ASH GAWAIN

ASHGAWAIN.COM

TABLE OF CONTENTS

MAP OF EARTH: 2100

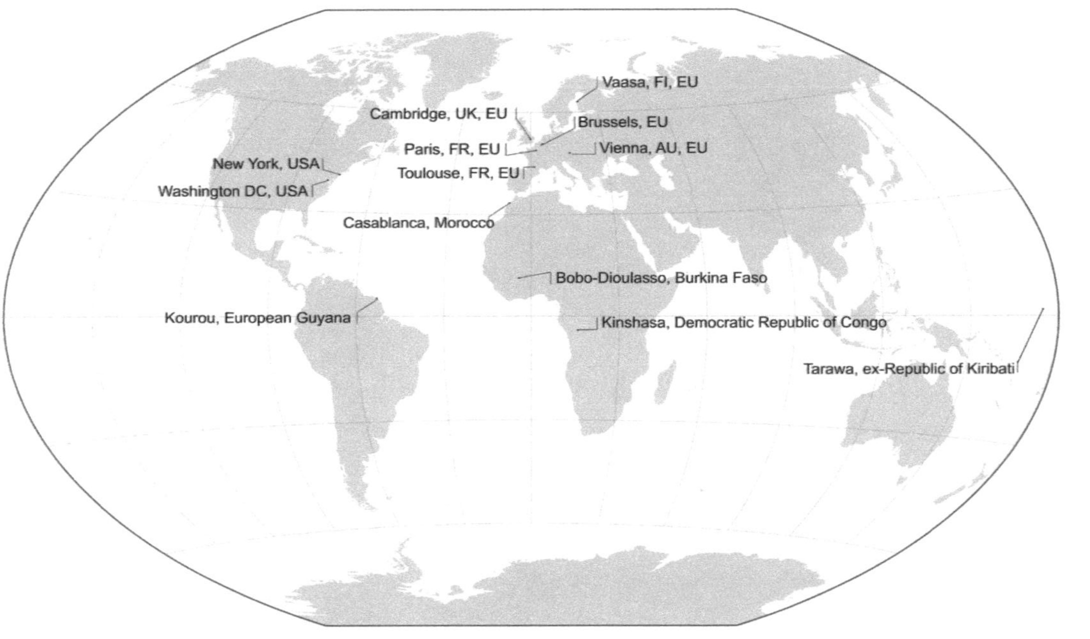

INTRODUCTION

In late August 2100, eight months after the return of the first interstellar exploratory mission to Alpha Centauri, two opinion pieces, published in two different papers, expressed two distinct views as to the future to give to the space race.

The first Op-Ed, published in *The Guardian*, had been written by Dr. Sheldon Cooper, the famous geologist from Cambridge University and author of *Feedback of the Earth* (2094). It was entitled '*The Chimera of Interstellar Colonization*'.

What is mankind on the geological timescale? Nothing. This statement, shocking for some, is all the more logical provided one is given the adequate perspective.

The Big Bang at the origins of the current universe occurred more than 15 billion years ago. Our solar system formed itself about 4.6 billion years ago from the gravitational collapse of nebulous molecular clouds, giving birth to the Earth. The first forms of life, probably in the shape of fungi, appeared about 2.5 to 3 billion years ago on our blue planet. However, life did not thrive as it was subjected to major and periodic 'snowball Earth' events, temporarily covering the whole globe with ice and snow, throughout the following two billion years.

Half a billion years ago was the last time our blue planet had turned white. It was only after this last snowball Earth episode that life on Earth could start to thrive and develop and evolve, but not without a few mass extinction events.

252 million years ago, under the Permian-Triassic transition, 96% of all marine species and 70% of all terrestrial vertebrate species became extinct. 65 million years ago, it was for the remaining dinosaurs to go extinct, thus allowing the subsequent flourishing of mammals. In both cases, the extinction was most likely caused by an asteroid impact, triggering a chain of super-volcanic eruptions.

The first humanoid mammals appeared about six million years ago, but our own human species, Homo sapiens, appeared less than 350,000 years ago. Our species could already have disappeared on a few occasions if it had not been for its geographical dispersion.

75,000 years ago, the Toba super-eruption, in Indonesia, brought about a 1,000-year-long winter, decimating all life in Eastern Asia. 39,000 years ago, the Campi Flegrei super-eruption in Italy brought about another volcanic winter, killing all human life in Europe, this time, and even leading to the extinction of our cousins, Homo neanderthalensis. In each case, had it not been for Homo sapiens individuals who had remained in Africa, our species would have been gone for good.

In that context, it is not too bold to state that mankind is negligible on the geological timescale. What is 350,000 years against 15 billion years? Yet, the overall belief among our civilizations is otherwise. The main monotheistic religions have all spread the beliefs that God had created the Earth for mankind, and that we human beings are thus entitled to exploit and spend and waste all earthly resources. This despicable anthropocentrism, which is nothing other than theological and philosophical arrogance, has had a disastrous impact.

If mankind is negligible on the geological timescale, it is not geologically negligible. The 1840 Industrial Revolution and its subsequent greenhouse gas emissions as well as exponential population growth have had so tremendous an impact on our Earth that the current geologic period is called Anthropocene.

Even though progress in nuclear physics, first with molten-salt reactors and then with fusion reactors, have enabled us to dramatically reduced carbon dioxide emission in the late 2050s, irreversible damage has been done. The sea level will keep rising for another thousand years. Worse, 60% of the animal species existing 200 years ago are now extinct, though only the most spectacular extinctions such as the panda or bonobo remain engraved in our memories.

We now know that the thermal expansion of the oceans and the melting of the ice caps have an impact on the rotation speed of our planet. Even if the resulting changes are about one millisecond per day, they are significant enough to affect the magmatic convections within the mantle of our Earth. The frequency of earthquakes and volcanic eruptions has already been observed to increase.

A brilliant student of mine has shown that the probability of a super-volcanic eruption within the next century is between 10 and 20% (Dörflinger et al. 2098). Even if mankind succeeds in managing the currently geophysically induced mass extinction, we may not stand a chance against a super-volcanic eruption of the Yellowstone caldera.

Sadly, in this grave hour, it seems that mankind is being carried away by a new anthropocentric dream: interstellar colonization.

In the mid-2070s, an eccentric billionaire financed a private venture to colonize Mars and try to find fossilized forms of life. The failure of this enterprise, of which there has been only one survivor, has convinced most people on Earth that only the colonization of a habitable planet should be attempted.

By 'habitable' is meant a planet that fulfills three criteria: It should have a gravity force within a 20% range of that on Earth in order to retain a thick enough atmosphere while allowing us not to weigh overmuch. It should have a magnetic field to protect its atmosphere and surface from solar radiation. Most importantly, it should have the presence of liquid water. There is no such planet other than Earth within our solar system.

The successful testing of the Alcubierre metric in 2094,

however, made faster-than-light travel possible and a first interstellar mission to the nearest star had successfully been conducted in 2099. Logically, a majority of people now believe we should engage in an intensive interstellar exploration in order to find another habitable planet.

This humanist dream is nothing but a chimera. The odds of finding a habitable planet within a decent range and in a decent time are minimal. Terraforming such a planet, should its atmosphere lack oxygen, would only be an everlasting and futile enterprise. Current research in that direction is, in my opinion, nothing but a waste of brilliant minds' time and public money.

We should instead prepare for a super-volcanic eruption and think, now, how we will be able to produce enough food and protect our species during a volcanic winter, while preserving the only thing worth saving about humanity: a civilization based on human rights.

Though Dr. Cooper certainly had a very valid point, his views were not shared by the World's Agency for the Regulation of Space Exploration and Colonization (WARSEC). At about the same time, the WARSEC director, Ralf Åhman, had indeed expressed a different opinion in *The Washington Post*. It was entitled 'The Hope of Interstellar Colonization':

Fear of annihilation has been a powerful driver of the conquest of space since the very beginning. At the start of the Cold War between the west and the east, back in 1947, it was the fear of nuclear annihilation that drove the United Sates and the Soviet Union to invest in their space programs. In 1957, Sputnik 1 was the first spacecraft to be successfully put into orbit and the Soviet Union showed to the world they could send nuclear strikes to anywhere on the globe. The United States responded with the Mercury, Gemini and Apollo programs and were the first to land a man on the Moon.

This fear of annihilation through nuclear apocalypse did not only lead, back then, to an unfathomable technical race, but also to an increased international cooperation in terms of outer space affairs. The space race led the UN General Assembly to create a Committee on the Peaceful Uses of Outer Space (COPUOS) in the early 1960s. Their first task was to demilitarize space by drafting four space-related Treaties with the assistance of the UN Secretariat's United Nations Office for Outer Space Affairs (UNOOSA).

This international cooperation led to new milestones and the last two decades of the 21st century will certainly be remembered as the decade when mankind claimed space. The deployment of the space elevators made it possible to bring heavy payload into orbit. The construction of the orbital station has led to a boom in commercial space activities. The creation of WARSEC, replacing UNOOSA subsequently to the successful testing of faster-than-light travel back in 2094, has encouraged the development of the lunar base, where aerospace shuttles and interstellar spaceships *are now manufactured in partnership with private space corporations.*

Last year, in 2099, the UNSS Forward led a first successful interstellar exploratory mission to the Alpha Centauri system, 4.3 light years away, under which a first exoplanet, which turned out not to be habitable, was scrutinized by mankind.

Mankind has now claimed its stake in space and is there to stay. Over the next decade, WARSEC will intensify our interstellar exploration, and our main goal will be to find a planet suitable for colonization.

Our ambition has been recently criticized by a famous Earth scientist, who believes efforts are being diverted from our preparation for a super-volcanic eruption on Earth. I shall, however, disagree with his criticism. Yes, member states of the United Nations should perhaps increase their cooperation on Earth to prepare for the plausible risk of super-volcanic eruption, in the very long term. This kind of cooperation, however, is not the prerogative of WARSEC.

WARSEC's only focus area is outer space affairs and one of WARSEC's missions, as defined by the United Nations General Assembly and with the approval of the Security Council, is to conduct an intensive interstellar exploration, with the hope of finding a colonizable planet.

Once again, these space exploration efforts are driven by a fear of annihilation, through super-volcanic eruptions this time. Even though we have no clear insight as to the probability of success, this does not mean we should give up all hope of finding a habitable planet.

I may, however, agree with Dr. Cooper and state that interstellar colonization should not be plan A to preserve human civilization. It is, however, definitely a plan B worth pursuing, if only to give humanity hope.

01: RUSH
(AUG 2100)

The WARSEC headquarters were located in Vaasa, Finland. Why was the United Nations agency in charge of space regulation located in a minor town on the west coast of Finland? This was something all new WARSEC employees wondered. Many came up with convoluted explanations, some assuming it was because its director, Ralf Åhman, had been born in Finland.

In fact, the reason had been simple. Back in 2095, when the location of the newly founded World's Agency for the Regulation of Space Exploration and Colonization had been discussed at the United Nations, Vaasa had turned out to be the only place all parties could agree on.

It was far enough from the locations of all other National Space Agencies, from NASA to the Japanese JAXA, to be perceived as neutral. It was far enough from all the headquarters of major private aerospace corporations, ranging from Boeing to Airbus and Comac, to be assumed to have no commercial preferences. In fact, it had been chosen because it was a remote location, not subjected to either tropical storms or earthquakes, while at the same time being within a reasonable distance from the USA, the European Union, China and the South Asian Union, which were the main contributors.

The fact that its director, Ralf Åhman, had been born in Finland was a mere coincidence, or the result of the random functions of the universe, as was usually said at WARSEC.

On Friday 27 August 2100, though, Ralf had hoped that Vaasa had been an even more remote location. A tunnel had been built under the Gulf of Bothnia, and Umeå, on the Swedish coast, was now accessible by train from Vaasa. This meant that Trondheim, in Norway, where his ex-girlfriend lived, was only 750 km (470 miles) away by train, six hours including the correspondence in Sundsvall.

This would not have been a problem if Solveig had not taken advantage of it to ask him to take care of their children for the weekend on such short notice.

The previous evening, he had taken a night train from Vaasa and arrived at Trondheim central station, in Norway, at 5:30 a.m. after a bad night's sleep. He had eaten an unhealthy breakfast at the Trondheim railroad station's McDonald's, and at 6:00 a.m., his ex-girlfriend had brought him the sleepy kids: their ten-year-old son Dag and their eight-year--old daughter Eleonor. He had taken them immediately to the next train to Sundsvall and they had slept most of the trip. In Sundsvall, they had taken the connecting high-speed train bound for Vaasa, Finland.

In the train to Vaasa, Ralf had tried to work a bit, but he had been constantly disturbed by his kids, mostly his son, who always asked weird questions:

"Dad, why are there some toilets onboard the AF5 Dachshund S, but not onboard the Chough glider?"

As a ten-year-old boy, Dag was, of course, interested in European aircraft. The AF5 Dachshund S was a small aerospace shuttle developed by Airbus Space, while the Chough glider was an assault glider with electric engines developed by Airbus Military. Dag would go on with his irritating questions:

"The AF5 Dachshund S can transport only six passengers and crew but has toilets, while the Chough glider can transport up to 24 passengers and crew, and they have no toilets."

Ralf was in no mood to answer. He considered his son. He had inherited blue eyes from both his blond Norwegian mother and ginger Scottish paternal grandmother. But his hair was afro, like his own father. His skin was lighter than Ralf's, though. Dag's sister, Eleonor, had brown eyes, and a darker skin complexion, though her shoulder-long hair was something in between blond and light brown, giving it a golden color.

Ralf was proud of his children, even though he was perhaps not spending enough time with them. He himself was a forty-four-year-old man, son of a ginger Scottish mother and a Finn of Somalian and Eritrean descent.

Dag went on: "I know that the AF5 Dachshund S can go to the orbital station and it takes eight hours. On the other hand, during the Moroccan war, the Chough gliders that deployed Legionnaires in Khouribga had to fly thirteen hours on their electric engines to come back to Europe."

This made Ralf even less willing to answer. Even if he was a UN diplomat, he was foremost a European citizen, and he could not help feeling ashamed for what the European Union had done three years earlier, when they had invaded Morocco. Luckily, President Bonavita had not been re-elected, and the new European president, Guido Niedling, seemed to be a decent and very reasonable person. That made him think of the upcoming election in the United States. As the polls stood, it seemed clear that the conservative Republican Barry Silverbane would be elected. He did not look forward to it, as it may have consequences on his UN agency.

Dag was still not tired of his metaphysical pondering: "I read that the pilots flying the gliders back to Europe had had to wear XL diapers. But since all astronauts also wear diapers, why put toilets onboard an AF5 Dachshund S?"

To Ralf's relief the high-speed train entered the tunnel under the Gulf of Bothnia, and Dag was attracted by the movie Eleonore was watching on her tablet.

Since Vaasa had been selected as the location for the headquarters of WARSEC, the public infrastructure had been booming under the impulsion of the town's megalomaniac mayor, a certain Petri Granfalk.

The good thing about it was that the first subway line had just opened, from Vaasa Central Station to Vaasa Airport and the nearby WARSEC campus, and it took them only fifteen minutes to arrive at Ralf's office, in WARSEC's main building.

The bad thing about it was that they had also built a gigantic, ugly arena, ruining the view from Ralf's office window, which overlooked the airport's runway.

It was 13:25 and Ralf was in a hurry. He had already postponed the meeting until 13:30 and this was not well perceived in a country such as Finland, where people usually did not work on a Friday afternoon in August.

He installed his kids in the sofa corner of his office, advised them to entertain themselves with their tablets, and hurried out of the room. In the corridor, he realized he was only wearing cream trousers, sneakers, and a purple polo shirt with the WARSEC logo. What the hell! It was Friday, and it was WARSEC, not the UN headquarters in New York. He rushed to the conference room.

When he entered the meeting room, he saw that everybody was there and waiting for him. The blinds on the south window had been lowered because of the low August Finnish sun. The projector was on and casting an image on the canvas screen.

The director of the Space Coordination Center was already standing by it. Glover Johnson was a short but muscular black American who had previously served in the US Navy, where he had reached the rank of rear admiral by specializing in the safety of compact fusion reactors. At almost forty-one, Glover was the *de facto* vice director of WARSEC. He was the only one in the room to wear a suit, a navy blue suit with a cream shirt, but no tie. All the others in the room had opted for their colored WARSEC polo shirts.

Sitting around the long rectangular table were Tatjana Aydemir, the director of the Lunar Coordination Center, and Thierry Diakité, her lead engineer, both of whom were wearing orange WARSEC polo shirts.

With them were the five main scientists behind the development of warp technology, all wearing red WARSEC polo shirts: Alice Fù, Tintin Mutombo, Anatoli Govorov, Mikko Andersson and Valeriya Limonov.

Rebecka Levi, the head scientist of the terraforming department, was also there and wore a light blue polo shirt with the WARSEC logo on it. Ralf took the seat between Mikko and Valeriya, who often avoided one another since their breakup onboard the *UNSS Forward*'s expedition to Alpha Centauri.

Glover Johnson started his presentation straight away, showing a slide with a timeline.

"2078, deployment of the first space elevator, on Tarawa Island, in the Pacific, operated by the Chinese and Japanese space agencies. 2084, deployment of a second space elevator in European Guyana and operated by NASA and the

European Space Agency."

Space elevators were 50,000 km-long geostationary nono-carbon tethers attached to orbiting asteroids to carry electrically driven capsules into space, making it easy to bring heavy payloads into orbit.

The ex-admiral went on:

"2085, start of the manufacturing of the orbital station, soon to be equipped with compact fusion reactors. 2091, deployment of the lunar base, with the Moon space elevator and the lunar refill station."

Ice had been found in the Shackleton Crater, on the lunar south pole. By hydrolyzing it, liquid oxygen and hydrogen could be retrieved from the Moon to refill the tanks of chemically propelled spaceships.

Glover had gone quickly through the list and was now saying: "2094, the first test flight of the *Alcubierre*."

As Glover mentioned the name of the *Alcubierre*, Anatoli Govorov raised his hands with his fingers in a V, making Glover laugh. The tall, hefty Russian physicist in his mid-thirties had been the engineer, and onboard the ship when the warp technology had been tested the first time. Alice Fù, who was sitting next to him, smiling, had been the captain. She was a slim Afro-Chinese chemist of about the same age as Anatoli, and she had been the one who had discovered the green matter, an exotic matter with negative-energy attributes on the quantum scale. She had been the recipient of the 2095 Nobel Prize in Chemistry.

Her discovery had greatly contributed to making faster-than-light travel possible, but it would have remained a chimera, if it had not been for the work of Tintin Mutombo, who sat next to her and also wore a red polo shirt. The thirty-year-old, tall Congolese theoretical physicist, whose French descent could be guessed from the lighter complexion of his skin, had come up with the unified gravity theory, reconciling the general relativity theory with quantum physics. This theoretical milestone had meant that it was now possible to use negative quantum energy to warp spacetime and have a spaceship travel faster than light. Tintin had done his PhD under Anatoli's supervision and both had shared the 2095 Nobel Prize in Physics.

The idea of warping spacetime for faster-than-light travel had been first proposed by Mexican astrophysicist Miguel Alcubierre, in 1994. However, back then, it had shown it would require an unreasonably massive amount of negative energy. In the 2010s, long before the green matter had been invented, the NASA's Eagleworks laboratories had shown that this amount of negative energy could be vastly reduced by shaping interstellar ships as cigars and by optimizing the thickness and oscillation of the warp field. This had been put into practice eighty years later, and both Mikko and Valeriya, now both in their early thirties, had been the main contributors. Mikko Andersson was a brown-haired Swede with Asian-shaped grey eyes while Valeriya was a short but stout Russian brunette.

Glover Johnson went on with the timeline:

"2095, WARSEC is created, and the decision is taken to further expand the orbital station, open it to commercial activities, and start manufacturing aerospace shuttles on the Moon.

"2097. WARSEC Ventures starts operating the lunar factory. Together with our partners Boeing, Airbus, Lockheed, and Comac, we manufacture our first aerospace shuttle prototype in August 2097 and get the first orders from Ryanair in December 2097, before the certification of both the Space Bear and the Space Hound in March 2098."

The Space Hound was a formerly cancelled Boeing project that had been resuscitated by WARSEC Ventures. It was a medium-sized aerospace shuttle able to carry up to 60 passengers. The Space Bear, a resuscitated Airbus Project, was a long and massive aerospace shuttle able to carry up to 670 passengers in its Ryanair version.

The ex-rear admiral continued his presentation: "February 2098: start of the manufacturing of the first interstellar ship, the *UNSS Forward*. April 2098: the orbital station opens to the public with three hotels operated by Radisson, Sheraton, and Vahlroos Travel, which also opens a space attraction park. We start mass manufacturing our Space Hound and, mostly, the Space Bear, which seems to be our best seller, as the EU Air Force, followed by the US Air Force and the Chinese Air Force, all wish to acquire some for suborbital transportation."

A single Space Bear could indeed transport two armed infantry companies to anywhere in the world in two hours. Combined with its vertical take-off and landing ability, it was attractive to the armies of this world. The sales to the EU, US, and Chinese military had meant a significant and fast in-flow of cash for WARSEC. However, it had not been uncontroversial for a UN agency to earn their money this way, but the subject was taboo in the room.

Glover was now pointing to the end of the timeline on the slide: "September 2098, commissioning of the *UNSS Forward*. January 2099, departure of the Alpha Centauri Mission. Exploration of the star system in the summer and safe return to Earth on 30 December 2099."

Glover Johnson had been pointing to Alice, Mikko, and Valeriya. All three had been part of the crew of the *UNSS Forward* on her first interstellar mission.

Ralf Åhman interrupted Glover: "Now we are in August 2100. Where do we stand?"

The director of the Space Coordination Center clicked on his remote control and said: "That's my next slide. First a few numbers. Commercial traffic to the orbital station since its opening two years ago has increased by 300% per year on average. As a result, we have decided to accelerate the further extension of the station. We will build two additional rings. We will also increase the number of circular gravity decks on each ring, from fifteen to twenty-three decks."

Glover went on: "The number of WARSEC employees has increased from fewer than 500 in 2095 to 1,500 in 2097 and to 6,500 now that the lunar factories are working at full speed."

Glover showed a graph with the evolution of WARSEC personnel, then went to the next slide, showing the financial resources:

"In 2096, the contribution of the member states stood for 80% of our budget, and our fees on satellite and suborbital flights for only 20% of it. Today the contribution of the member states stands for less than 10% of our budget. We have indeed succeeded in multiplying our income more than tenfold, thanks to the sales of our aerospace shuttles manufactured on the Moon. We have also started earning income by taxing commercial space activities."

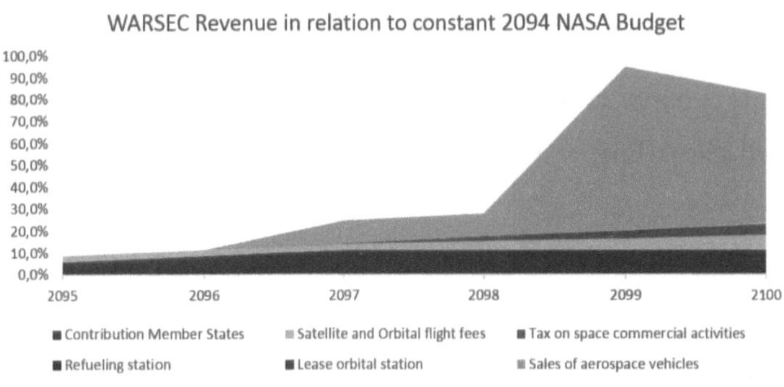

Figure 1: WARSEC Revenue by type of income.

Ralf looked at the graph and commented: "The fees on satellites and orbital flights as well as the taxation of commercial activities, now account for the same amount as the contribution of member states. That's good, but still not enough."

Glover acquiesced: "You are right. Currently, most of our income is coming from the sales of aerospace shuttles. It has brought us a lot of cash, but it won't last. When most of the airline companies have acquired aerospace shuttles, be they ours, or those from V-Space, the market will contract."

"We shouldn't worry about it too much now."

It was Tatjana Aydemir who had spoken. The forty-five-year-old director of the Lunar Coordination Center was a short, dark-haired German with blue eyes. She was wearing an orange polo shirt, the color of the WARSEC engineers. All the meeting participants were now looking at her.

She clarified her thoughts: "It will take more than ten years for the market to be fully saturated with aerospace shuttles. This is both our analysis and that of V-Space. Meanwhile, we will start selling warp-able spaceships instead. We have already our first customers."

"This is correct," Glover said. "Both NASA and the Chinese Space Agencies will acquire two Forward class ships to conduct scientific missions within our solar system."

"It is not our role indeed to launch scientific missions to the moon of Saturn," Ralf noted. "The NASA will be happy to do it when they have their own warp ships."

Glover went on: "Then, Vahlroos Travel will also acquire some Forward class ships to bring tourists to Mars. They should open a tourist center on the red planet by 2104".

"This means," Tatjana added, "that WARSEC should have a source of income secured at least for the next twenty years. By then, there may be enough commercial space activities for us to earn enough income from their taxes alone."

Though a UN Agency, WARSEC had been given the right to tax any commercial space activities, in accordance to the Vienna Treaties of 8 December 2094.

After Glover had covered the financial situation and prospects of the UN space regulation agency, he sat down and let Tatjana Aydemir give a short exposé of the current production at the lunar factory.

She first mentioned that the production of aerospace shuttles had diverted resources from the manufacturing of interstellar ships. She briefly mentioned the coming 'Neo' version of both the Space Bear and the Space Hound, to be launched within five to eight years. She then gave an update on the manufacturing of the interstellar spaceships.

"As you know, two Forward class ships are currently operational, the *UNSS Forward* and the *UNSS Fridtjof Nansen*. The *UNSS Ernest Shackleton* will be commissioned in December this year, and the *UNSS Roald Amundsen* will be operational in April 2101. By January 2102, we should have seven Forward class ships operational for interstellar exploration."

Forward class ships were medium-sized cylindrical spaceships, 75 meters (246 ft) long and 32 meters (105 ft) in diameter. They were equipped with three circular gravity decks revolving around a 0-G core and cargo bay. They could transport up to a hundred passengers and crew and were meant primarily for exploratory missions.

Ralf raised his hand and said: "I have made it clear to the UN secretary-general, Mrs. Hira Dorjee-Sherpa, that we won't be ready for the next exploration wave before January 2102. She agrees with us. However, as you have all seen in the news, we may soon have a new US President in disagreement with this."

Glover Johnson, who was the only US national in the room, sighed and said: "You are so diplomatic, Ralf. Barry Silverbane will indeed most likely be the new US president, elected in November this year. As you know, he calls WARSEC personnel for 'pussies', and believes we should rush into more intensive and accelerated interstellar exploration."

Tintin shook his head and said: "I am not embarking on any interstellar cruise if there are no rescue Forward class ships in back-up to provide assistance. I don't want to starve to death in the Tau-Ceti system, waiting five years for a rescue."

"Don't worry, Tintin. The ships will all have their greenhouse and their mini-farm. You will be able to grow your food."

It was Rebecka Levi who had spoken. The Israeli-Palestinian scientist was a tall, thin agronomist with black curly hair. She had also been working with the deployment of greenhouse and farming areas within the orbital station.

"We won't launch any suicide mission anyway," Ralf said. "But we will have to follow up the development."

He turned to Tatjana: "What about the *Eleonore Roosevelt*?"

The *UNSS Eleonore Roosevelt* was to be the first interstellar colonization spaceship built.

Tatjana clicked on her remote control and showed the next slide: "I was about to come to that. We will start manufacturing the first spaceship of the Ambassador class in two weeks. She should be commissioned next summer. As you see, she is the size of a European aircraft carrier, that is to say, still smaller than a US aircraft carrier."

Glover, who had served in the US Navy, smiled. On the slide, a picture showed a schema of the large cylindrical colonization ship. It was 240 meters (787 ft) long and 80 meters (263 ft) in diameter, and had eight circular gravity decks revolving around the 0-G core.

"I still think we are making a mistake," said Tintin.

Everyone in the room knew his thoughts, but they let him give his reasoning once more: "Our current spaceships are still using the green matter and cannot warp faster than ten times the speed of light. In two years, the new purple matter will be available for industrial use and will enable us to design and build new ships able to warp spacetime with displacement velocity up to 200 times the speed of light. I still believe we should put on hold our colonization spaceship manufacturing and wait ten years until we can build faster ships."

Tatjana objected: "As Ralf wrote recently in *The Washington Post*, our role is to give hope of future interstellar colonization. If we wait another ten years before designing a colonization ship, we send the wrong signal. Besides, what if we find a habitable planet in the next exploration wave?"

"The odds are pretty thin," Tintin commented. "I think we are only wasting precious time and, in the end, we won't have any faster spaceship before 2012. V-Space will beat us in the race."

Thierry Diakité raised his hand. The athletic black man, who also wore an orange polo shirt, was a robotics engineer and had developed the robots assisting with the manufacturing of spaceships on the Moon. He said: "No worries on that aspect. I still have acquaintances working at V-Space, and they are still stuck on their vertical atmosphere entry approach. We know it won't work."

Both Tintin Mutombo and Thierry Diakité had previously worked at the Vahlroos Corporation's subsidiary V-Space, the main site of which was located in Bobo-Dioulasso, Burkina Faso.

Back then, they had been associated with a project to build a warp-able spaceship with atmosphere entry capabilities. Both Tintin and Thierry had disagreed with the chosen approach of having the ship warp vertically straight into the atmosphere.

According to them, the spaceship would not be able to stabilize upon warp-out, and would most likely crash. Even if artificial intelligence could be used to stabilize the ship upon re-entry, the passengers would be subjected to such a G-force that they would all certainly die.

Ralf Åhman got up from his chair and went to the canvas screen.

"I would not worry too much about V-Space," he said, as he invited Tatjana with a gesture to retake her seat. "As you know, upon Vahlroos Corporation's insistence, the United States have requested the International Court of Justice, to evaluate the very legality of our organization. According to Michael Vahlroos, their CEO, WARSEC should not be allowed to tax commercial space activities and private space corporations should not need to apply to us for exploitation rights. His position is that it is in total disagreement with the previous Outer Space Treaty and Moon Treaty. The International Court of Justice will give its ruling tonight, and this poor Michael may well be disappointed if I am not mistaken in my interpretation of international law."

Ralf Åhman also announced that he wanted to give a short update on the current research on terraforming, and invited Rebecka Levi to take the floor next to him. The Israeli-Palestinian agronomist had no slides to show and decided to be concise:

"Over the last eighteen months," she said, "I have mostly worked with two PhD students from Cambridge, whose doctorate is being funded by WARSEC. One is a geologist, and we have worked together to see how we could force an oxygenation event on a planet with the presence of liquid water but the absence of oxygen. The other one is an economist, and we have worked with Ralf to study the practicality of such a terraforming operation, should we find a planet to colonize. The research has been quite satisfying, except for some silly conflicts with their respective supervisors, delaying the publication of some articles. I will have more to show you in March next year. Hopefully, we will be able to hire these two researchers next spring after their respective PhD defenses."

Ralf jumped in: "Most of you already know the economist. This is Sanne van der Maas, the only survivor of the Martian colony."

The engineer Thierry Diakité had designed the insect-like robots that had built the rudimentary rocket Sanne had used to reach the Martian orbit in order to leave the colony and come to Earth. Alice Fù and Anatoli Govorov had been part of the crew of the *Alcubierre*, back in 2094, which had met her in orbit of Mars, and brought her to Earth at warp speed. Though Sanne van der Maas had been only eighteen at the time, she had also been involved in the 2094 Vienna Conference, and had worked closely with Ralf and Glover.

When the meeting was over and they eventually left the conference room, Ralf noted that Anatoli was still limping. He asked him: "How is your leg?"

The tall Russian smiled and replied: "Much better than nine weeks ago. They have just removed the plaster, but I lost all the muscle in my right leg. I need to exercise a bit. My back is still hurting, though."

"Solo-climbing in the French Alps with no experience was not the smartest thing to do," Glover commented as he was heading for his office. "You were lucky those two alpinists saved you and you were lucky you had a helmet on."

Anatoli shrugged: "That was not luck. I always have my helmet on. But all the rest was silly indeed."

The accident had been filmed by some climbers and had become viral on social media, giving bad press to WARSEC for a short while. Luckily, it had rapidly been forgotten with the Summer Olympics and the presidential campaign in the USA.

Ralf had no time to worry about it. He needed to rush to his office to pick up his kids. They had not done much sport today, but the following day was Saturday, and Ralf intended taking them to the swimming pool to exercise.

02: THE V-YACHT
(AUG 2100)

Sophie Couillard was sitting behind the pilots in the Albaspace Neo's cockpit. The narrow, long, windowless aircraft with curved delta wings was now approaching Saint-Bart Island, in the Caribbean. It had taken only twenty-seven minutes from Bobo-Dioulasso, in Burkina Faso, where the V-Space premises were located.

The Albaspace Neo was the best aerospace shuttle in the world. It was a newer and better version of the older Albaspace, of which Sophie herself had been the project director, before being promoted to general manager of V-Space, one of the Vahlroos Corporation subsidiaries. The hydrogen-powered aircraft was equipped with four CUBIC-R engines. The hybrid air-breathing rocket engines were meant to serve as reaction jets at low speed, as ramjets at high speed, and as rockets in space or when the air flow did not contain any oxygen anymore.

But the Albaspace Neo was not only built to reach the

orbital station, it was also designed to reach the Moon from Earth in only eleven hours. To that end, it carried a compact fusion reactor to power the onboard electromagnetic drive. The so-called EM-drive would propel the shuttle solely on electromagnetic impulse when out of the atmosphere, making it faster than traditional chemically propelled ships. Like the Space Hound and the Space Bear from WARSEC, the Albaspace Neo was equipped with vertical take-off and landing capability, a must to land on the Moon.

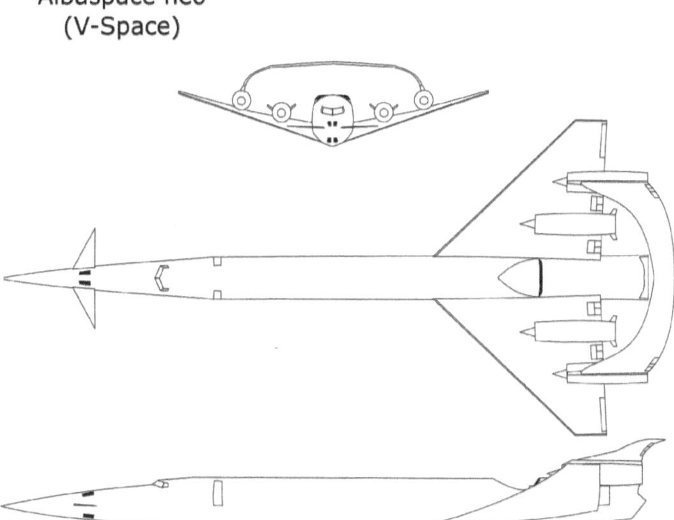

Figure 2: The Albaspace Neo developed by V-Space has the same design as the Albaspace, which is used as Air Force One by the US president. Like the Albaspace, it has no windows and the cabin is equipped with a multitude of screens. The Neo version, however, is equipped with an EM-drive and has vertical take-off and landing capability.

Less than 6,500 kilometers (4,050 miles) away from Burkina Faso, Saint-Bart had been too close to Bobo-Dioulasso for the Albaspace Neo to have used its suborbital flight capability. Instead, it had followed an atmospheric flight path and relied on its scramjet, squeezed in at the rear of its fuselage and below the overarching bent aileron. With it, the aerospace shuttle had shot through the sky at Mach 22.

The journey had been fast and smooth and, while the night had been falling in Bobo when she had taken off, it was still a sunny early afternoon in the Caribbean.

From the cockpit, which had the only windows of the aircraft, Sophie spotted the utility carrier, anchored in the bay, two kilometers off the island. It was a ninety-meter (296 ft) long rectangular ship meant to house Michael's private exploration submarine, his two helicopters, some ultra-rapid boats, and jet-skis. In short, all he needed for his too short and too seldom but well-deserved holidays. Or so he claimed.

The whole roof of the ship was a landing deck, and the Albaspace commenced its vertical landing maneuver. Further away, Sophie recognized Michael's yacht, which was modestly called the *V-Yacht*.

As the Albaspace Neo landed on the deck, Sophie was quite proud of her company V-Space. Transportation time has been greatly reduced thanks to their Albaspace shuttles. The world was moving forward. She did not like the idea of being summoned to his yacht, though. What did he want?

Michael Vahlroos was the CEO of the Vahlroos Corporation, one of the most dynamic technical companies of their time. His subsidiaries ranged from the boring, but safe, capital intensive Vahlroos Investment and Vahlroos Property, to the exciting and risky V-Fusion, first to have commercialized compact fusion reactors, V-Space, of which Sophie was the general manager, and Vahlroos Travel, which operated in the field of space tourism.

Apart from being the general manager of V-Space, Sophie had also been a director of the board for both V-Fusion and Vahlroos Travel for three years now. This was not too bad for the forty-two-year-old aerospace engineer originating from Montreal, in Canada.

On this Friday 27 August 2100, Michael had summoned her, and she had no idea why.

As soon as the Albaspace Neo had landed on the deck, Sophie went down the airstair and found herself with her trolley bag on the deck. The tall and athletic blond general manager of V-Space was wearing a long green dress and a straw hat. She covered her blue eyes with a pair of sunglasses and headed for the hangar downstairs. The Albaspace Neo took off as soon as she had cleared the deck.

A steward directed her to the rear ten-meter-wide landing deck where two personnel-carrier drones were standing. She recognized the drones developed by the V-Lab, another subsidiary of the large Vahlroos Corporation. She was asked to board one. She did it reluctantly and the electrically powered drone took off, propelled by its ducted fans. The mini aircraft set course toward Michael's private yacht, located only two kilometers (1.3 miles) away.

She hated the drone. She had once been onboard a similar one when an engine failure had occurred. The parachute had correctly deployed, and the inflatable rafts had kept it on the sea surface. She had nonetheless had to wait for two hours, floating on the ocean, before being rescued by the US coast guard. She would have preferred any other transportation means, but Michael was always insisting on promoting new technologies.

The unipersonal drone landed on the front landing deck of Michael's yacht, just below the jacuzzi deck. The forty-six-year-old CEO was standing up there, in his swimming trunks, wearing sunglasses. Michael Vahlroos was a blond man of average height with a normal weight, but without any visible muscle.

"Hi, Sof," he waved, "I have a bottle of champagne, meet me in the jacuzzi."

Sophie carried her trolley bag up to the jacuzzi deck and put it under the table. She had her bikini on under her dress, which she quickly took off.

"First I need to put some sun cream on," she said.

"I can help you," Michael said, and he took her tube, put

some cream on his hand and started spreading it on her back. Meanwhile, she spread sun cream on her arms, chest, and belly. She suddenly felt his hands go into her bottom bikini and his reproduction organ rub against her buttocks.

"I will be naked in the jacuzzi," Michael announced. "Don't feel obliged to keep your bikini on."

She turned around, and Michael was standing naked. He headed for the bathtub. Sophie followed him, keeping her swimming clothes on. "It's OK. I like wearing my bikini. Especially when I know you have a crew of eight working on this ship."

A few years earlier, Michael had more or less forced her into a sexual relationship, which she had found hard to decline as she was constantly single and also had sexual needs. No other men she found interesting were interested in her. Intelligent and shy men were scared by her tall and athletic figure. Athletic and sexy men were scared by her intelligence.

"What news from V-Space?" Michael asked as he poured some champagne into a glass for Sophie. "The sales for the first two quarters have been outstanding. Where will we land for Q3?"

"The third quarter will also be above budget," Sophie replied, accepting the champagne glass. "The Albaspace Neo is selling beyond expectation, and it benefits Vahlroos Travel as space tourism is booming. We plan to open the lunar attraction park already in April next year and everything is going according to plan. We will have the Moon Hotel and the Lunar orbital station."

"That's good for Vahlroos Travel indeed. Cheers!" Michael said raising his glass. "You took a good initiative last year."

Sophie Couillard had sealed a partnership with WARSEC, through which V-Space co-financed the development of smaller deployable space stations meant to be used in the event of interstellar colonization. In exchange, V-Space would be allowed to use the first manufactured stations to welcome tourists first around the Moon and then around Mars.

Sophie went on: "By January 2102, Vahlroos Travel should have their first Forward class ship. This will further boost the sales of the Albaspace Neo, as tourists will flock to travel at warp."

She took a sip of her champagne.

"What about competition?" Michael asked.

"Our competitive intelligence tells us WARSEC will develop a Space Bear Neo within four years. However, this should not be a threat. Since they still have to buy compact fusion reactors from V-Fusion, they will not be that competitive in terms of pricing. They should keep it for their own usage. They have already purchased three of our Albaspace Neos, but they need more convenient ships in the event of a planet colonization."

"Good to hear," Michael smiled. "You're good, Sof. You're that good!"

She felt him untie the strings of her bikini bra and bottom.

She did not mind, as long as she remained seated in the bath tub.

"You're so good, you look better without a bikini," Michael added.

This was Michael's typical awkwardness with women. Sophie decided to continue with her business exposé: "Concerning the V-liner, things are also moving forward. We have hired brilliant new engineers, and we may have a way to negotiate the atmosphere entry. The idea is to fragment the entry trajectory, doing a multitude of short warp jumps. It should ease the trajectory guiding, but we still need to make more progress."

"Good, good," Michael said, now patting Sophie's legs under the water. "I knew you would solve it. You are so good, Sof."

She let him pat her. What was she going to do anyway, now that she was on his yacht? It would just be another opportunity for bad sex, or so it seemed. She went on:

"Progress has also been made with the development of the purple matter for commercial use. It's now our feeling that we will be able to complete the development of the V-liner by the end of 2103. It will be ready much before the WARSEC have their own Space Bear Neo."

"You're good, Sof. That's why you're the GM of V-Space."

Sophie now felt how Michael grabbed her around her hip and lifted her to have her sit around his legs. His manhood was as erected as the Washington Monument. She did not mind. He was silly but doing it in a bathtub was not that unpleasant. She moved herself forward and let him penetrate her.

She smiled and whispered into his ear: "Make me CEO instead. CEO of both V-Space and Vahlroos Travel. You would remain only CEO of the other subsidiaries. For space business, I'm the best you've got."

He smiled back.

"I don't doubt it."

They kissed. Sophie started to rock herself on Michael's body, holding him behind his back.

Michael's smartphone beeped.

It was lying by his glass of champagne, on the side of the tub.

She was riding him, but he took his smartphone anyway and peeked at it. She felt how his manhood softened and collapsed. What a douche! She jumped away from his lap and sat back in the pool.

"The bastards!" Michael yelled, looking at his smartphone and not even noting that Sophie had dismounted him. "The fucking bastards."

"What is it?" Sophie asked.

"The fucking International fucking Court of fucking Justice! They have given their ruling. I just received an alert. I had summoned you here to be with me for the occasion, but I was not expecting this!"

"What happened?"

"The bastards! They just declared themselves incompetent! Because the Vienna Treaties were signed by sovereign states, they declared themselves incompetent to assess their legality."

Michael stood up in the jacuzzi, completely naked.

"That's outrageous. That's just outrageous. The world is becoming communist! WARSEC has full sovereignty over space resources!"

Sophie Couillard was used to Michael's outbursts. They were his trademark, in a way. Michael was a Calvinist Evangelist, and a strong believer, with all its psychological implications. After his parents had died in the Big Two earthquake, which had ravaged San Francisco back in 2081, he had inherited a small fortune and turned the property investment company which Vahlroos Corporation had been into a leading technological company.

He had himself been one of the engineers to develop the first compact fusion reactors, when he had worked at Lockheed. However, his newly founded V-Fusion had been the first company to successfully commercialize CFRs. He had seen his success as a blessing from God.

As a result, when the Vienna Treaties had been signed in 2094, he had taken it very personally. According to him, WARSEC should not have been granted authority over extraterrestrial resources and they were a threat to free enterprise.

Sophie, who still sitting in the Jacuzzi, gazed a short moment at Michael's genitals, which were just in front of her face, before she looked up and said: "Calm down, Michael. WARSEC is no communist organization. They encourage private initiatives in space, and Vahlroos Travel has been the biggest winner so far."

Michael eventually sat down back in the jacuzzi.

He almost sobbed: "They should not have a monopoly on interstellar exploration."

This did not soften Sophie, who now said in a more determined manner: "Can we get serious? Have you read the reports from the *UNSS Forward* about the first interstellar journey to Alpha Centauri?"

"No, I haven't, but that's not the point."

"I have read them, and that's the point. Impossible to grow fresh food onboard. One member of the crew even got scurvy on the way back. Scurvy in 2099! Not to mention the crew relationship issues on board. The mission has officially been called a success, but it was no victory march. Believe me, it's right to let WARSEC spearhead the way in interstellar exploration. We have a key role to play regarding space economy, WARSEC can't do it without us, but we should clearly let them lead the way."

"How dare you?" Michael exclaimed, standing up again in the jacuzzi. "Do you see that yacht over there?"

Sophie looked in the direction in which Michael was pointing. There sailed a gigantic yacht, perhaps a hundred and fifty meters (500 ft) long.

"That's the yacht of the founder of the Church of Quantology," Michael explained, his private parts still hanging. "The guru of that cult has become a billionaire by luring countless adepts into believing they can be in different quantum states at the same time. He is an insult to science, he is an insult to entrepreneurs, and yet, he is more successful than I am."

"Successful?"

"He has a bigger yacht than mine," Michael explained as he sat down back again in the jacuzzi. "I feel I have been blessed by God to do something useful with my life. Not like that Gerry Cruiser in his filthy Church of Quantology yacht. I have a divine role to play."

"A divine role?"

"Look what's happening in the EU. That disgusting leftist president, Guido Niedling, wants to introduce a global tax on capital under UN supervision. It will affect wealthy people, like me, like us. If President Fang could be re-elected, she would endorse his proposal."

"President Fang cannot run for a third time," Sophie said calmly. "Silverbane is gonna be elected president."

"And I'm happy with that" Michael said as he reached for his champagne glass. "Silverbane is the man we need to calm down all those leftists around. Could you really imagine a UN agency for the coordination of an international tax on capital, for the so-called redistribution of wealth? Could you imagine that? It would be even worse than WARSEC."

Sophie decided not to answer. She took a few more sips from her glass of champagne.

"It's my divine mission to prevent this," Michael went on has he put his glass of champagne back down at the side of the tub. "Tax and regulations cannot be allowed to impact and distort destiny. That would be too unfair."

Michael started sobbing, and Sophie assumed it was her role to pat him on his shoulder.

03: Career Changes
(Fall 2100)

The European Union Air Force Academy was located in Cranwell, in the UK, which was actually not a United Kingdom anymore, but the 'United Commonwealth of South Britain'. It had become a Republic in 2097. The training program at the Air Academy was three years long. The last year of the training consisted in the specialization in one of the Air Force branches, ranging from fighter jets and attack helicopters to transport aircraft and even assault gliders.

Out of the hundred and fifty cadets of the class of 2101, seventy-five had been assigned to the transportation branch. Among these, Aisha Barjaoui and twenty-nine other cadets were to specialize in heavy transport.

Unlike most of her fellow cadets, Aisha Barjaoui had two artificial legs. Unlike most of her fellow cadets, Aisha Barjaoui had not been born a European national. In fact, she had had a non-typical career.

She had been born and raised in Morocco, in a poor family. At seventeen, she had become pregnant while having an affair with a rich Chinese expat in Casablanca. Back in 2095, abortion had been illegal in Morocco and Deng had helped her to go Ireland, where abortion laws were the most permissive in Europe. She had been denounced to the Moroccan authorities, though, and had faced imprisonment should she return to her home country. As an undocumented immigrant in the EU, she had decided to join the European Foreign Legion, where she had served gallantly in European Guyana, Kirghizstan and even Morocco, her home country. Her own regiment of legionnaires had been part of the European invasion of Morocco, back in September 2097, something she was not particularly proud of.

During the Moroccan crisis, both her mother and ex-lover had been killed in an anti-Chinese riot, while her father had been killed in the subsequent bombing of Casablanca by the European Union.

As for Aisha's outfit, they had been landed in stealth assault gliders near Khouribga, a hundred and twenty kilometers inland, close to some phosphate mines. The legionnaires had seized the military airport, but they had received only partial reinforcement and had eventually been bombed by their own European killer drones, that had been subject to an unfortunate bug. She had lost half of her squad and the other half had been wounded, but it was not in Khouribga she had lost her legs.

In fact, Aisha, who back then had been only a sergeant, had

played a major role in the negotiation of a ceasefire with the Moroccan Army and had led the evacuation of the wounded, earning the rank of lieutenant.

Aisha had lost her legs a few months later doing something she had called the most stupid thing in her life: ice climbing when it was raining. The ice screws she had placed to secure herself on her ascent had been unsafe, as the rain had weakened the ice. When she had fallen on some bad ice, the ice screws had not held. The thirty-five-meter (115 ft) fall had cost her both legs. She had, however, been granted European Union citizenship.

Her former captain from the Legion, who had been seriously wounded at Khouribga, had advised her to apply to the Air Force instead and she had started at the Academy in August 2098.

She had turned out to be the best pilot of her year and could have chosen to join the fighter branch if she had wanted. However, her former captain, Antoine Léger, who was now employed as a space safety specialist at WARSEC, advised her to apply to the heavy transport branch instead. And she had been convinced by his arguments.

This was how the short but muscular pilot on artificial legs had joined the heavy transport branch.

In August 2100, the thirty cadets of the heavy transport class flew over sixty hours on the Airbus 800M, a four-engine turboprop transport aircraft. Aisha also found an opportunity to try to fly a Chough glider, of the same kind as the one which had landed her in Kirghizstan and Khouribga. It was fun, but incredibly slow. She was happy she had not been forced to become a glider pilot.

From September onward, the thirty cadets were assigned to only two types of aircraft: the huge four-engine cargo jet A590C and the Airbus 940V, a four-rotor vertical take-off and landing aircraft. A cadet asked why they were to specialize in two completely different kinds of heavy aircraft. Aisha was thrilled by the answer. Captain Léger had been right.

The EU Air Force was planning to train a first group of space transportation pilots, which would be picked from the fifteen best cadets of the heavy transport branch. Since the Space Bear was the heaviest aerospace shuttle with vertical take-off and landing capabilities, they wanted the cadets to excel at both flying a heavy cargo jet such as the A590C and making vertical take-off and landing with A940V.

There was only one A590C and two A940Vs for the thirty cadets, so they spent a lot of time on simulators. They were not learning how to fly anymore, but how to escape anti-aircraft fire and missiles. It was not as easy as on a Dachshund, Aisha thought. The A590C performed well as it was quite fast and incredibly maneuverable for its size but landing vertically with the A940V under heavy fire would be like being a sitting duck.

Aisha hoped she would never have to do that.

One of the advantages of being in heavy transport was that one got the chance to travel a lot, especially with the A590C, transporting cargo to Spain, France, Italy, Greece, and even Iceland.

At the beginning of October, Aisha Barjaoui had been lent to an active heavy transport squadron for a large airborne exercise in southern Germany. She was only the second officer onboard, but still! It was impressive to fly in close formation with twenty-three other heavy transport, escorted by twelve AF5 Dachshund. They were flying at 3 km (10,000 ft) above the ground, and when they were close to the target, they suddenly dropped to 800 m (2,600 ft).

"Cockpit to loadmaster," Aisha called on the interphone. "Drop zone in 5 minutes. Open the cargo door."

Aisha switched a button to turn the red light on in the cabin. She knew that the paratroopers were getting ready. She had her eyes fixed on the GPS and the altimeters.

"We are almost there," the captain said.

Aisha saw on the GPS that they were above the dropping zone and turned the light to green. From the open cargo door of the heavies in front of them, she saw four armored vehicles being dropped out of the aircraft, followed by sixty paratroopers. Using the surveillance cameras, she checked the situation behind the plane.

"Impressive, isn't it?" said the crew captain with his heavy

Italian accent. "Having said that, I would not like to be a paratrooper."

"Neither would I," Aisha replied, focused on steering the plane.

She had seen enough of it in Khouribga.

The first officer suddenly pointed at the screen: "Damn it. Two paratroopers have collided with each other, they are completely entangled… oh, yes. They've managed to get loose, but one is falling quite fast."

"At least 2 months in a hospital for that one," the captain said. "Lieutenant Barjaoui, you made a very good choice in joining heavy transport. In case of an airborne assault, we are on the right side of the sky."

And the captain laughed as Aisha steered north to follow the formation of heavies back to Stuttgart.

At the end of October 2100, Aisha got a longer leave and decided to check on her Cambridge friends. Once again, it was raining. Fuck England. The only positive thing about that country was that she had become very good at flying with instruments. Perhaps it was the reason why the Air Academy was located in Cranwell. Luckily, she would leave this rainy hell by January.

Her Cambridge friends had arranged to meet her in the indoor climbing gym, near Parker's Piece. In the hall, she found Samir, Sanne, and Amina. Aisha had met Samir and Sanne back in the summer 2095, when she was homeless and lost in Europe following her abortion.

It was Samir Benyamina who had advised her to join the European Foreign Legion. He was a mid-height, thin French man with black curly hair and had now been living in Cambridge for five years. He had first come to Cambridge under his compulsory Civil Service, where he had served two years as an orderly in some healthcare institutions. Samir had then studied robotics for three years at the local Community College. At twenty-three, he had now graduated and was looking for a job as an engineer. Meanwhile, he was still working as a cook in a local pub.

Sanne van der Maas had also done her Civil Service in Cambridge, but as a mathematics tutor for high-school kids. The very tall and athletic brunette with messy, short hair was also the only survivor of the Martian colony. She had been born on the red planet twenty-four years earlier, at the very start, long before the supply of bone reinforcement medicines and D-vitamins had been compromised by the bankruptcy of the Martian show. This had enabled her to grow more or less normally. Her parents had always forbidden her to leave their Martian hut under daylight in order not to expose herself to solar radiation, and this had been her luck. She had been the only one not to die of a cancer of or of bone disease. She had eventually been rescued and brought to Earth in 2094, under the coordination efforts of what was then the United Nations Office for Outer Space Affairs, the precursor of the WARSEC.

After her Civil Service, Sanne had remained in Cambridge, where she had studied economics. She was now doing a PhD in space economy, which was funded by WARSEC.

The last of Aisha's climbing friends was Amina Dörflinger, and she was also the best climber Aisha had ever seen. Originally from Switzerland, Amina had competed in climbing and even won a bronze medal in lead climbing at the 2096 Riga Olympics. At twenty-six, she was now to start the last year of her PhD in Earth science, also funded by WARSEC. She was doing research in terraforming.

The mid-height, slim, and ripped Swiss climber was now reaching the top of the wall. She did not clip the rope in the top anchor carabiner and just let herself fall, her shoulder-length dark hair flying behind her. The rope eventually stopped her fall at the next quickdraw, and Sanne hauled her quickly down to the ground. When she had landed, Amina's deep blue eyes noticed Aisha.

Aisha came forward and asked: "Where is Emily?"

"She was working at the hospital this morning," Samir replied. "But she will come soon."

Samir's girlfriend was a trained nurse.

"She is pissed at Samir," Amina replied as she removed the knot from her harness. "So she is avoiding us."

"Why is that?" Aisha wondered.

Sanne removed the belaying device from her harness and explained: "Samir has applied to WARSEC as a robot engineer.

He was called to the first tests at the center in London. He did well, so now he has been called to Vaasa, in Finland, to do some further tests."

"You want to work for WARSEC?" Aisha wondered.

"Why not?" Samir replied. "Sanne and Amina are already promised employment there after their PhDs. This summer, as we were doing some mountaineering in the Alps, we rescued a Russian astronaut doing some solo-climbing."

Sanne jumped in: "The solo-climber happened to be Anatoli Govorov, the 2095 co-recipient of the Nobel Prize in Physics. He advised Samir to apply to WARSEC, when he learnt about his background."

Samir went on: "So I did the test. Not very difficult. Four hours of programming, one hour of IQ tests, one hour of psychological tests, and two hours to write an essay about ethics and decisions in a committed environment. It was just a very long day. But now I've been called to the next step of the selection process."

Aisha complimented Samir and asked: "When is the next step of your selection process? I mean, in Finland?"

"First week of November," Samir answered. "We will have physical tests, a comprehensive teamwork test, a psychological evaluation and two personal interviews."

"They take their recruitment seriously, at WARSEC," Aisha said. "It's more serious than the Air Academy."

Samir shrugged: "They kind of have to. Even if you get

hired, if you don't meet the proper standard within the first nine months of your employment, you can be fired with only two weeks' notice."

"In their defense," Amina said, "an organization such as WARSEC has to be psychopath-proof."

"But I am still not sure if I want to join WARSEC," Samir said. "It doesn't pay as well as private companies. So, if I get a better job offer, I will decline WARSEC."

"Have you got job offers so far?" Aisha wondered.

"One in London," Samir replied, "but, come on, who on Earth would want to move to London? It's too expensive to live there, and Londoners are arrogant, rich assholes. Even worse than Parisians, and believe me, I know what kind of bastards Parisians are."

"He also got an offer in Dublin," Amina said.

"Dublin is a very nice city," Aisha commented.

"Yes, but My Lady Emily does not want to move to Dublin," Amina said, irritated. "She basically does not want to move out of Cambridge. She should have done her European service like everyone else, instead of using her studies as a nurse as an excuse to get exemption."

"That's true," Sanne said. "It's not good to spend one's life on the same spot. Cambridge is not even a great city. Of course, there's a nice social life here and a good climbing gym. But life is so crappy expensive. Look at us. We have decently paid PhDs, and we are sharing a student flat. Should we stop being students, we would have to pay through the nose to rent a tiny room in the cottage of a rich asshole, whose only trouble in life has been to inherit from his or her parents."

"In Vaasa," Amina went on, "there is space. WARSEC provides you with your housing. There is a climbing center downtown. There is even a huge sports arena that can house twice the population of the town!"

Aisha smiled and said: "I've heard of that one. This Mayor Petri Granfalk is now a world celebrity."

"As for Sanne and me," Amina said, "we will be employed without having to be part of any selection process. We are said to have both written outstanding theses. Especially mine. I basically show it's possible to force an oxygenation event on a planet with a carbon dioxide atmosphere and liquid water in less than thirty years. This means that interstellar colonization becomes realistically feasible."

"I thought you did not care about mankind and their survival," a voice said.

It was Emily who had just arrived. Samir's girlfriend was an athletic ginger-haired English girl.

"I still don't," Amina replied. "I still don't believe that interstellar colonization can work or that mankind can survive. On this, I am fully aligned with my supervisor Dr. Sheldon Cooper. But if I can be paid and given housing for doing research, going to space, and spending time in a spaceship where I can work out as much as I want, then I'm signing up immediately. Besides, there are not many job opportunities within science anyway."

"You are still talking about WARSEC, as I see," Emily said. "And you, Aisha? Any plans to go to space?"

Aisha smiled and said: "As a matter of fact, yes. Next January, for the first time, the Air Force Academy will train fifteen cadets for space transportation, and I am one of them. Even better, the first part of the training is in Vaasa with WARSEC. The second part is in Toulouse, with the European Space Agency. So I get to leave this rainy country for snow and, later, sun!"

They all congratulated Aisha, except Emily who was not in the mood to see all her friends willing to leave Cambridge for some space adventures.

Aisha went on: "That's why we got to fly on both the A590C and the A940V. They wanted to test the cadets' ability both to fly heavy traffic and to take off and land vertically. The Space Hounds and Space Bears have VTOL capabilities, as they have to land vertically on the Moon."

"So, you are gonna go to the Moon?" Emily asked.

"So will Samir, if he gets in at WARSEC," Amina added. "The manufacturing units are on the Moon."

"And so could you," Sanne went on. "You are a fit nurse. You can get in their medic program whenever you want."

"But I don't want to. Damn it, I don't want to climb today. Bye." Emily said, and she left.

"*Putain, elle commence à être chiante*," Samir said. ('She's starting to be fucking irritating.')

The next Tuesday, Aisha Barjaoui was lying on the side of the burning frame of the crashed A940V. Her legs were covered in blood and completely broken. She was unconscious. The thick, heavy smoke was dangerously close to her.

At last, the para-rescuers came. One of them started examining her.

"No, Eriksen, no!" a voice yelled.

"Use your brain, Eriksen! What is the most imminent threat?"

"The fire and the smoke?"

"Correct, Eriksen," the voice yelled. "Drag her, hold her legs up, thirty meters [100 ft] that way."

Aisha Barjaoui felt she was carelessly dragged along the ground. At least she was further away from the burning aircraft and the smoke.

"Evaluation, Eriksen."

"Two legs broken. Wide open. Bones in pieces. Has lost a lot of blood," Eriksen said. "I'll use a tourniquet."

"Yes, Eriksen. What next?"

"I can try to sew the arteries back together."

"Don't be silly, Eriksen! That lady has already lost too much blood. By now she has already lost her legs, but you don't want her to lose her life. Come on, IV, move your ass!"

Aisha started to be annoyed at that Eriksen. Were all

pararescue students so incompetent? He tried to place an IV and failed as he was shaking so much. He made two other attempts.

"What the hell are you doing, Eriksen? You're gonna turn her arm into the arm of a drug addict!"

Eriksen finally managed to set an intravenous catheter, but went too deep and it started to bleed. In the end, Aisha could not stand it. She woke up and punched Eriksen in the face.

"*Helvete!* ['shit!']" he said. "Aisha, is that you?"

It was Torbjørn Eriksen, from the European Foreign Legion. The brown-haired Norwegian o had been Aisha's mortarman, and the only other legionnaire of her squad to make it through Khouribga unhurt. He had been with her when she had had her ice climbing accident.

"Torbjørn!" Aisha exclaimed. "What the hell are you doing here?"

"Got fired from the Legion in June last year," he answered. "They said I was not fit for combat anymore. I volunteered for the Pararescue corps instead. After saving your butt at the ice wall, I thought I would be more useful as a medic. And so far, I have made it through the pipeline."

"Do you think this is tea-time?!" The instructor yelled at both of them. "Eriksen, set this bloody IV and evac her now."

Following Captain Léger's advice, Aisha had volunteered to earn a few extra euros by acting as a severely wounded victim on catastrophe simulation for the pararescue students. She had done it three times already and had liked it. She had met two other former legionnaires who had lost an arm and a leg respectively at Khouribga. They had remembered her for organizing the evacuation of the wounded.

Later that evening, they all met at the base's cafeteria together with Torbjørn Eriksen. The pararescue instructor went to their table.

"Do you know this Eriksen?" he asked the three crippled actors.

"Yes, sir," the one-armed man replied. "From the Legion. In Khouribga, he helped with the evacuation of the wounded."

"Did he?" the instructor asked.

"Sergeant Barjaoui was in charge, though." The one-legged former legionnaire said. "Sorry, I meant Lieutenant Barjaoui."

Aisha started laughing.

The chief sergeant instructor looked at Aisha with wondering eyes.

She explained: "We were under fire from our own drones, and the radio communications were jammed. The only option was to link up with the enemy and use their land lines to ask for help. So, I removed the top of my uniform, to be sure that the Moroccans didn't fire at me. And I made a dash for their lines."

They all saw Torbjørn blush.

"Behind me, I heard a guy panting and saying '*Arle på, arlse på*'. The guy outran me, heading to the Moroccan position.

It was Torbjørn, in just his underpants, running toward the enemy."

"At least, they did not open fire on us," Torbjørn defended himself. "And they let us use their phone."

"For sure they were surprised!" Aisha admitted "But the best part was later. Our white Norwegian friend turned completely red as he was badly sunburnt."

They all laughed.

After dinner, Aisha told Torbjørn she had pictures from their time in the Legion to show him. They went to her room. As a lieutenant and the most senior female cadet, she had a room to herself. She showed him a few pictures of when they were mountaineering together with Lieutenant Hoffman and Sergeant Uwilingiyimana, now both dead.

"*La Meije*!" Aisha said, smiling at a picture. "A wonderful summit."

Aisha complained it was too hot and removed her shirt, showing only her bra.

"You are even better trained than before, Aisha," Torbjørn said.

"What about you? Come on, show me your muscles." Aisha retorted. "I've seen some pararescue students train in the pool. They have totally fuckable bodies."

"God, I hated the water acclimation," Torbjørn said, smiling and taking off his shirt.

"Now, the pants," Aisha said. "Like in Khouribga."

At the same time, Aisha was slowly removing her pants, but kept her prostheses on.

"You failed an IV today, sergeant Eriksen," Aisha said. "And you shall be punished."

"Yes, madame."

"Come and lick me."

Torbjørn was definitely not a good lover, but Aisha saw potential if he were properly coached. She let him spend the night in her room, but did not sleep well. Partly because of the too narrow bed, and mostly because of the recurring ghost pain in her amputated legs.

The following morning, when they woke up, they saw briefly in the news that the new American President Elect was Barry Silverbane, the Republican candidate. There were some demonstrations in the States, with people holding signs reading '*Not my President*'. They did not pay more attention to it.

Torbjørn Eriksen's was Aisha's first flirt since she had lost her legs and she was happy. He was perhaps not the smartest man on Earth, but he was a good guy. At least, he liked her for who she was and did not mind that she was a cripple. Not like that idiot Alpine ranger Éric Legrand, she thought.

At the beginning of December, Aisha introduced Torbjørn to her friends in Cambridge. He was also a good climber, and they met again at the climbing gym. This time, again, Emily was nowhere to be seen.

"She dumped Samir," Amina explained. "Left him for a man-midwife."

"She could not stand that I was accepted at WARSEC," Samir added.

Aisha congratulated Samir on his admission to WARSEC and asked more about the selection program.

"It went fine," Samir replied. "The funny part was the teamwork exercise. We were six on a spinning module and had to solve programming tasks while being disturbed by multiple alerts, smoke, and so on. If you are a trained mountaineer and fine climbing in a committed environment, you will not find it that hard."

Sanne smiled: "What I like, when I listen to Samir, is that nothing is hard for him. Anyone would think that just anybody could join WARSEC. I am just curious: out of the six in your spinning modules, how many were finally accepted?"

"Only myself and another one," Samir replied.

After a four-hour climbing session, they went back to Amina and Sanne's student flat. Amina always kept a stock of bottles of wine. She had some Prosecco and decided that Samir's selection by WARSEC was worth popping a cork.

"Cheers," she said, after pouring the bubbly wine into five tea mugs.

"To space," the others said.

"And to the Moon, for me," Samir said.

"It's too bad that we got that new Republican US president," Sanne said.

"Why?" Aisha wondered.

"Haven't you read *The Chained Palmiped*?" Sanne asked.

The Chained Palmiped was a weekly satirical paper, still printed on actual paper. It was the English sister paper of the French speaking *Le Canard Enchaîné*.

"I have seen that he wants to abolish the Federal Service President Fang had just enforced," Samir replied. "In my opinion, that's too bad for them, if they favor congregationism over integrationism. But I shall not judge domestic US affairs."

"Yeah, that also," Amina said. "The real bad thing is that they want to pressure the UN to launch the next interstellar expedition earlier than planned."

"You mean earlier than February 2102?" Torbjørn wondered.

"Indeed," Sanne said. "According to *The Chained Palmiped*, Silverbane plans to threaten to stop contributing to the WARSEC budget, unless they start their next exploratory missions as early as April next year."

Amina grimaced: "I had been told I would be on one of the next interstellar missions. But if they pull forward the launch of the missions, I will never be part of it."

"Don't worry," Aisha said. "WARSEC will never be able to launch all their four missions in April. So far, only the *Forward* and the *Nansen* are fully operational. The commissioning of the *Shackleton* has been postponed to February, and the *Amundsen* will be operational only in June, as it stands. There has been some delay."

"You seem to know a lot about the WARSEC spaceships," Amina noted.

Aisha shrugged: "I want to be a space pilot, remember?"

04: FINNISH WINTER
(JAN-MAR 2101)

Moving out of Cambridge had not been easy for Samir Benyamina. He had first had to move out of his student flat, getting rid of tons of things he and Emily had accumulated. It was all the more heart-breaking, since Emily was temporarily moving back to her father's house. She could not even take with her the furniture they had acquired. They had sold all of it to students moving in to flats nearby.

The only point of friction between her and Samir had been the sharing of their climbing equipment. Emily wanted to keep most of it. In the end, Samir had agreed to keep only his personal gear, and half a dozen quickdraws, as well as a few nuts and friends. Emily had kept all the ice screws.

After moving out of his student flat, he had spent a few nights in Amina and Sanne's flat, before going to Paris to spend the Christmas holiday at his father's, even though they did not celebrate Christmas in his family. His youngest brother Abdelkader was counting the months: He would soon be eighteen and had only six months and two weeks left before moving out for his Civil service. He would serve in a kindergarten in Krakow, Poland.

During his stay in Beaudottes, in the Paris suburbs, Samir's obese father would spend the day lying on the couch watching TV, and barely talked to his children. When he did, it was to criticize them. They knew nothing about life. They had to think about the after-life instead of being materialistic. He was certain Samir would burn in hell for going to space and playing God.

Samir's older sister, Soraya, on the other hand, was very proud of Samir. She was now working as an engineer in Umeå, in Sweden, still together with her Swedish boyfriend. She was also happy to have a sibling moving to Northern Europe, not far from where she and her Anders lived.

At the end of December, Samir followed Soraya and Anders to Umeå, taking the same flight to Stockholm. In a way, he was quite excited. It was only the third time only he had flown. Before his selection process in Vaasa a few weeks earlier, he had never flown. When he had traveled to Algeria as a kid, it had always been by boat. At last, he was taking the plane like an average middle-class materialistic loser, as his father would call it. It felt great.

From Stockholm, they took the high-speed train to Umeå, where Samir spend New Year's Eve at his sister's.

The year 2101 began and he, for the first time in his life,

had a steady job. Not bad for a twenty-three-year-old kid from Beaudottes. On Sunday 2 January, he took the train through the tunnel under the Gulf of Bothnia to Vaasa. His new life was beginning.

Samir was soon disenchanted. Vaasa was cold and dark. The sun would rise at ten in the morning and set slightly after three in the afternoon. How could people survive there? He discovered the answer soon enough: they drank.

During the first four weeks of his employment, Samir had to complete a great many online courses, through which he committed to understanding major safety rules and procedures.

The engineers were working in what was called an 'activity-based office'. They had no fixed desk. It was a bit like at the community college. Every morning, one would pick up an available spot, connect one's laptop to the network and complete the assigned tasks. Putting a bunch of nerds in a room without introducing them to each other was not the best way of having them socialize, Samir thought bitterly.

When the first weekend came, he decided to go to town and check out the city. It would certainly have had a nice skyline if the gigantic arena on the horizon had not spoilt the view.

At 14:30, it was already darkening, and Samir went to Vaasa's climbing gym to check it out. It was not as big as the one in Cambridge, but it was well designed and organized. And it was definitely much better than what he had seen in Paris.

As he was on his own, he started bouldering. He was not too bad, he thought. Some climbers were talking English, quite a few were talking Swedish, but the majority were talking Finnish, a language that seemed to come straight out a fantasy movie. He understood virtually nothing of what they were saying. When he was solving a complicated boulder problem, some Finns were showing their thumbs up and saying to him either *"bra jobbat"* or *"näyttää hyvältä"* which Samir guessed meant 'good work.'

An athletic-looking girl with what he had identified as a Finnish nose asked him:

"Minä olen yksin. Haluatko kiivetä minun kanssa?" ['I am on my own. Do you want to climb with me?']

Seeing that Samir was lost, she spoke Swedish instead: *"Jag är själv. Vill du klättra med mig?"*

"I'm sorry. I don't understand neither Finnish, nor Swedish," Samir replied.

"Where are you from?" the girl asked him in English.

"Paris, France, and Cambridge, UK." he answered.

"Do you lead climb?" she asked. "I would like a climbing partner."

"Sure," Samir replied. "I have my harness in my bag. I will get it."

"What's your name?" the blond girl asked him, reaching out her hand. "My name is Ida."

"Name's Samir," he answered, shaking her hand. "Let me grab my gear."

Ida had a rope, and they started lead climbing. After they had completed a few routes, Ida asked him:

"What are you doing in Vaasa? Are you one of the space people?"

"Indeed", Samir replied. "First week in Finland. And you?"

"I'm a Finnish teacher, in high school."

"How can kids learn that language?" Samir asked. "It really sounds complicated."

She laughed.

"I could teach you a little bit," she said. "Tonight, I am meeting some friends, we are going out. Do you want to come?"

"Why not?"

Parties in Finland started early, Samir was told. At five-thirty they went to Ida's flat not far from the city center, so that Samir could leave his bag, since he had no time to go back to the WARSEC campus.

"What's in here?" Samir asked, pointing to a weird cabin inside one of the rooms.

"This is a mini sauna," Ida replied. "Very common in Finland, even in small flats. Do you like saunas?"

"I've never tried," Samir conceded.

"I want to shower anyway," Ida said. "I'll put the sauna on, we have the time. We have to meet my friends at 19:00."

"But I don't have swimming gear with me," Samir objected.

"In Finland," Ida replied as she took off her shirt, "We go to the sauna completely naked. I will open a bottle of wine."

A moment later, Ida came back completely naked, with a bottle of white wine and two glasses.

"Why are you waiting to take off your clothes?" she asked. "Shall I do it for you?"

"It's OK," Samir said, "I can manage. It's just that… I was not expecting this."

"Don't worry," Ida said. "It's completely innocent. Just two grown-ups drinking wine naked in a sauna. Normally it's beer. But beer makes one fat. We climbers can't afford beer."

"Agreed."

"Just to reassure you," she added, "I'm not going to rape you."

Half an hour later, as they were showering, Samir did not feel he had been raped, but it hadn't been completely innocent either. They had already drunk a whole bottle of wine between them when they later met Ida's friends in a bar. Samir was introduced as a new '*Ranskalainen*' (Finnish for 'French') from the space people, who was a good climber. He rapidly noted that Finnish women talked much more than Finnish men.

In his WARSEC welcome package, he had read that Finland had been the first country in the world where women had obtained the universal right to vote. It had happened as early as 1905. Seeing how much Finnish women talked, he had no trouble understanding why.

In the meantime, he did as the other men did: he listened politely to the babbling ladies while sipping his vodka.

Later that night, after spending a short time in a heavy metal night club, Ida took him back to her place. There were so drunk, though, that they both threw up several times on the way home. When they finally reached home, they were so loaded that they just collapsed on her bed. The next morning, Samir had a horrible hangover, but Ida seemed in perfect shape. She was exercising in her living room.

"It was a good night, wasn't it?" she asked. "Shall we go again to the climbing center?"

The following week, Samir continued with the boring online courses, but at least he spent three nights downtown at Ida's. However, the drinking bothered him. It seemed that Finns were less affected by alcohol than he was. Had they naturally evolved to manage vodka better than other human beings?

During his third week, Sami had a crash course in robotic applications related to the manufacturing on the Moon Base. It was quite simple. They basically used only two types of robots, legged and caterpillared, with the same operating system and architecture.

The week after, he had another crash course in space assistant robots, the ones that were being used to work on the orbital station or onboard the starships. Samir found out that the whole of the robot architecture had been optimally designed. Once one had understood the ground principles of one of the robots, one was at ease with the four types of robots used by WARSEC. That was brilliant.

Meanwhile, all the WARSEC personnel was encouraged to take some basic evening classes in Finnish. In the corridors, posters promoted the learning of the Finnish language. On one was a picture of a shirtless beefy man with long black hair, and it read: *"Don't learn Dothraki, learn Finnish instead."* On another poster was a middle-aged couple with pointed ears, and it read: *"Don't learn Elvish, learn Finnish instead."*

Samir decided to skip these classes as they clashed with his climbing activities. Ida was trying to teach him the basics anyway.

On Monday 31 January 2101, he started what would be a four-week training course in space safety. Aisha Barjaoui, from the European Air Force, was on the same course. WARSEC's space safety courses were indeed open to all air forces, space agencies, and aerospace corporations.

Aisha explained that she had spent the month of January in Toulouse, France, where she had completed a hundred hours in simulators, for the three types of aircraft she would learn to fly into space: the *AF5 Dachshund S*, with an S for space, the *Space Hound* and the *Space Bear*.

"Looking forward to the training being over," Aisha told

Samir. "They won't let us fly into space for real until we have completed at least the *Basic Safety Courses 1* and *2*."

To Aisha's positive surprise, their safety lead instructor was Antoine Léger, her former captain in the Legion. His face still looked badly burnt from Khouribga, but he had had a new hair implant. As a safety specialist, he wore a green jumpsuit. Engineers, like Samir, wore orange, pilots like Aisha wore pink, and scientists wore light blue. There were also some of the WARSEC administration who would fill no particular function in space but who took the courses because they could. They wore purple.

During the first few days of the training, their ability to handle G-force was tested. All the participants managed 5G without any difficulties. Samir asked Antoine if they could test their limit and the latter answered "*Pourquoi pas*?" ('Why not?') Samir was gratified to see that he could handle 14G before passing out. A moment later, he saw that Aisha made it to 23G before losing consciousness. How the hell did she do that?

For the rest of the first week, they practiced how to dress in the different kinds of space suits: red atmosphere-escape-and-entry suits, white space-sorties suits and light-pink lunar suits.

The whole of that week, Antoine insisted on the importance of following the safety procedures. They would spend the following week in a depressurized hangar and would be subjected to the Armstrong limit if anything went wrong with their suits.

The second week was indeed spent in a replica of the Moon Base installed in the depressurized hangar. They were sleeping in replicas of the buried lunar habitation modules and got proficient in putting on their moon sortie suits, checking they were properly pressurized, using the air locks and doing all kind operations on the fake lunar soil.

Because the lunar suits could only be pressurized to 0.3 atmosphere in order to give the astronauts a certain agility, they had to make do with a dioxygen concentration of 40%, and it equated to being at an altitude of 4,000 m (13,200 ft) on Earth.

For both Samir and Aisha, who had mountaineering experience, it was not an issue, but most of the other trainees found it exhausting.

All the more since the 35% oxygen concentration in the lunar habs pressurized at 450 millibar was equivalent to being at 2,700 m altitude [8,900 ft] when resting. The reason was to enable the astronauts to speed up the time required to put on their lunar suits without risking a pulmonary edema.

They also simulated fire drill in their huts, as well as sudden depressurization of one of the sections of a Moon hut, and how to react by retreating to pressurized safety chambers.

By the end of that second week, even Samir was exhausted. Ida would wait until his training was over, he decided. He went to the corridor where guest participants, including Aisha, were quartered. The non-WARSEC course participants were mostly from the EU Air Force and the US Air Force, with a few from the Chinese Space Agency.

"Beware of the Armstrong limit," he grumbled. "Beware of the fucking Armstrong limit."

"Samir! Can you tell me what the Armstrong limit is?" Aisha said, imitating Antoine's voice.

"Sir, yes sir," Samir joked back. "The boiling temperature of water is a function of the atmospheric pressure. At one atmosphere, water boils at a hundred degrees Celsius [212 °F]. With an atmospheric pressure of only 6.3 kilopascals, water boils at human body temperature that is to say at thirty-seven degrees Celsius [98 °F]."

"At what altitude on Earth does the atmospheric pressure decrease to 6.3 kilopascals?" Aisha asked, still imitating Antoine Léger.

"Between 18 and 19 km [62,000 ft]!" Samir replied, still imitating the tone of a soldier answering to a Sergeant Major.

"What happens to your body if you are beyond the Armstrong limit?" Aisha asked.

"Water in my mouth and lungs will cook instantly. I feel a burning sensation in my mouth before passing out and dying of lack of oxygen. This is why I should always, repeat always, wear a pressurized suit beyond the Armstrong limit, be it on a plane flying at 30 km [98,000 ft] altitude, or being on the Moon, on Mars, or God knows where mankind has had a bad idea to go despite the inhospitable pressure."

They all laughed in the corridor.

"At least, next week, we get to fly in 0G."

The third week of the course, after dressing in their atmosphere escape suits, they assembled on the tarmac of Vaasa Airport, next to a massive aerospace shuttle. The eighty-meter-long (262 ft) Space Bear was bigger than any other aircraft on the airport, with its large delta wings on the roof and its two massive CUBIC-R engines.

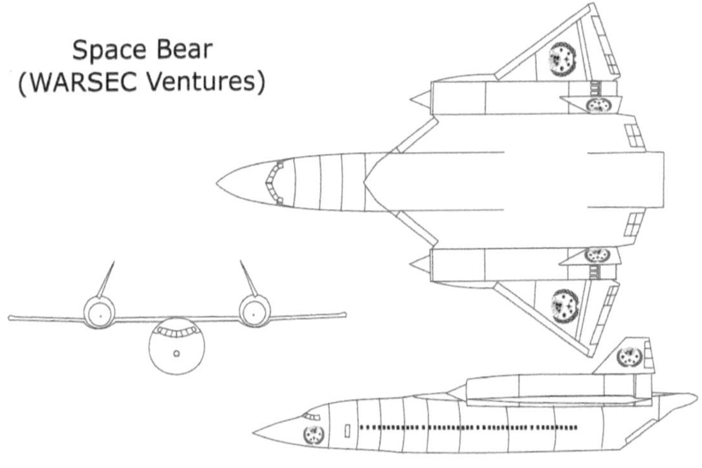

Figure 3: The 80-m long Space Bear is manufactured on the Moon by WARSEC Ventures. Originally an Airbus project, in can carry a payload of 50 metric tons. Here with the WARSEC Logo.

The course participants boarded the shuttle through the rear cargo door and went through an additional air lock before they could sit down in the cabin. Even though the cabin was pressurized, they were told to keep their suits on.

A moment later, the large aerospace shuttle took off and slowly reached the altitude of 15 km (49,000 ft), where it levelled. The hydrogen-powered aircraft then accelerated, and both Samir and Aisha were pushed back in their seats by the subsequent G-force.

Samir heard that the engines now sounded different. They had reached Mach 3, and the hybrid CUBIC-R engines were no longer serving as regular reaction jets, but as air-breathing ramjets instead. They were soon dashing at Mach 7 and the Space Bear started to steer upward again, more and more vertically.

Through the window, both Samir and Aisha could see the atmosphere darken.

Then they heard a loud sound. The hybrid CUBIC-R engines were now serving as non-air-breathing rocket engines. The liquid hydrogen was being combusted with the help of an additional supply of liquid oxygen. The Space Bear was now shooting vertically out of the dark mesosphere.

Another fifteen minutes and all the space trainees smiled in their red pressurized suits: they were at last in space, and in weightlessness.

They remained in low orbit for more than twelve hours.

The engineers had to practice solving diverse programming problems, while the pilots had two simulators onboard the Space Bear to test flying a White Parrot. Antoine Léger, who was not wearing a suit, but only a radio headset, waited until everybody had pooped in their diapers before he authorized the pilot to land back in Vaasa.

"That's part of the program," he said in his headset. "If you can't poop in a diaper, you have no right to be in space."

It was not nice to use a diaper as a grown-up. It was horrible to take it away after pooping in it. Two of the WARSEC newly recruited engineers even quit as they believed it was inhumane to have to use diapers at work.

In the third week, they did three orbital sorties in all.

"You know, Aisha," Samir said during the third atmosphere entry, as they were all sitting in their red atmosphere-entry suits. "When I worked as an orderly, I got used to changing diapers for elderly people. But if someone had told me it would be only another three and a half years before I had to poop in one myself, I would never have believed it."

Aisha was more philosophical: "We do what we have to do to go to space."

"The worst thing," Samir answered, "is that now, when I am back on Earth, and far from the closest toilets, I wish I had a diaper on me."

Everybody laughed onboard the Space Bear. Samir had

forgotten he was on the open radio channel.

Then came the fourth and final week. They finally went all the way to the orbital station, and it was an eight-hour flight from Vaasa.

In 2101, the orbital station was a 240 m (287 ft) long structure consisting of four gravity rings around a 0-gravity core. Each gravity ring had a 150 m (492 ft) diameter and contained fifteen circular gravity decks revolving on magnetic rails, to simulate the Earth's gravity. The gravity ring at the front of the station was the WARSEC ring. Then was the ring reserved for the respective space agencies of the United Nations member states, as well as for private aerospace corporations. The two other rings were for space tourism and contained hotels, restaurants, and even a space attraction park.

Around the gravity rings were the space terminals where the interstellar ships and aerospace shuttles could dock.

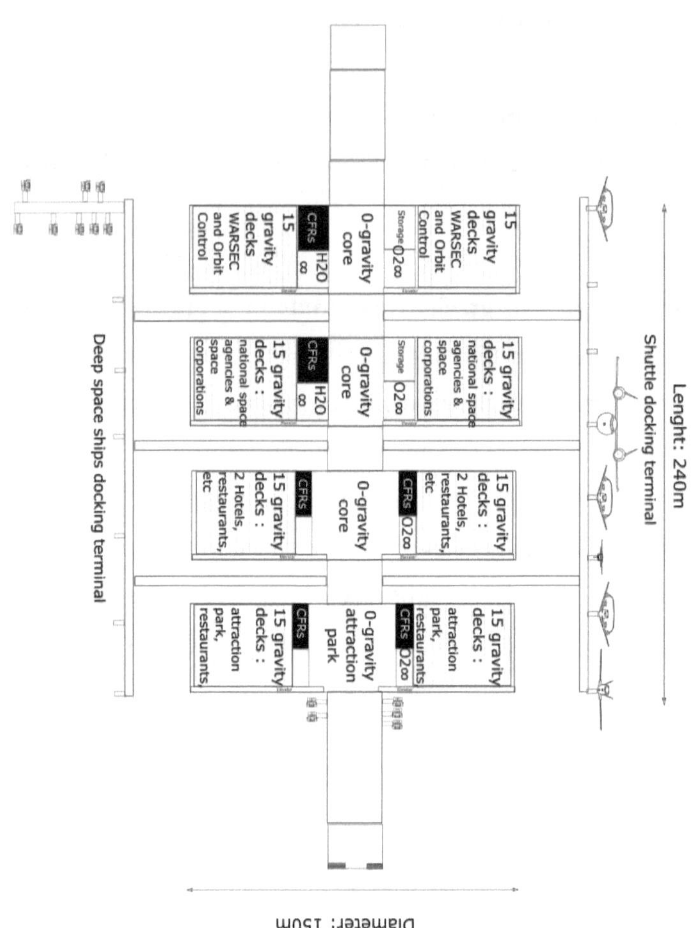

Figure 4: The orbital station in 2101 as it is being extended.

As the Space Bear was commencing its approach maneuver to the orbital station, most of the trainees were gazing at the glowing Earth with amazed eyes. But both Samir and Aisha were looking at the Moon, instead.

"In April, I will be there," he announced.

"You'll probably get there before me," Aisha admitted.

In the station, there were quartered in the WARSEC gravity ring. The fifteen circular gravity decks all had concave floors and convex ceilings, and it was a strange feeling to walk on them. One felt slightly dizzy at the beginning, but got used to it.

The decks were revolving around the 0-G core at different speeds in order to approximately simula te the Earth's gravity. Deck 1, the inner deck, was performing 5.2 rotations per minute while deck 15, the outer deck, had a rotation speed of 3.4 turns per minute. For obvious reasons, the gravity decks had no windows, lest its occupants be prone to motion sickness.

The following day, they all did their first space sorties. Samir was slightly apprehensive. This time it was for real. There was no hangar door that could be opened in an emergency to pressurize the environment. Their space suits would be the only thing separating them from the void of space.

With his suit on, he floated his way into the air lock. Four other trainees were with him, including Aisha.

They closed the air lock's inner door.

They all checked one more time their suits were correctly pressurized. Next, Aisha opened the air lock's outer door. They were floating in the doorway and, outside, safety specialists were waiting for them, some attached to cables, other flying in their small white maneuvering units.

Aisha floated out, and Samir followed her. It was like climbing. The best way not to be scared was to remain focused. Samir barely looked at the glowing Earth beneath him. It was too scary. Instead, he focused on what he had been asked to do for this first sortie: to follow a set of ladders around the space station.

They had small safety tethers and would lock them on some rails. It was like a via-ferrata and equally boring. Aisha soon found out how to make their first sortie more fun. For each arm traction on the ladder, they tried to propel themselves as far as possible, making use of the weightlessness. They had their safety tethers and it was totally safe.

Next, Aisha was "bungee jumping" in outer space using her safety tether to be dragged back to the station. A supervising space safety specialist asked her to calm down.

The first sortie lasted two hours. But they would do another one in the afternoon with more intelligent tasks. It had been decided that the orbital station would be extended and have six rings instead of four. Most importantly the ring diameters would be increased from 150 meters (492 ft) to 250 m (820 ft) so that each gravity ring could hold twenty-three circular gravity decks instead of fifteen.

As a result, both the aerospace shuttle and deep space terminals had to be moved further away from the 0-gravity core, and new corridor pipes had to be installed first. The trainees were given the task, under the supervision of their space safety specialist and the space construction workers.

Both Aisha and Samir loved it. In their four days at the space station, they totaled twenty-five hours of space sorties each, and both would have gladly done more if it had not been against the regulations.

By Friday 25 February 2101, the space trainees had all successfully completed their *Basic Safety Course 1*.

There were four other courses before they could obtain the rank of safety specialist. As a trainee pilot, Aisha was to remain on the station for *Basic Safety Course 2* to learn how to spacewalk autonomously in space.

Her second course was only two weeks long. After that, she would be back in Toulouse to fly AF5 Dachshund S and Space Hounds, which she looked forward to. However, she would also have to take *Basic Safety Course 3* to learn how to lead space evacuations and, most importantly, she would have to take *Advanced Safety Course 1*, which included a jump with a parachute from the orbital station. She did not look forward to it at all.

Before leaving the orbital station, Samir got a chance to watch Amina's PhD defense on WARSEC's intranet broadcast, in the WARSEC ring's cafeteria, together with Aisha.

The WARSEC director himself was in Cambridge to attend Amina's defense, and her supervisor, Dr Sheldon

Cooper, looked rather proud.

After doing a thirty-minute presentation, Amina was bombarded with questions by her opponents, but seemed to manage them quite well. Neither Samir nor Aisha understood all the technicalities, but the main conclusion was that oxygenizing a planet was possible, provided it was done correctly.

Samir was back in Vaasa on Saturday 26 March. For the following month, Samir went back to his Vaasa routine, with the exception that Ida had dumped him. However, he was soon seeing her friend, a certain Sirpa, also blond, and also with a Finnish nose.

At WARSEC, he was introduced to several simulators to train how to handle the lunar manufacturing robots. One of the supervisors, Thierry Diakité, thought that Samir was performing really well.

Samir remembered him from when he had collected Anatoli Govorov's camping car and dog in Chamonix, in the French Alps.

In late June 2100, Anatoli had been staying in the same campsite as Samir and Emily. Back then, he had a small brown kokoni dog he would usually leave with some fellow Russian campers while he went do some hiking and try some solo-mountaineering. While Samir and his girlfriend had been climbing on the *Arrête des Cosmiques* ridge, Anatoli had tried to go past Emily and fallen on a snow cornice, breaking a leg and dislocating a shoulder in the process. Samir and Emily had rescued him, and Anatoli had put them in charge of his camping car and kokoni dog, until Thierry Diakité and Tintin Mutombo, two of Anatoli's friends, had come to Chamonix to collect them both.

One evening, Thierry brought Samir to the table where Anatoli was sitting, in the cafeteria. Tintin Mutombo was also there. So was Ralf Åhman, the UN diplomat Samir remembered from his time in the European Service. He had been at the funeral of Gareth Fraser.

The fourth man, he recognized from the pictures. It was Glover Johnson, the Coordination Center director, and he had personally sent an email to Samir after the rescue of Anatoli, suggesting he should apply to a position as a robot engineer at WARSEC.

They were all from senior management at WARSEC. Why was Thierry taking him there?

"Samir! At last," Anatoli greeted him. "I never had a chance to thank you."

"No problem," Samir answered shyly as he sat down next to him.

"Glover," Anatoli said, "Don't be pissed off. Samir has the solution to your problems."

"I'm sorry," Samir said. "I don't know what you are talking about."

Anatoli laughed out loud and said: "Samir, I've heard you

have been quite successful with local girls. You are the perfect coach for Glover. His wife has found a nice Finnish boat captain and is filing our poor Glover a divorce."

"I'm sorry, sir," Samir said to Glover.

Anatoli went on: "Samir here has been dumped by a ravishing English girl. But he has found some rebound here in Vaasa. You should do the same, Glover."

Glover gestured Anatoli to be quiet and said: "My main problem is that she does not want to take care of our child. Rika is three and a half years old, and she wants me to take care of her on my own. Sincerely, she should take care of our child."

"That's a common issue nowadays," a voice said. "A hundred years ago, divorcing parents were fighting to keep the child, now they are fighting *not* to keep the child. Hi, Samir."

It was Eamon Windsor. The thin, dark-skinned man used to work as a psychiatrist at Addenbrooke's hospital,

"Hi, ex-king," Samir said.

Samir had met him during his Civil service, at Cambridge. Back then, he had barely been aware that Eamon was in fact Prince Eamon and heir to the throne of South Britain. When his mother had died in 2096, he had been crowned king of England.

That his father should have been Pakistani, and that he himself had republican ideas, had not made things easy, and he had been under high pressure to abdicate. At his instigation, the crisis had been solved by organizing a referendum, asking the South British nations whether they wished to have a constitutional monarchy or a republic. South Britons had voted for the republic and King Eamon had handed over his position as head of state to the new president elect on 19 September 2097, the same day the European Union had invaded Morocco.

After serving as the last king of England, Eamon had joined WARSEC as a medical officer and had been part of the crew on the first interstellar expedition to Alpha Centauri in 2099. He had made himself even more famous by releasing a video cast called: 'Doctor's log'.

Eamon sat down opposite Samir at the long rectangular table, but the director of the Space Coordination Center was still absorbed by his personal problems:

"Ralf is lucky," Glover went on, looking at the WARSEC director. "He only has to take care of his kids when he wants to."

Ralf Åhman grimaced and said: "I'm not the most exemplary father."

"Neither am I, god damn it," Glover retorted. "Laura is a sailor. She will most probably earn the right to see our child *only* when she wants to. I will lose, and I will have to take care of Rika on my own."

"I'm sure you will manage it," Eamon said. "If you can manage the whole safety program of WARSEC, you will manage a three-year-old kid."

"Don't worry," Ralf said, smiling. "Rika is the easy part. Our next challenge is also American, but is called Barry Silverbane."

"Your new President is crazy," Thierry told Glover.

"I did not vote for him," Glover said defensively.

Thierry looked at Glover: "I know that, but still. Barry Silverbane has been in office for six weeks and has already threatened to stop the US contribution unless we push for a new exploration wave next month."

"Yes, I know," Glover said. "But I am confident Ralf and the secretary-general will work out a diplomatic way out."

Glover, Tintin, Eamon, Samir, Anatoli, and Glover all looked at Ralf Åhman.

The WARSEC director shrugged and said in a very low but both serious and sarcastic voice:

"If we launch our interstellar missions by the end of April, astronaut lives will be put unnecessarily in danger, Mr. President. Among them, American lives, Mr. President. Mr. President would certainly not like to put American lives in danger, wouldn't he? Therefore, we believe Mr. President is willing to work out a compromise. We could start our mission on September 1st. That is to say, still five months ahead of schedule, but in safe conditions, to protect American lives. What would Mr. President say?"

They all laugh, except Ralf.

"Don't laugh," Ralf said seriously. "Face-saving outcome is the key to successful negotiations at the UN. If you don't like it, don't work for the UN."

05: SPACE APPRENTICE (APR-JUN 2101)

Toward the middle of March, Samir Benyamina was informed that he would depart for the Moon Base on Wednesday 6 April 2101, and would remain in space until 6 July. There, he would spend periods of two weeks in a row on the Moon working twelve hours a day, followed by one week's rest onboard the orbital station.

When he was onboard the orbital station, he was more than advised to spend his time taking the *Basic Safety Course 2*, to learn how to spacewalk on his own, and the *Basic Safety Course 3* to learn how to organize the evacuation, protection, and rehabilitation of a spaceship. It was always useful. He was also advised to spend time with the robot engineers on the station to see how they use the assistant robots.

On the Moon, he would have the chance to take a course in *Advance Safety 2* to practice how to lead the evacuation of a lunar hut or organize its rehabilitation. That way, at the end of his first space mission, he would be qualified for going on an interstellar mission. The *Advanced Safety Course 1*, which consisted in jumping with a parachute from the station, was not required for engineers. Anyway, it was too expensive, and only senior staff, in addition to pilots and safety specialists, were allowed to take it.

When Tintin Mutombo explained all that to Samir, he thought that he'd better do what they said lest he be fired before the end of his probation period.

On April 5, Sirpa explained to Samir that it had been a pleasure meeting him, but since he was now going away for a three-month mission, she wanted to try some new space boy. There was an interesting rotation at WARSEC, she explained, and they were all pretty fuckable. "*Merci pour le moment,*" she said in French to Samir ('Thanks for the moment.').

Samir was now pretty used to being dumped and did not care that much. Besides, some of the female astronauts looked pretty interesting.

Thierry Diakité was on the same flight as Samir. It was an Albaspace Neo. No pressurized clothes were needed, and they just sat next to one another in their orange inner suits. As the plane was waiting on the tarmac, Thierry briefly mentioned his first lunar rotation:

"When I first went to the Moon, I had to take the space elevator. We were transporting the robots to the lunar facility.

It took an eternity to get there. With this Albaspace Neo, it will take only eleven hours. WARSEC has only three of these."

The take-off onboard the Albaspace Neo was the smoothest Samir had ever experienced, and twenty minutes later they were in low orbit around the Earth climbing toward the orbital station.

The Burkinabe engineer added: "You are lucky, Samir. Before, we had to either stop first at the orbital station or dock into modular EM-drives. The Albaspace Neo has a CFR with a built-in EM-drive. We will land on the Moon in ten and a half hours!"

"At least we've got time to enjoy the weightlessness", Samir said.

They were no windows in the cabin of the Albaspace, but by watching the screen, Samir saw that the aerospace shuttle did several orbits as it climbed its way up to the altitude of the orbital station.

As they flew closer to the station, the screens in the Albaspace displayed images of the larger spaceships that were orbiting nearby. There was the *Orion*, from NASA, and a few other spaceships from the Chinese Space Agency. He recognized the *Alcubierre*, which had done the first warping of spacetime on 17 September 2094. And then, there were three starships of the Forward class.

Thierry pointed at the screen: "The *UNSS Forward*, which has been to Alpha Centauri, is over there. And there you have the *UNSS Fridtjof Nansen* and the *UNSS Ernest Schackleton*. For some reason, the starships of the Forward class all bear the names of explorers of some kind. For now, they're the names of polar explorers. There is also the *UNSS Roald Amundsen* being finished on the Moon. She will be fired into orbit in two days. You will see, quite impressive. The next Forward class ships to be manufactured will be the *Louise Arner Boyd*, the *Amelia Earhart* and the *Barbara Hillary*, but they won't be started before October."

"The first ships you named. That's the four ships for the next interstellar exploration wave. Where will they be going?"

"The *Forward* will go to Sirius," Thierry replied. "The commander will be Mikko Andersson. Anatoli Govorov will take the *Shackleton* to Epsilon Eridani. The *Nansen* will go to 61 Cygni, under the command of Valeriya Limonov. Last, but not least, Tintin Mutombo will take the *Amundsen* to Tau Ceti."

"Will you be on one of the missions?" Samir asked.

Thierry smiled and said: "No way! I'm not interested. I don't want to spend two and a half years of my life onboard one of these ships. If I go on an interstellar journey, it has to be for a real colonization project, not a vague exploration mission. I have more important things to do."

"Like what?"

"You will see when we are there," Thierry replied. "The Forward class was only the first class, for exploration missions. But I have also been working on the Ambassador class. A much bigger starship class, for colonization. The first one, the *UNSS Eleonore Roosevelt,* will be put into the lunar orbit by the end of May."

"How big is the *Eleonore Roosevelt*?

"240 meters [787 ft] long, 80 meters [262 ft] in diameter. Eight circular gravity decks. 115,000 square meters area [1.3 million square feet] with simulated gravity and 400,000 cubic meters [14 million cubic feet] in the cargo bay. Room for 600 passengers and crew for a colonization mission. That's what I call a real interstellar ship."

"And why not build even bigger?" Samir joked.

Thierry smiled and actually replied: "We do have some other projects in the pipeline. The Quantum class will be 800 meters [2,650 ft] long and 250 [820 ft] meters in diameter. But it won't be manufactured before there is an actual planet to colonize. You know, the whole WARSEC project is a bubble."

"What do you mean?"

The Albaspace Neo had just followed its last orbit at accelerating speed and was now propelling itself to the Moon.

Thierry resumed his explanation: "The fast growth we are experiencing now is economically sustainable only if we find at least one planet to colonize. If there is a planet to colonize, you can channel commercial activities to space and levy a tax on it. Currently, the main income of WARSEC comes from the selling of aerospace shuttles, but the market will be saturated within a decade or two at most. If an actual colonization project is started, then we can sell interstellar ships to private companies to operate on the newly opened commercial routes. Otherwise, there is a risk of the whole WARSEC project going bankrupt."

"The next interstellar missions will be launched in September. Do you think they will find something?"

"I haven't the faintest idea," Thierry replied. "I'm a robotic engineer and skilled mathematician, not an astrophysicist. There is a high probability this mission will fail, though. The real purpose of these missions is to calibrate some exploratory robot programs. That way, the next step will be to send exploration warpedo drones to explore other stellar systems faster."

The Albaspace Neo landed smoothly on the Moon Base and taxied to the lunar port gate. Thierry commented that it did not exist when he had been to the Moon for the first time. When Samir unstrapped himself from his seat and started to walk away toward the front door of the aircraft, he felt how light he was. At first, he had trouble walking.

Adjacent to the lunar port, half buried under the surface, there was the lunar hotel. The roof was covered with layers of water tanks and lunar gravel to protect its inhabitants from solar radiation.

"Property of Vahlroos Travel," Thierry said. "V-Space was my former employer. I would have liked working there if the CEO had not been an asshole. Have you heard of Michael Vahlroos?"

"The CEO who has his picture on the top covers of many books, saying how good he is?"

"That man," Thierry confirmed. "Well, he is a stupid asshole."

In the lunar port, they were asked to put their lunar suits on, and then were taken out through an air lock to the lunar surface.

As he was walking on the Moon, Samir felt an immense thrill. He, the little drug dealer from Beaudottes, was walking on the Moon! How lucky he had been! He was forever grateful to the European Civil Service. Without it, he would not have been forced out of Beaudottes. Had he not been in Cambridge, meeting Sanne, he would probably not have thought of applying to a community college to learn robotics. Without it, he would not have made it to WARSEC.

In front of the lunar port, several mini self-driving lunar buses were waiting. As Samir and Thierry boarded one, the latter pointed at what looked like some six-story-high grey lunar dunes on the other side of the lunar landing pad and explained:

"These twelve lunar dunes are, in fact, manufacturing hangars. That's where the Space Bears and Space Hounds are manufactured. The hangars are covered with multiple water tanks and lunar gravel to protect against solar radiation. The hangars are not pressurized, and you will have to keep your suit on."

"What about the interstellar ships: where are they manufactured?" Samir asked as the self-driving minibus set itself in motion.

Thierry pointed further away and said: "They are built in deep cylindrical holes over there. They are assembled vertically with a complex system of 3D-printing arms on a modular crane. Then, they are put into orbit using boosters."

Their self-driving lunar bus took them down into a broad tunnel.

"It has been bored by tunnel boring machines," Thierry informed Samir. "Our habs are all buried in this gallery to offer protection against the solar radiation."

In the tunnel, their minibus stopped in front the air lock of a hab, and Thierry led Samir into the habitation module.

Samir did not sleep that well that first night on the moon, though. Was it the lesser gravity, or was it the fear that somehow his lunar hut would be suddenly depressurized, and he would have to put his escape suit on? At some point, he felt the ground shake violently.

The following morning, at breakfast, all the astronauts were laughing.

"Did you hear last night?" Thierry asked. "A meteorite crashed just two kilometers away from the lunar base. It was not a big one, only the size of a motorcycle, but still!"

Samir did not think that was funny. If he also had to be

aware of meteorites, working on the Moon seemed to be even more exposed than high altitude climbing.

Later that morning, Thierry showed Samir his station in one of the large lunar dune-like hangars. He was to supervise twenty robots and manufacture a Space Bear. The required parts had already been dispatched the previous week. Thierry then left Samir on his own.

Samir did not understand why he had no supervision. He had gone through the assembly procedures but was not sure why he had twenty robots instead of twelve. The pre-programmed assembly tasks were not meant for twenty robots. He called Thierry on the wireless, who just asked him to think up a better assembly program. He had not the time to help him.

Samir assumed he would be fired if he could not deliver and decided to set himself to the task. While he was monitoring twelve of the robots starting the manufacturing of the Space Bear, he started to go through the assembly program.

While he was supposed to work only twelve hours a day, he spent his first nights as well trying to optimize the program. Luckily, in the hut, Thierry would answer his questions.

"Don't panic, you're not completely on your own during the day," Thierry said. "The supervisors are monitoring all the engineers and robots, for the sake of safety. Since you are the only one to be working on this Space Bear, special care is dedicated to you. So far, you have not made a mistake."

Samir finally redesigned the whole assembly process for twenty robots, optimizing the recharging of the robots' batteries and their multitasking. At the end of his first two weeks, he was rather proud of himself. He had assembled a whole Space Bear and performed the control checklist.

"Assembly time, two weeks…" Tatjana Aydemir read when they were in one of the habitation modules turned into an operation room. "Is there a mistake? Samir, have you filled in the log properly."

"Yes, I have," Samir replied hesitantly. "Have I done something wrong?"

The short, dark-haired director of the Lunar Coordination Center looked at Samir suspiciously and said: "Space Bears are supposed to be assembled in four weeks, with an extra week to bring the components and an extra week to do the quality checklist."

"He had twenty robots instead of twelve," Thierry jumped in. "Anatoli told me that Samir could have great potential. I was checking…"

Tatjana looked at Thierry and said: "Please, keep me in the loop. The log looks good, but we still have the regulatory one-week inspection."

"At least he proved my point," Thierry remarked. "Increase the number of working robots by sixty-six percent, and you can double the productivity."

"Yes," Tatjana said. "But not everybody can handle twenty

robots at the same time."

The following day, Samir and Thierry left the lunar base for their first one-week rest onboard the orbital station. They boarded a White Parrot with sixteen other astronauts. The SX-White Parrot was a fifteen-meter (15 ft) long double decker space-only vehicle developed by NASA, and there were twenty passengers onboard.

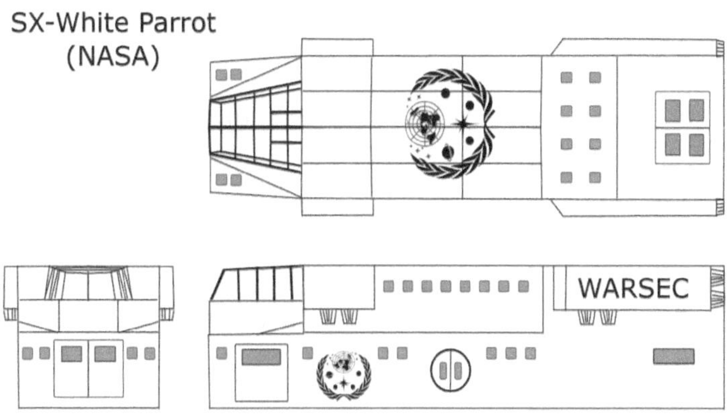

Figure 5: The SX-White Parrot, here with the WARSEC logo.

The take-off was shaky but the spacecraft soon reached the lunar orbit, where it docked into a modular EM-drive. Now propelled with electromagnetic impulse, the spacecraft started its eight-hour-long flight for the orbital station and the passengers were told they could get out of their space suits.

"Don't be mad at me," Thierry told Samir as they were finally floating comfortably in inner suits. "I'm doing you a service. On your return, you will be assigned to the team working on the *Eleonore Roosevelt*. And when we are at the orbital station, I want you to take your *Basic Safety Course 2* so that you can be proficient in spacewalking. Since you have already spent two weeks on the Moon, you only need to take the short version of the course, which is just one week. That means we will be able to assign you to the last integration steps of the *Roosevelt*. And if you continue like this, you will raise from Level 3 to Level 4 by July, which will be good for your salary."

WARSEC employees were ranked within the organization depending on their so-called 'level'. The paygrade was a function of the level.

"What level are you?" Samir asked Thierry.

"I'm level 6. Tintin and Anatoli are Level 7. Tatjana is level 8, Glover is level 9 and Ralf is level 10. Level 11 will be the UN secretary-general, Hira Dorjee-Sherpa."

During his first few months in space, Samir had almost no leisure time. He took advantage of his first 'rest' week to qualify as an autonomous spacewalker and an evacuation specialist in space. During his next rotation on the moon, he qualified as an evacuation specialist on the lunar base.

The work on the *UNSS Eleonore Roosevelt* was quite demanding, but this time he was working in a team with a great supervisor. The *Roosevelt* was standing on a 100 m wide (328 ft) level platform, dug 250 m (820 ft) deep below the surface, and covered by a huge canvas to protect her from lunar dust.

On May 27th, 2101, the canvas was removed, and six huge rocket boosters were attached to the side of the colonization starship.

On May 29th, Samir was onboard the *UNSS Forward*, flying above the Moon, when the *Eleonore Roosevelt* was put into orbit. He felt quite some pride as he saw the huge starship he had worked on reach the lunar orbit. He was also quite excited to spend some time onboard the *Forward,* even though, he would not travel at warp with her. They were simply towing the *Eleonore Roosevelt* to the Earth orbit, where the compact fusion reactors and most of the avionics would be integrated.

As they were flying toward the Earth, he saw two Space Hounds of the EU Air Force docked into their respective modular EM-drives and heading for the Moon. He was told later that one of the pilots was Aisha Barjaoui, who was to do a two-day session of touch and go to the lunar base.

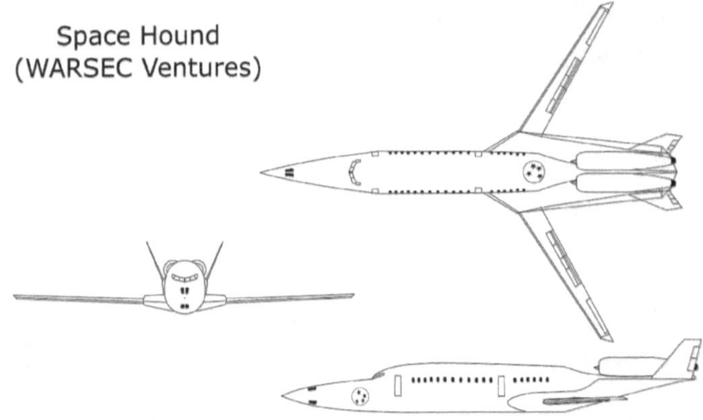

Figure 6: The Space Hound, here with the EU Air Force logo, was initially a Boeing project.

At the orbital station, he got some news from Earth. Amina had started in April at WARSEC and had taken her *Basic Safety Course 1*, but Samir had missed her on the station. Sanne had completed her PhD in the middle of May and was to start at WARSEC in June. Samir had no regrets about having missed her defense. Economics was even more boring than geology.

During the following six weeks, Samir worked intensively with the integration of the *Eleonore Roosevelt*. Even in his official rest weeks, he volunteered to help, as the starship was now anchored to the orbital station.

Like the cylindrical ships of the Forward class, the *Eleonore Roosevelt* of the Ambassador class had no windows, and he would work fourteen hours in a row without being distracted by other activities around the ship.

Meanwhile, Thierry seemed to be slightly more absorbed by politics. Down on Earth, the presidential elections were taking place in Burkina Faso, his native country, and he had forgotten to vote. His former schoolteacher, Lenka Sawadogo, was one of the favorites of the candidates in the presidential race. She eventually was elected as Burkina's president on June 13th. Thierry happened to find it easier to focus on the starship after the elections were over.

On July 1st, the nuclear reactors of the *Eleonore Roosevelt* were successfully started. On July 4th, 2101 and to the pride of the US astronauts, the *UNSS Eleonore Roosevelt* successfully tested her chemical propulsion and her EM-drive by flying around the Moon and returning to the orbital station.

Samir had the honor of being onboard the *UNSS Eleonore Roosevelt* for her maiden conventional flight.

When he was back at the orbital station the following day, he saw Aisha. She was to do her parachute jump from the station to fully qualify as a space pilot.

"One last jump, and I am certified," she said. "See you on Earth."

Later that day, Samir got to know that Aisha's jump had gone fine. The next day, as he floated into the Space Bear taking him back to Vaasa, he had a last look at the long *Eleonore Roosevelt*.

When the space shuttle finally entered the atmosphere on July 6th, he had the feeling of having accomplished his duty.

06: SWEDISH SUMMER
(JULY 2101)

The next morning, when he was back on the WARSEC campus in Vaasa, Samir Benyamina was awakened by knocking at the door of his one-room apartment.

"Samir… Samir…Samir…"

He looked at his smartphone. It was 10:07 a.m. Finnish Time on Thursday 7 July. He finally managed to get up, and opened the door of his room. Standing in the corridor were Sanne and Amina.

He greeted them with a quick hand gesture and said: "Hi, Dr. Amina, hi, Dr. Sanne. Sorry, I slept really badly. The sun is always up in this place, and they don't even have shutters."

"Was it better on the Moon?" Sanne asked

"The lunar habitation modules are all underground to protect us from solar radiation so, yes, it was better on the Moon," Samir answered. "How were your first few months at WARSEC?"

"I'm certified *Basic Safety 1* and *2*," Amina replied.

"I've not been yet into space," Sanne said. "But, as an economist, I am not a priority either."

"We just wanted to be sure you were OK," Amina said. "If you want, you can meet us in the geology department."

An hour later, Samir went to the research building of the WARSEC headquarters and looked for the geology department. When he found it, he was surprised to see that most of the researchers were women, and all extremely good looking and athletic. Damn it, he should have studied geology.

Amina was sharing an office with five other researchers. On the door was a road sign signaling it was forbidden to park dinosaurs. Under it, a caption read: "*This space has been velociraptor free for 2.19 x10^10 days and counting. Don't mess it up.*"

"Let's have a coffee," Amina said. "I will message Sanne, her department is downstairs. We can go on the balcony, there is a nice view over the runway and the awful arena behind."

They went to the balcony and Amina and Samir flopped on to one of the sofas. A fine breeze was blowing, but it was sunny. Samir inhaled and exhaled slowly, so as to enjoy the open air.

A moment later Sanne arrived, together with another woman, a certain Rebecka Levi, who introduced herself as an agronomist. She had been working a lot with Amina on her PhD. Both sat on the sofa opposite Samir and Amina.

"How is space farming going?" Sanne asked the agronomist.

"It's going fine," Rebecka replied. "The first farming deck in the WARSEC ring will be fully operational at the end of November. By next year, we will have even our own orbital-produced wine."

"Orbital-produced wine," Samir wondered. "That must be disgusting."

"It most likely will be," Rebecka admitted. "But it was a special request from Ralf, the director. According to him, he is certain people will be willing to pay a high price for wine produced in orbit. And since WARSEC is all about merchandising…"

"Come on, Rebecka," said Sanne. "We have no choice. WARSEC needs money to finance interstellar exploration and colonization. There is nothing wrong if some people want to buy disgusting but expensive wine."

"You are right," Rebecka admitted. "Stupidity nearly led mankind to its end, but in the end, if human stupidity is properly channeled, it can be used to raise funds to save it. Mankind will, in the end, be saved by its own stupidity. How ironic."

"I love this woman," Amina commented. "Almost as cynical as I am."

"Anyway," Rebecka went on, "We have also installed some farming sections onboard the Forward class ships so that they can grow their own vegetables, fruits, and berries. We will even have some chickens to produce eggs and give them some fresh meat."

"Thank you, Rebecka," Amina said. "That way I will not be

constipated from only eating rice."

"You are going?" Samir asked.

"Sorry," said Amina suddenly. "Yes, I am going to Epsilon Eridani, onboard the *UNSS Ernest Shackleton*. Rebecka will be onboard as well, so we won't starve to death."

"That will be an interesting journey," Rebecka said, smiling.

"Who will be the commander?" Samir asked.

"Your solo-mountaineer friend: Anatoli Govorov," Sanne replied.

"Eamon Windsor, your other friend, will be the ship's doctor," Amina added.

Samir was thoughtful: "Two and a half years…That's quite a long while still."

Sanne decided to change the subject: "What will you do for your holiday?"

"I don't know," Samir said. "I have no mountaineering partner this year. Perhaps I will visit my sister in Umeå, and then my little brother in Poland."

"Hmm, Umeå?" Amina said. "It's on our way to Swedish Lapland."

"Are you going there?" Samir asked.

"We have only one week of holiday this summer, since we started so recently," Sanne replied. "Mikko Andersson, one of the pilots on the Alpha Centauri missions: he's a Swede from Lapland. He recommended we do something called the Dag Hammarskjöld trail. It starts in… Let me check."

She took her smartphone and displayed a map.

"It starts in Nikkaluokta, in the Kiruna municipality and goes all the way to Abisko, on the Torneträsk lake. It's a five-day hike. 120 kilometers (75 miles)."

"And we can take advantage of this tour to summit the northern top of the Kebnekaise, Sweden's highest peak."

"How high?" Samir wondered.

"2,097 meters," Amina replied (6,880 ft).

Samir laughed.

"Don't be an arrogant French climber!" Sanne said. "Did you know by the way that the Kebnekaise was first summited by a French geographer?"

"Exactly," Amina confirmed. "Charles Rabot, in 1883. If it was good enough for him, it is good enough for you."

The following Saturday, Sanne, Amina, and Samir were on the train from Vaasa to Kiruna in northern Sweden. To Samir's dismay, they were accompanied by Mikko Andersson, who obviously had a crush on Sanne, and Anatoli Govorov, who decided to join them at the last minute. They both had their dogs, the big husky, Apollo, and the little brown hairy kokoni, Calypso.

From Kiruna, a bus ride took them to Nikkaluokta, the start of the trail.

In the bus, Anatoli was complaining to Mikko: "These rules are incredible. Because you are a Sami, you can have your

Apollo running free, but because I am not a Sami, I have to hold my Calypso on a leash."

"That's because of the reindeers," Mikko explained.

The Sami people were the native inhabitants of Lapland, spanning Norway, Sweden, Finland, and Russia. Reindeer herding was an important part of both their culture and economy.

"Come on, Mikko," Anatoli said. "Your husky can easily kill a reindeer, my kokoni would just run away. These rules don't make sense."

"We Sami have been discriminated under constant attack by the Swedes for half a millennium, so we can well have these rules." Mikko replied, irritated. "However, since you are my friend, and if we are checked, I will say your kokoni dog is a Sami dog as well."

The first part of the hike was rather uncomfortable, as there were a great many mosquitoes, but as they gradually gained altitude, it became more pleasant. The first night, they camped close to the Tarfalla research station, except that there was no night: the sun would not set.

The weather was still fine the following day, as they made it over what used to be a glacier to the highest peak of Sweden.

"It's only rock," Samir complained. "Not a single square meter of ice."

"Don't blame me," Amina said. "Blame global warming."

To Samir's admiration, the little brown Kokoni made it to the top without having to be carried.

"Russian made," Anatoli explained proudly. "The little Moscow street dog who has been in space, at warp and on the Kebnekaise."

They went down the mountain on its western slope to join the Dag Hammarskjöld trail. Here and there they found some meditation places.

"Meditation…" Anatoli commented. "That's for Ralf Åhman and UN diplomats. Let's get the hell out of here."

Samir was gradually getting to appreciate Anatoli. He was not as useless as one might have believed after his climbing accident in Chamonix. He was still a recipient of the Nobel Prize in Physics. Mostly, he was a true integrationist. He would not bother about anyone's origins or social background before befriending them. He had no problem spending his holidays in a cheap camping site in Chamonix, or camping in the wild in Lapland rather than sleeping in the more expensive cabins.

Samir enjoyed all the more the *Dag Hammarskjöld* trail since they barely had any rain.

"We have been quite lucky," Mikko explained. "It's not usually like that."

"Have you seen the horror movies *The Lone Hiker* and *The Lone Hiker Hikes Again*?" Anatoli wondered.

Samir, Amina, and Sanne all laughed.

"Sure, we have," Sanne replied. "During our Civil

service, in Cambridge."

"Well," Mikko said, "The stories are set here."

"Let's hope we don't stumble upon a serial killer," Samir said.

"Don't worry," Amina replied. "I have done my military service in the Swiss Alpine Rangers. I can handle serial killers."

They all laughed.

Finally, on Thursday 14 July in the morning, they arrived at the Abisko tourist station where they had booked two nights.

After taking a shower, Samir met the two girls sitting at one of the outdoor tables, with five pints of beer on it. The two dogs were attached to the table on a leash.

"We have a beer for you, Samir," Amina declared.

"Thanks," said Samir. "Where are Mikko and Anatoli?"

"I don't know," Sanne replied. "They finally had some network coverage. Both had many missed calls from the WARSEC office."

"Has something happened?"

"I guess so," Amina replied. "We will know soon enough."

A moment later, Mikko and Anatoli appeared on the terrace, both with serious faces.

"What happened?" Sanne asked.

"A car accident, in Vaasa," Mikko replied. "A drunk Finnish driver, assisted by badly coded autopilot software, ran over four of our robot engineers who were mountain-biking."

Samir had always thought that mountain-biking was a stupidly dangerous sport, and this comforted his thinking.

"Is it serious?" Amina asked.

"Luckily," Anatoli said, "there have been no fatalities, and their lives are not in danger. However, they were all four selected for the interstellar mission."

"It causes a problem," Mikko explained. "We still have too few engineers with the safety qualification requirement for an interstellar journey."

"Why?" Samir wondered. "I have them, and I have spent only three months in space."

Anatoli looked gravely at Samir: "You are the first engineer to have passed all the safety requirements in one mission. Glover Johnson is strictly against forcing one's body to the limit. But since he was kept on Earth with his divorce issue, Thierry was fairly free to test how far he could go with you."

"That means Samir could join the expedition?" Amina wondered.

"Actually," Mikko said, "He is number four on the replacement list. He is single, has no children, the right qualifications and very high service grades. But Samir, no pressure, you don't have to accept. And, most of all, you don't have to give your answer now. We need your answer before Monday evening, though."

"On which expedition would I be?" Samir asked.

"We will have to reorganize our crew," Anatoli said. "But you will most likely be with me on an exploration of the Epsilon Eridani system."

"I see," Samir said.

"The departure date is set for September 1st," Anatoli added. "To my knowledge, it has not been postponed. That means that we will go to the orbital station on Tuesday 26 July, in twelve days. We will be back on Earth in February 2104, after a quarantine spent in orbit."

"That means a very short holiday for you," Mikko went on. "If you accept, you will not get any bonus. However, you will have two and half years of untouched salary when you are back. You have just been raised to Level 4. You will be ranked to Level 5 when you come back. That means you will be entitled a two-room apartment, instead of your current pantry."

"Thank you," Samir said. "I will have to think about it."

A moment later, as Mikko, Anatoli, and Sanne went into the restaurant to get some lunch, Amina whispered to Samir's ear:

"If you come onboard the *Shackleton*, I will sleep with you."

07: STAR SYSTEMS NOT FAR AWAY (JUL-AUG 2101)

On his journey back from Abisko, Samir Benyamina stayed in Umeå to spend the weekend with his sister Soraya and her boyfriend.

His little brother Abdelkader had now moved out of his father's home to start his Civil service in Poland. Samir had, therefore, no special reasons to return to Paris. None of his siblings liked Fat Ali. They would just let him die alone. How ironic it must be for his asshole father. Ali had had six children, hoping some of them would take care of him when he grew old. In the end, all six had fled from him. All his siblings were now safe, away from the bad father.

Samir was single and had nothing holding him back on Earth. On Sunday evening, he called Anatoli to tell him he would join the mission to Epsilon Eridani. On Monday, he took a flight to Krakow to visit his little brother Abdelkader.

There, the slavants were not housed in converted containers like in Cambridge, but in construction barracks. They had more space, but Samir felt it was less cozy. His brother seemed to really enjoy it, and by looking at the girls doing their service there, he understood why. On Thursday, he flew back to Vaasa.

As he was leaving for a two and a half years mission, he had to move out of his one-room apartment. He didn't have much, and he stored most of it in Sanne's room. She was, however, less happy to have inherited all the skis and climbing equipment from Amina. Besides, Mikko had somehow convinced her to take care of his dog, Apollo. She did not understand why people would get a dog if they could not look after it.

On Tuesday 26 July 2101, Samir Benyamina, Amina Dörflinger and the rest of the crew of the *Amundsen* boarded a Space Bear to the orbital station at Vaasa Airport. Sanne van der Maas wished them a safe flight. She would be at the orbital station together with Ralf Åhman at the end of August, to assist at their departure.

Onboard their Space Bear was also the crew of the *Amundsen*, who would explore the Tau Ceti system. The crew members were easily distinguished by the color of their flight suits. Anatoli Govorov and Tintin Mutombo wore pink. Eamon Windsor, the doctor, wore blue, Samir wore orange, and Amina light blue. Anatoli had taken his bitch, Calypso, with him. The kokoni dog was now eight years old, but she would go to

Epsilon Eridani with him.

On the eight-hour flight to the orbital station, Samir did not talk much, though he was sitting beside Amina. He was focused on his tablet with his headset.

"You seem nervous," Amina asked him.

"I have to review all the procedures quickly," Samir replied. "I don't have a primary role onboard the ship, but I have to be able to help everybody. Deployment of the telescope, launch of satellites or probe. In case of damage, repair of the structure. What to do in case of a reactor meltdown. It's endless."

"I'll let you study," Amina replied. "I will watch some *Star Trek* episodes."

They spent the next four days at the orbital station, loading their starship and planning a three-week pre-interstellar journey program. Part of the crew had been on the interstellar journey to Alpha Centauri, and Samir was quite relieved to see that he was the most junior engineer onboard. All the others were more experienced than he was.

He was under direct command of Iman Nassirbakli, the chief engineering officer who had been on the *UNSS Forward*'s first interstellar mission. The bald Iranian engineer was level 6 and also served as the *Shackleton*'s XO, or executive officer. He was Anatoli's second in command.

He dispensed Samir from helping with the loading of the ship. He wanted him to review all the procedures he would have to know without being interrupted or disturbed.

Adodoola Agboola, an athletic girl from Niger, was the other robot engineer. She was also Level 4. Iman's team also consisted of two nuclear engineers, Ava Pearson from Canada and Zhinia Bhullar from Pakistan. The two system engineers were Aaron Mizrahi from the Israeli-Palestinian Republic and Andrea Cermak from the Czech Republic. The two structure engineers were Ivo Hübler from Austria, and Pedro Simoes, from Portugal. Rebecka Levi, also from the Israeli-Palestinian Republic, though technically onboard in her capacity as a farming engineer, and answering to Iman, wore the light blue suits of the scientific team.

At the orbital station, there was a simulator to learn how to fly a starship of the Forward class. All the members of the crew were to spend at least two hours on it. They did not have to know how to fly it but should have a passing understanding of the main control panels. The only thing every crew member was required to know was how to stop the warp drive if needed. It was pretty straightforward. They trained under the supervision of the two pilots, Lucy Li from China and Natalia Bielski from Poland, and the two navigators, Gabor Horvath from Hungary and Nu Singh from India.

The engineers' and pilots' space sortie skills were tested one last time by the crew's safety specialists: Hans Doer from Germany, André Dumonteil from France, and James Young, an Afro-American from Illinois.

The medical team was led by psychiatrist Dr. Eamon Windsor from the UK. It consisted of two space paramedics: the Afro-American Dylan Moore and the Caucasian-American Carter Ross, both from Kansas. They took care of the scientific team on a few spacewalks.

Though Amina saw herself as a geologist, she was technically the geophysicist of the team. The geologist role was filled by Dr. Chen Wang from China, who had made himself worldwide known for testing the *beornine* and go into hibernation during the Alpha Centauri mission.

According to the famous videocast by Dr. Eamon Windsor, Chen had allegedly got tired of all the bad movies available onboard. In fact, as he explained to Amina, he had seen it as a good opportunity to lose weight, while doing nothing. Indeed, the beornine he took enabled one to keep one's muscles while burning one's fat during a longer hibernation sleep. One burnt on average one kilo of fat per week spent in hibernation. The issue with the beornine was that one kept aging, though. So if one did not want to sleep one's life away, there was no real advantage of going into hibernation, except if one wanted to lose weight, as Dr. Wang had done.

There was also one planetologist, Dr. Akira Nakano, from Japan. The other four scientists were all astrophysicists: Dr. Dan Singh from India, Dr. Stella Christopoulos from Greece, Dr. Peter Lindqvist from Sweden, and last but not least, the chief science officer Dr. Synøve Solberg from Norway. Dan

Singh, Chen Wang and Synøve Solberg had all been onboard the *Forward* on the Alpha Centauri expedition.

Among the rest of the crew, only Iman Nassirbakli and Dr. Eamon Windsor had past interstellar experience.

On Monday 1 August, they boarded the *UNSS Ernest Shackleton* to start a three-week training period. They first warped to Mars to practice the deployment of the telescope and of satellites.

When Anatoli and his two pilots, Lucy Li and Natalia Bielski, activated the Alcubierre metric, both Samir and Amina felt a deep thrill. They were now true space explorers! When they arrived in Mars's orbit, they were greeted on the radio by Mikko Andersson, who was already there with the *UNSS Forward*. The crews of the *UNSS Nansen* and the *UNSS Amundsen* were meanwhile practicing in orbit of Venus.

In the first week of their pre-interstellar exercise, they practiced launching warpedoes 65 and intercepting them. Radio waves could not go faster than the speed of light in space, which was not convenient for communicating from a star system located ten light years away. As a result, WARSEC had developed the torpedo-shaped drones nicknamed 'Warpedoes.'

While Forward class ships could travel only ten times faster than the speed of light, Warpedoes 65 could travel sixty-five times faster than the speed of light. By traveling at warp 65, it meant they would take only 59 days and a few hours to carry a message from the Epsilon Eridani system back to Earth.

As they were practicing with their warpedoes, Samir had the impression it was like a giant intrastellar ping pong.

The *Forward* and the *Amundsen* orbiting Mars would send their warpedoes to Venus, where they would be intercepted by the *Nansen* and the *Shackleton*, which would in their turn send them back to Mars. Every day, they also had a one-to-two-hour fire drill. Nobody liked it.

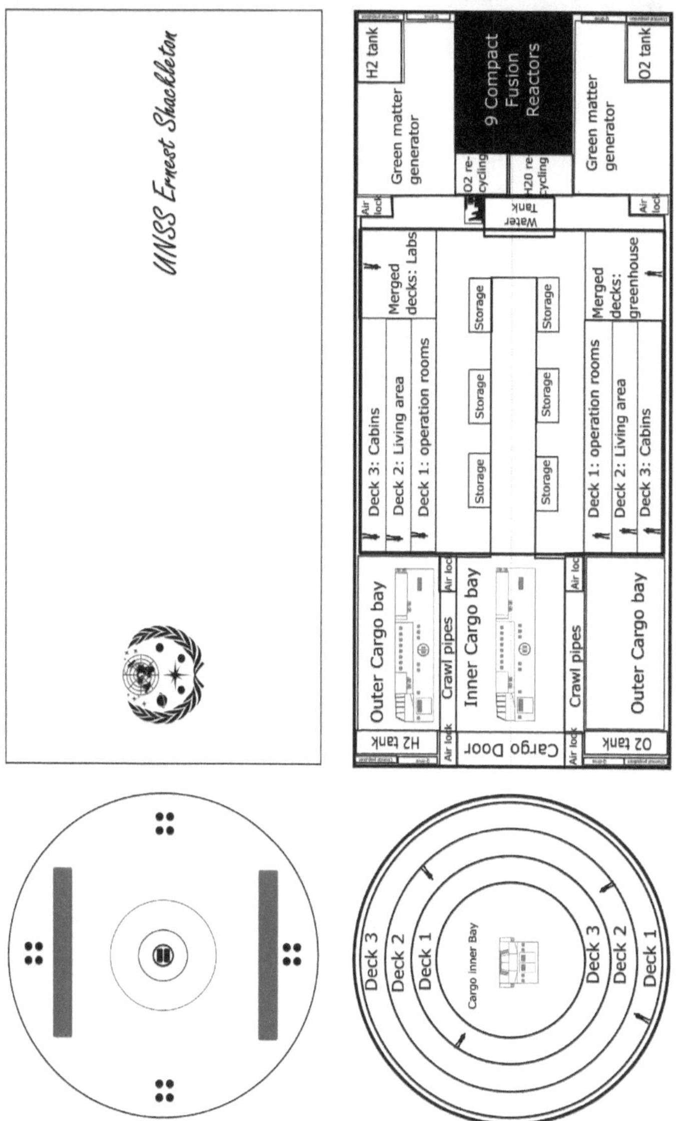

Figure 7: The UNSS Ernest Shackleton of the Forward-class.

In the second week, the *Shackleton* warped to Saturn. This time they were completely on their own, and they practiced what Samir thought was the scariest exercise in his whole life. They simulated a full evacuation of the spaceship after substantial damage.

"Drill... Drill... Drill..." Anatoli said over the intercom. "A meteorite has hit the front of the ship. The 0-G core is depressurized. Four compact fusion reactors damaged. Explosion risk imminent."

As Samir put on his evacuation suit, he saw nuclear engineers Zhinia and Ava calmly turning off the damaged reactors from the operation room, while safety specialists James and André brought them their escape suits.

Iman led the other engineers and the pilots out of the gravity ring and into the 0-G core, through the safety air lock. It was not actually depressurized, but they wore their escape sorties suits nonetheless for training purposes, and floated their way to the cargo bay.

After going through the cargo bay's air locks, Samir and Adodoola each floated their way to the two warpedoes they each had to looked after, while Iman, the two system engineers, and the two structural engineers started loading the two White Parrots with food. Natalia and Gabor jumped in to the pilot seats of one of the Parrots, while Lucy and Nu took command of the second one.

They were soon joined by the two nuclear engineers Ava

and Zhinia, escorted by the safety specialists, all dressed in their space suits.

"The ship is secured," Chief Security Officer Hans Doer said on the radio. "It won't explode in our faces."

The scientific team and the medical team were soon there to board the White Parrots, and Anatoli Govorov, the ship's captain, was last to float his way into the cargo bay.

Adodoola opened the cargo door and floated her way out, steering her fifteen-meter long warpedo. Samir followed her with his. He was happy to be escorted by James Young, one of the space safety specialists.

Outside, Samir did not like it. Some people would probably have liked to orbit Saturn. As far as he was concerned, it was nothing more than a gigantic yellow-brownish gas planet with an aggressive ring. It looked as if it would swallow them all.

The two White Parrots followed them out, and they regrouped. Anatoli ordered Samir to attach his warpedo onto one of the White Parrots, while Adodoola was to send hers to Earth, to inform them of their simulated situation.

"Next step is to retrieve at least one, and at best two nuclear reactors to power the White Parrots," Iman said. "Samir, Zhinia, Ava, André, and Hans. On me."

This was over-cautious. In fact, their ship had two modular EM-drives in the cargo bay, to be used by the White Parrots. The two EM-drives were each powered by a compact fusion reactor. But they had to train for the most complicated scenario and attempt to salvage two of the reactors of the *Shackleton*.

André Dumonteil brought Samir a jet-propelled backpack so that he could steer himself to the front of the *Shackleton*. While Hans Doer and Ava Pearson headed for the side air lock, to come back into the ship, the others headed to the front of the vessel. Together, they worked on extracting one of the ship's nuclear reactors.

The operation was interminable and Samir was constantly gazing at Saturn beneath him.

"You engineers are funny," Synøve said on the wireless. "When you are on Earth, you look at the stars, but when you're in space, you only look at the closest planet beneath you."

She and the other scientists were waiting calmly onboard one of the White Parrots and had nothing else to do than chit-chat with the working engineers.

"What's wrong with that?" Adodoola asked back on the radio.

"Take a deep breath, all of you, and admire the sky in stars."

Samir took a few deep breaths and started looking at the Milky Way instead. He would probably have enjoyed it, if he hadn't been so scared. It was true. When he was on Earth, he would look at the Moon. When he was on the Moon, he would only look down at the Earth. Perhaps he was not as true an explorer as Synøve.

"What I'd rather admire is two salvaged working nuclear reactors," Iman retorted on the radio. "You are disturbing my team, with your poetic bullshit."

"Iman, Iman, Iman," Synøve went on. "Always following the procedures. Even when you are at a party: Beer and wine you're fine, wine and beer, oh dear! You will never have a beer, after a glass of wine."

"Of course not," Iman replied, "I don't want to throw up."

"Red and white, all right. White and red, you're dead," Synøve kept on. "You will never drink red wine after a glass of white wine."

"Of course not, it makes you puke. I'm not Scandinavian."

"What about sex?" Synøve went on. "Do you follow the procedure?"

"What would it be?" Iman wondered, still working with Samir on reactor number three. "Describe it for me, and I will tell you."

"Ooh la la," Zhinia said on the wireless.

"Kissing, stroking, fingering, licking, docking," Synøve replied.

"You know that all the wireless communications could be being recorded on Earth?" Rebecka said on the wireless.

"Who cares?" Adodoola replied. "We will be away for two and a half years, and it will be forgotten."

They finally got two nuclear reactors out of the ship, fully operational. The two White Parrots docked into them.

The engineers could climb onboard the two space-only vehicles to take a break. Samir, Adoodola, Iman, and Aaron went into the White Parrot where Anatoli and half of the scientific team was located.

"Well done," Anatoli congratulated them. "With the compact fusion reactors, and the food stored, we can now wait one year for assistance. Let's now simulate a repair of the ship. If we can save her, it means we can wait three years for assistance, and in a more comfortable environment that these White Parrots."

"Come on, engineers," Synøve said, "Fix that ship. A White Parrot is not convenient for sex, and one year without sex, that would be horror."

"You could not live two days without sex," Iman retorted.

"You, an Iranian, say that?" Rebecka joked.

"What about Iranians?" Iman wondered.

"Everybody knows Iran is the country where people are the most sexually liberated in the world," Rebecka added.

"That's true," Aaron said. "That's the positive outcome of a sixty-year-long regime forbidding sex. It resulted in the craziest country in the world as far as sex is concerned."

"People always do most what they are told not to do," Eamon admitted. "Reverse psychology. It was the same with the UK. Victorian sexless England resulted in the most sex-addicted European nation for a while. Meanwhile, in Sweden, where youngsters were encouraged to have sex at a young age, they barely had any at all."

"That was a very interesting topic," Iman said grumpily. "Why don't we resume the exercise?"

The simulation of the repair of the ship took an eternity. Samir hated it. He had to use his diaper several times. Having glucose and salt water directly injected into one's blood under the space suit as a survival meal was not a wonderful gastronomic experience either. They eventually 'rehabilitated' the ship and placed the nuclear reactors back into it.

The whole exercise took forty-two hours, after which Samir was exhausted. Anatoli was, however, quite pleased. Everyone had performed decently, and talking bullshit was to be encouraged to decrease the amount of stress.

After the exercise, they were granted two days' rest before Anatoli took the *Shackleton* to outer space, a hundred Astronomical Units from the Earth. An Astronomical Unit (AU) was the equivalent of the distance between the Earth and the Sun.

There, again, they practiced deploying their telescope and sending and intercepting warpedoes. The interception was much more time-consuming, as it took longer to locate the received probes.

The *UNSS Shackleton* was finally back at the orbital station on Monday 22 August. As soon as the ship was docked, the whole crew went to the restaurant at the Radisson hotel.

"We'd better enjoy good food while we can," Anatoli said. "We have one week left at the station."

Over the following days, they went through numerous departure checklists. Samir and Adodoola had to check they had enough spare parts to fix all their robots and devices if needed. They triple checked the redundancy batteries and went through their stock of different kinds of powders to feed the 3D-printers.

Once, when she was eavesdropping on them, Amina commented:

"When I hear you talk about iron and aluminum powder, you almost sound like drug dealers."

"We have a lot of different powders, but no cocaine," Adodoola replied with a smile.

As the departure day approached, VIPs started to turn up at the orbital station. The whole senior leadership of WARSEC arrived at the station on August 27th, and Sanne van der Maas was with them, wearing a purple flying suit. "The color of the useless space people," she joked. Glover Johnson was also there with his soon-to-turn-four-year-old daughter Rika.

The following day, the four interstellar crews gathered in the station's large concert room, with concave floor and convex ceiling, to be presented to journalists.

The journalists were reminded that the four crews would only explore star systems that were not very far away.

The *Forward*, under Mikko Andersson's command, would travel to Sirius's binary star system, only 8.6 light years away.

The *Shackleton*, under Anatoli Govorov's command, would explore the Epsilon Eridani star system, 10.5 light years away. The *Nansen*, under Valeriya Limonov's command, would probe the 61 Cyny binary star system, 11.4 light years away. Finally, the *Amundsen*, under Tintin Mutombo's command, would reach Tau Ceti, 11.9 light years away.

Glover concluded the session with a short speech:

"Ladies and Gentlemen, space explorers. Your ships, the *UNSS Forward*, the *UNSS Fridtjof Nansen*, the *UNSS Roal Amundsen* and the *UNSS Ernest Shackleton*, are all named after polar explorers. Like polar explorers in their time, you, interstellar explorers, will be cut off from all human civilization and with no possibility of immediate assistance. You have to remain careful when committed."

"Remember. There are two kinds of polar explorers. The '*Scotts*' and the '*Shackletons*'. In 1911, English explorer Robert Scott led an ill-prepared expedition to try to beat the Norwegians to the South Pole. They did reach the pole, though they came second, and they all died. In 1915, Ernest Shackleton, also an Englishman, attempted a trans-Antarctic expedition. The expedition aborted at an early stage with their ship, the *Endurance*, sinking off Elephant Island. They never reached their objectives, were cast away off Antarctica, but the whole crew survived."

"Survival has to be put ahead of the success of the mission. Returning safe and sound is more important than reaching the stars. In case of doubt, always remember: you will have to decide if you want to be the next Shackleton or the next Scott. The answer should be easy, I believe."

Dr. Eamon Windsor stood up and added:

"And if any of you mess up with the safety procedure, then you will be sentenced to watch Ridley Scott's two movies *Prometheus* and *Alien: Covenant*. Believe me, you don't want to waste an hour of your life watching these movies, so behave!"

The four crews laughed heartily.

Ralf Åhman had booked dinner for all the crews at the Radisson. After the dessert, they were approached by some celebrities. There were actors from the *Star Wars* franchise posing and taking selfies with some of the WARSEC crew. Anatoli and Tintin seemed to enjoy that, but Samir, Amina, and Adodoola kept a respectable distance from all the flashing smartphones.

"You are right," Iman Nassirbakli said. "These celebrities. They don't care about you. They won't even remember your name. They will just tell their friends: 'That's me and a guy going on an interstellar mission.'"

"Samir… Amina…" a voice called.

It was Aisha Barjaoui. She wore a flight suit from the EU Air Force. With a gesture, she invited them to stand up from their table and come with her to the bar. As she walked on the concave floor of the restaurant, Samir noted she was not fully at ease on her artificial legs, at least not on the gravity decks.

Sanne, who had been sitting at the same table as the WARSEC senior leadership, also joined them.

"What are you doing here, Aisha?" she asked, as they were standing by the bar and waiting for four Irish coffees.

"I'm in the VIP space squadron," Aisha replied. "In short, I fly EU politicians around."

"No kidding?" Samir wondered. "Do you like it?"

"It's not that I had a choice, really," Aisha replied. "When our class was graduating from the Air Force Academy, the European president was there. Of course, as I was one of the fifteen new space pilots, I was personally presented to him."

"And he fell in love with you?" Amina joked.

"Almost," Aisha grimaced. "An immigrant woman, former legionnaire with artificial legs and who has, moreover, been awarded the *Dag Hammarskjöld* medal for service on a peacekeeping mission… He insisted on having me as one of his personal pilots."

"Can he do that?" Sanne asked.

"Obviously," Aisha replied. "Not that I'm complaining. I have been promoted to the rank of captain and I fly to a lot of new destinations. I get to sleep in fancy hotels."

"Does the president travel in space a lot?" Samir wondered.

"It's the first time he's come here since I started in July," Aisha replied. "He seemed to like the Space Bear and made it his new EU Flight One."

"I see why we pay taxes," Sanne commented. "Well, if you

want to take advantage of your visit to the orbital station, I can arrange for you to spend time in our simulators. That way, perhaps, you will want to join WARSEC in a few years."

As she took her Irish coffee from the barwoman, Aisha smiled and said:

"Why not? By the way. The EU president is here at the station, but in a fancier restaurant this evening. He will shake your hands tomorrow before you board the *Shackleton*."

Out of the 116 astronauts to embark on the four interstellar missions, thirty-two were from Europe, and EU President Guido Niedling had insisted on greeting them before their departure. They were in the orbital station's concert hall, and it was Tuesday 30 August 2101.

"Hello and good luck, son," the EU president said to Mikko Andersson.

"I don't rely on luck, but on my team, Mr. President," Mikko retorted.

"Good call, son," the president replied

Then he came to Samir.

"Where are you from, son?" he asked.

"Born in Marseilles, raised in Beaudottes," Samir answered.

"I don't know Beaudottes," the President replied. "It must be a nice place. Good luck, son."

At last, he came to Amina.

"And where are you from, miss?"

"They must have made a mistake," Amina replied. "I'm from Europe, but not the European Union… I'm Swiss."

"Who knows…" the president said. "Perhaps Switzerland will have joined the EU by the time you are back."

The very same afternoon, Samir and Amina said farewell one last time to Aisha and Sanne, and boarded the *Shackleton* with the rest of the crew. The *UNSS Ernest Shackleton* undocked from the Station, and the whole crew went through the three-hour-long final departure checklist. When they were ready, they set course for the Moon's orbit, using the EM-drive.

They spent Wednesday 31 August orbiting the Moon together with the three other exploration ships. The *UNSS Eleonore Roosevelt*, of the Ambassador class, was also orbiting nearby.

They practiced one last fire drill and went through two long pre-interstellar journey checklists.

"It's all about following checklists," Amina said to Samir when they had a break. "A kid could do that."

"You say that, because you are here as a scientist; you have almost nothing to do."

"I still take care of the dog," Amina replied. "And you are all happy that I do it."

She had indeed been spending a lot of time with Calypso, the brown kokoni bitch.

The departure time slots had been scheduled between 11:00 and 13:00 UTC on Thursday 1 September 2101.

The *UNSS Road Amundsen*, led by Tintin Mutumbo and bound for Tau Ceti, was first to leave at 11:00. At 11:30 it was the turn of the *UNSS Fridtjof Nansen* and Valeriya Limonov's crew to leave for 61 Cigni.

"OK, we are next," Anatoli said calmly. "Nobody wants to drop out at the last minute?"

Nobody answered.

"OK, I take that as a no. Good. Let's go through the final warp ignition checklist."

Only the nuclear engineers and the pilot team were involved in that checklist. Samir sat back and relaxed at his station, in the 0-G core, close to the front nuclear reactor.

"Hi, Samir, can I keep you company? There is too much tension in the control room."

It was Amina.

"Sure."

"I was thinking of something," Amina said. "There is a lot of empty space on this ship. We should build a climbing gym. At least to do bouldering. We could build it on the greenhouse deck."

"Sure," Samir smiled. "We've got the 3D-printers. I can easily print out some grips if you help me design interesting climbing problems."

"Then," Amina continued, "We have no alcohol on board,

but we grow potatoes and grapes. I'm pretty sure we can find a way to make some vodka and wine."

"Hmm," Samir replied. "You know how to talk to an engineer!"

Amina caught Samir's hand and smiled:

"It's gonna be a good, good trip."

"*Warp in five seconds,*" they heard on the interphone. "*3…2…1…Now.*"

Samir looked at Amina

"And now we are at warp."

"This checklist was much ado about nothing," Amina replied, smiling. "Have you ever tried a 69 in 0-G?"

"No."

"Let's be experimental and try it. We can go into a White Parrot."

"It's gonna be a good, good trip indeed," Samir replied, as he followed Amina to the cargo bay.

08: VIP TRANSPORT
(DEC 2101)

The AF5 Dachshund S-VIP was parked on the tarmac of the EU Air Force base at Melsbroek, north of Brussels, the capital of the European Union. At the beginning of December 2101, a low-pressure front had covered all of Western Europe, and heavy rain was pouring over the cockpit.

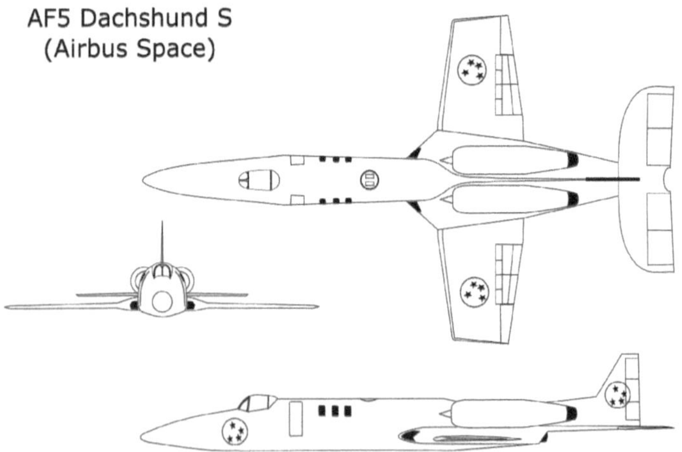

Figure 8: AF5 Dachshund S with the colors of the EU Air Force.

Inside, Captain Aisha Barjaoui was pre-programming the flight computers and reviewing the departure checklist.

"They are late."

Lieutenant Caroline van Groot, from the EU Air Force, was to act as a stewardess on this VIP flight to the orbital station. She was wearing her fine Air Force uniform with a skirt, while Aisha wore a flight suit.

"Aren't you supposed to wear your parade uniform on a VIP flight?" Lt. van Groot asked.

"Yes, in theory..." answered Aisha, still focused on her checklist. "But I don't want to. First of all, I don't have nice legs to show off. "

She thought a short instant about her artificial legs, before adding:

"Then, he is not the president, but only an ambassador. He is not German, but Finnish. And, last but not least, these Dachshund S-VIP are so uncomfortable that I'd like at least to be in comfortable clothes."

"Yes, but they are the fastest aircrafts."

The Dachshund S-VIP was a modified version of the standard European Fighter AF5. It was longer and the fuselage was slightly broader, to allow a navigator to sit beside the pilot. The internal bomb bay had been replaced by a tiny cabin meant to take three passengers and a flight attendant. They even had a small lavatory cabin.

"You've never been in space, van Groot?" Aisha asked

the lieutenant.

"No, captain. It will be the first time. I have only done suborbital flights."

"Next time," Aisha said, "I would recommend you swap your skirt for a pair of trousers. We will be in weightlessness for the majority of the trip, if you see what that implies. Why have they put you on this flight?"

"All our ministers and officials now only want to take space flights. I was redundant on the regular VIP transport squadron."

"Will you receive basic space safety training?"

"Yes, I will be sent to WARSEC next spring. Oh, a car is parking next to us. They are coming."

Caroline went out of the aircraft to welcome the two men with an umbrella at the foot of the airstair.

"Thank you, madame," the older man said when he was onboard.

"Welcome on board, Mr. Ambassador," said Caroline as she was closing the cabin door. "Please make yourself at ease."

The two men certainly mistook the invitation, as they took off not only their coats and jackets but also their ties, their shirts, their shoes and trousers. The ambassador revealed a somewhat overweight body, while the man who looked like his assistant, though he was thin, was clearly not exercising enough, to Lt. van Groot's military tastes.

"I'm sorry, sirs. May I ask you what you are doing?" she asked.

"Putting ourselves at our ease," the ambassador replied. "Changing to more comfortable clothes. The Dachshund S-VIP is uncomfortable enough. Besides, there are no Germans nor French onboard the planes, and all the space people at the orbital station look down on people wearing suits. Always adapt to your environment. That's the key to survival, also for ambassadors."

Aisha rose from her pilot seat and went into the cabin.

"It is my duty to inform you that you have only one pilot onboard," she announced. "Should you require an extra pilot, we would have to wait for another five hours."

"I know," the ambassador said as he got some soft pants out of his trolley bag. "I don't want to wait, that's why I requested this special transport."

"Yes, sir," Aisha said. "Please put your pants on, take your seats and fasten your seat belts, we have a departure time slot in five minutes."

"Yes, captain," The ambassador said.

"We don't have safety instructions?" the ambassador's assistant asked.

"Pretty straightforward," Aisha replied. "The cabin is also an escape pod. In case of an accident, it will release and land with a parachute. We will be with you all the time. Then we will have to wait for the Navy or the Air Force. By the way, I will make a fast take-off, so it's gonna be a bit hard the first twenty-five minutes."

Aisha went back to her seat, followed the engine ignition checklist, called ground control, and started to taxi toward the runway. Conventional take-off was faster than vertical take-off. She would just make a dash for the sky. She was tired of the rain.

"EU VIP 5, you are clear for take-off," a voice said on the radio.

Aisha looked at the time. It was 09:06 UTC. She slowly pushed the two gas throttles forward, and the Dachshund gradually gained speed on the runway.

"V1..." said the flight computer, *"V2..."*

Aisha pulled the side-stick, first gently and then much harder. They took only 6 minutes to reach the altitude of 20 km (66,000 ft) where she levelled the plane. They were far above the clouds, and she smiled at the sun.

"Pilot to the cabin," she announced in the intercom, *"commencing gravity escape maneuver."*

She liked to do the gravity escape maneuvers manually and set the autopilot in stand-by mode. She pushed the side-stick, still at full-throttle. When the Dachshund had reached Mach 3, she switched the CUBIC-R engine configuration to ramjet mode. The acceleration force kept her stuck to her seat. At Mach 6, she ignited the scramjet and started gently pulling up the side-stick. Meanwhile, she switched the CUBIC-R engines to rocket mode. At 60 km (217,000 ft) of altitude, she ignited the rocket engines and, ten minutes later, they had reached

110 km (361,000 ft) and were in weightlessness, bound for the orbital station.

However, she left the rocket engines on for another ten minutes and it was 09:39 UTC when they could, at last, enjoy the silence of space. She eventually switched the autopilot back on.

"Expected arrival time, 12:25," she said on the interphone.

"Well that will be my new record," the ambassador said as he floated his way into the cabin and sat down on the navigator seat beside Aisha. "Do you mind if I keep you company?"

"As long as you don't try to fly the shuttle, sir." Aisha answered.

"You despise me, don't you, captain?" the ambassador said.

"I don't know you, Mr. Ambassador," Aisha replied. "Please remember that this cockpit is equipped with a cockpit voice recorder. Anything we say is fully recorded."

"Only the last thirty minutes," the ambassador corrected. "And the CVR will be listened to only in the event of a crash. What are the odds of a crash, captain?"

"One in a hundred million," Aisha answered.

"I will take that risk," the ambassador said.

"Beware," Aisha retorted. "Some people do win the lottery."

"I know what you think," the ambassador went on. "Again, one of these politicians using an expensive trip to the orbital station, again a waste of the taxpayers' money while your skills could be better used elsewhere."

"I was not thinking at all," Aisha replied. "I'm focusing on flying this aircraft."

"The autopilot does that just fine," the ambassador replied. "I have been appointed EU Ambassador to the World's Agency for the Regulation of Space Exploration and Colonization. For some reason, the new European president has also made this position part of the cabinet. So, I have to commute between Brussels, Vaasa, and the orbital station. Now the AF5 Dachshund S-VIP is the fastest planet-to-orbit shuttle. The president lets me use it."

"We all have good reasons to use a Dachshund."

"I know who you are, Captain Barjaoui," the ambassador went on. "We've met before. You were corporal back then. It was in Kirghizstan, I gave you the *Jean Monet* medal, on behalf of our beloved president at that time, Mme Bonavita."

"Kirghizstan…" Aisha said. "Was it you? I threw that medal away."

"You did?"

"After Khouribga, a hundred legionnaires were given the *Jean Monet* medal for defending phosphate mines against nobody, while refusing to assist their comrades in arms in distress. Fuck the *Jean Monet* medal."

"I don't blame you. Kirghizstan was a finer hour for us. I was the EU Ambassador to that country, back then. I did not play a great role in that crisis, though you perhaps remember that the lights on the ground were suddenly switched off before your gliders landed at the Airport. That was my little contribution."

"What was your name again, Mr. Ambassador?"

"Punainen, Esko Punainen."

"Sorry, Mr. Punainen. I really could not recall your name."

"Call me Esko. Once again, I'm not French, I'm only Finnish," the ambassador replied. "No need to call me 'Mister or Sir.'"

Through the cockpit windows, they could catch a glimpse of the Tarawa Space Elevator, far away.

"I can guess what you want," Esko asserted. "You want to join WARSEC. To be part of the ongoing interstellar exploration."

"Perhaps."

"But you are stuck here with me," the ambassador replied.

"Not stuck. We are flying to the orbital station."

"We can work out a deal," Esko said. "I know the director of WARSEC very well. I can ensure that you get access to some extra WARSEC training."

"I already have," Aisha retorted. "I happen to know one of the junior economists, assistant to the director. I have already been given access to their Forward ship simulator. Forty-two hours of simulator already, I spend so much time in the orbital station shuttling politicians."

"Not bad," the Ambassador replied. "Well, if you become my regular pilot, I will also make the proper introduction to the WARSEC director himself, and ensure you get a hundred more hours of simulator, while allowing you to elude the President's company. In a few years, you can just apply to WARSEC and they will hire you. All you need do is not to tell anyone at *The Chained Palmiped* that I am spending too much of the taxpayer's money."

"There is a cockpit voice recorder onboard," Aisha said.

"I take that as a yes," The ambassador replied.

At the orbital station, Esko Punainen kept his word. While both his assistant and the flight attendant checked in at the Radisson hotel, he led Aisha to the WARSEC ring and found the director's office. Ralf Åhman was there. The EU Ambassador seemed to know him indeed, and they exchanged a few words in Finnish. In his office, Aisha realized that the Space Coordination Center director, Glover Johnson, was also there, as well as the UN secretary-general, whom she had met before.

Hira Dorjee-Sherpa was a blind Nepalese diplomat who had held the highest position in the United Nations Secretariat since September 2094. She had been renewed for a second term and her mandate expired in December 2104. The secretary-general sometimes wore earGlasses enabling her to 'see' despite her birth blindness through electric impulses sent to her earlobes. Not this time.

Esko introduced Aisha Barjaoui to Ralf Åhman, Glover Johnson and Hira Dorjee-Sherpa as a European space pilot with artificial legs who was also a former legionnaire, and recipient of the *Dag Hammarskjöld* medal for her service in Bishkek.

"A legionnaire who becomes a pilot," Glover commented.

"That sounds like a new Eugene Bullard."

Aisha realized she still had not checked Eugene Bullard on Wikipedia. Her Wing Commander in Cranwell had also mentioned him, after she had happened to punch two racist French cadets. She would really have to find out who this Eugene Bullard was.

"Captain Barjaoui," the secretary-general asked. "Your legs? Did you lose them in Khouribga?"

"No, Madame Secretary-General," Aisha replied. "A mountaineering accident. I was in Khouribga, though. I was lucky not to be hurt."

"I remember your voice now," the secretary-general said. "You were the one who gave me the black boxes of the killer drones in my hotel room."

"I don't know what you mean," Aisha lied.

"Don't worry, your secret is safe with us," Hira said. "Even Esko would not say anything to the Europeans."

"You know what I thought of our former president," Esko replied. "Anyway, should the EU Air Force fire her, you would be the first to hire her."

A moment later, Aisha was heading for the simulator rooms. Sanne van der Maas had already ensured she had visitor access shortly after her visit to the station in late August. One of the simulators was free for the next twenty-hours, and she had somehow managed to book it.

While many officials had come to the Orbital Space Station to watch the departure of the *UNSS Eleonore Roosevelt* for a four-week long mission in the near interstellar space, Aisha focused on what mattered to her: practice how to fly a spaceship of the Forward class. She had been hoping for this moment throughout her flight and had studied the documentation the three previous evenings.

She wanted to see if she had progressed. She spent three hours on her own and was quite satisfied with her progress. She was no longer taken aback by the huge mass of the spaceship, which was fifty times heavier than a loaded Space Bear, which was itself thirty times heavier than an AF5 Dachshund S.

"Again, squatting in our simulator room?" a voice asked. "You are from the EU Air Force, yet I am told you are always using the simulator."

Aisha recognized Alice Fù, the Afro-Chinese commander of the mission to Alpha Centauri. Alice had also been the inventor of the green matter, which was used for faster-than-light travel. But Aisha had known about her even before she had become a star. Alice had been the ex-girlfriend of her lover Deng Hoang, whom Aisha had been seing in Casablanca, back in 2094. Alice Fù was wearing the WARSEC pilots' regulatory pink suit.

"I'm Captain Aisha Barjaoui, from the European Air Force," Aisha replied, showing her ID badge. "Sanne van der Maas made me part of an exchange program, granting me partial access to the simulator. This has just been confirmed by Glover

Johnson, and Ralf Åhman gave me full access to the simulator. I may use it as long as there is no training, which is the case now."

"Indeed," Alice said. "There are not many warp pilots left. The others are either onboard the four *Forward exploratory* ships, or on *Eleonore Roosevelt,* or resting on Earth. I guess I am the only one at the station."

"May I continue to practice?"

"I can even practice with you if you don't mind," Alice said.

Aisha skipped dinner that night and checked-in at the Radisson at 02:00 UTC. The following morning, in the windowless restaurant, she went to the coffee machine like a cruise missile. After she had drunk her first mug, her mind became clearer. She spotted the Air Force Lieutenant together with a NASA astronaut, looking as if they had had a less innocent night. The ambassador's assistant was sitting at another table, his eyes down on an electronic tablet. Aisha refilled her coffee mug, found a copy of *The Chained Palmiped* and sat down at a table on her own.

"You don't eat anything for breakfast?"

It was the ambassador, Esko Punainen.

"I have a French breakfast," She replied. "A mug of café au lait with a copy of *The Chained Palmiped.* Interesting articles about that big earthquake in Rome last Sunday. Many lives could have been saved if the mayor had listened to some geologists."

"Christmas holiday approaching, you don't want to scare the tourists, you don't listen to the experts, and hop, 15,000 dead."

"I was in on a rescue mission in Nice with the Legion, after the 2096 earthquake," she said, "Putting bodies in bags, it was not nice."

Esko changed the subject: "Ralf Åhman, the WARSEC director, called me. They would like you to be in the WARSEC briefing room in twenty minutes at most. You may want to eat more breakfast."

09: Space Castaway
(Dec 2101)

Esko Punainen led Aisha to the WARSEC briefing room, carrying with him tons of wiener bread and Danish pastries he had taken from the Radisson. Ralf Åhman, Glover Johnson, the UN secretary-general Hira Dorjee-Sherpa, as well as Alice Fù and other officials from various Space Agencies were there. They all pulled serious faces.

"As you all know," Ralf Åhman started, "One of the missions of WARSEC is to scan space for incoming celestial bodies of significant size, also called cruisers, that may crash on Earth. In that aspect, it seems that we have failed, as we received this morning a warning call from NASA."

A woman dressed in a NASA uniform stepped forward on the concave floor and said: "Last night, our orbital radar spotted an incoming celestial body of a mass of 250 megatons and at a distance of 0.9 million kilometers. Given its current speed and course, we have calculated that it will hit the Earth in the Atlantic Ocean between Iceland and Scotland in about 92 hours. The consequences of such an impact would be catastrophic, causing multiple tsunamis hitting all the coastal cities on both sides of the Atlantic. It would also cover the atmosphere with dust, causing dramatic global cooling, and could also aggravate the planet's volcanic activity."

There was a silence in the room.

"We have no proven methods of diverting such a large asteroid," Glover said. "One of the possibilities that was considered at WARSEC was to send communication warpedoes to the asteroid and have them warp out inside it. It should trigger a seismic quake within, enough to deviate it slightly from its course. This would be enough to have the asteroid miss the Earth, as long as we can do it within the next fifteen hours."

There were some whispers of relief in the room, and Aisha saw Esko Punainen eat another croissant.

"However," Glover went on. "Our four operational ships of the Forward class able to carry warpedoes are on an interstellar mission, and cannot be called to help. The *UNSS Eleonore Roosevelt* of the Ambassador class is currently at warp to the near interstellar space. They will be 500 Astronomical Units away, meaning any radio message would take 70 hours to reach them. We have sent four communication warpedoes. Being conservative, they should be back to Earth orbit twelve hours before the impact."

There was again a silence in the room, and the UN secretary-general took the floor briefly.

"At this distance, a powerful nuclear explosion may still divert the asteroid," Hira Dorjee-Sherpa said. "My staff is, as we speak, calling for an extraordinary meeting of the Security Council behind closed doors. I will ask for a temporary suspension on the ban of nuclear weapons in space and ask the member states in the possession of nuclear bombs if they are willing to assist WARSEC with detonating a nuclear bomb on this asteroid. This will be our plan B."

"Our plan A," Glover said, "will be the *Alcubierre,* the spaceship that tested the warp drive. She is still operational. Her cargo bay cannot contain communication warpedoes, but we can program them to go there on their own. When we are on the spot, we will try to aim at the asteroid as precisely as possible."

"To avoid any panic on Earth," Hira Dorjee-Sherpa added, "We ask you to respect an embargo on all information concerning this incident. Together with the Security Council, we will think of the best timing and appropriate way of communicating about it. Thank you."

When the short briefing was over, Glover Johnson and Alice Fù went straight to Aisha.

"We are currently short on people," Glover said. "Alice is currently our only warp pilot at the station. She told me you do OK on simulators. Our few assistant pilots available are all the bus-driver kind of pilots. I need someone with a fighter pilot background, in case the warpedo technique does not work."

"Can it fail?" Aisha asked.

"It may, unfortunately," he said very quietly. "It has never been tried, and we have no accurate warp technology. The chance of success is less than 10%."

"Why don't we wait for a nuclear bomb?" Aisha asked.

"Diplomacy is not fail-safe either," Glover replied. "Besides, it goes at far below warp speed. Follow me."

Glover Johnson led Alice and Aisha to the elevator, taking them out of the WARSEC ring and into the 0-G core of the station. They floated their way past security to the terminal, where the *Alcubierre* was anchored.

"We triple checked, Alice," an engineer in an orange suit said. "Nuclear reactors fully operational, the recently added EM-drive tested. A bit low on chemical propellant, though. You may want to top up the tank at the Moon refueling station."

"Understood, thanks," Alice replied.

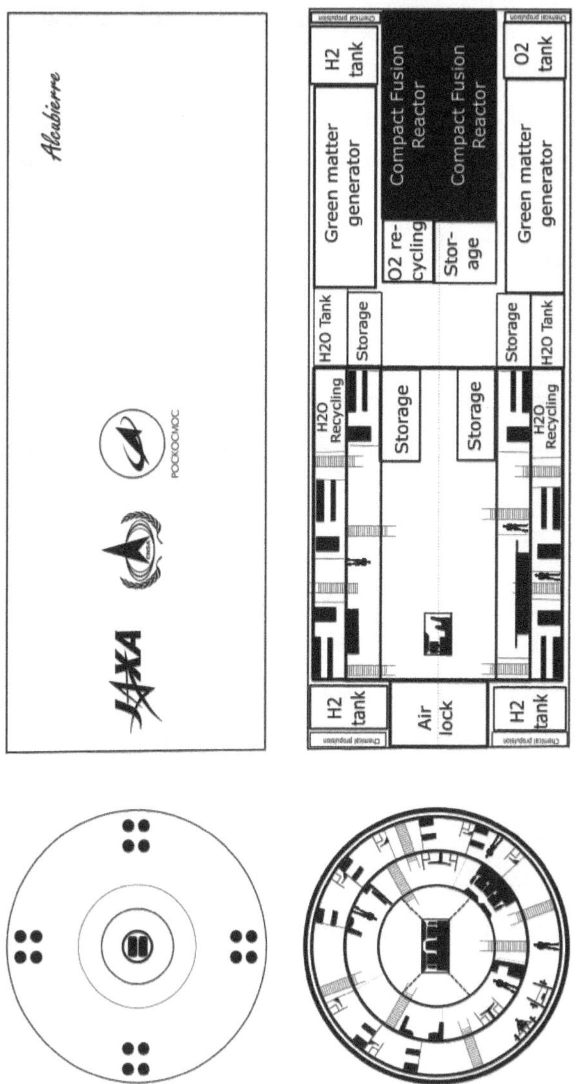

Figure 9: Drawing of the Alcubierre as it was in 2094. In 2100, EM drives were added to it. In 2101 it is still the property of the Japanese, Chinese, and Russian space agencies, not WARSEC.

They boarded the *Alcubierre* through the back hatch and closed down the air lock.

"All right," Glover said. "That's the three of us. We stay in the 0-G core and use the secondary control station here. Alice, you are the commander. Aisha, you are the pilot. I am the nuclear engineer."

"Don't you want to swap your green suit for an orange one?" Aisha joked.

I'm perfectly fine in green," Glover replied. "We should have gotten you a pilot suit, instead of your European Air Force suit."

"I will do just fine,"

They strapped in to their respective seats. In front of them, they could see the window of the reach hatch, and everywhere around, they had screens giving them visual and technical information on the ship and its surroundings.

Alice commenced the departure checklist, and Aisha was a bit slow at the beginning. Both her crewmates showed patience, and Glover was smiling at her in a way that suggested 'rather safe than sorry'.

When they undocked from the station and started using the chemical propulsion to navigate away, Aisha was immensely thrilled. An instant later, they started the EM-drive and orbited around the Earth at full speed to gain enough momentum to reach the Moon.

"That part is like for a Space Bear," Alice commented. "Except that the *Alcubierre* has a mass of 16,000 tons, while a loaded Space Bear has maximum mass of only 350 tons. Always keep that in mind."

"Yes, Madame," Aisha acknowledged.

"Just call me Alice," she replied. "You did well at the beginning. I thought for an instant I would need to retake the control when we were undocking, but you corrected immediately."

"I was surprised by the mass, indeed," Aisha said. "It needed much more correction. I had improved on the simulator lately, but I will keep working on it."

"I will let you do the refill at the Moon station."

They reached the Moon Elevator's refill station six hours later, and Aisha successfully docked the ship without Alice having to take back control. While they were filling up, Aisha cast a glance at the Moon 200 kilometers [124 miles] below. The Moon had been formed from the collision of a planet-sized celestial body with the Earth long ago. Of course, the now incoming asteroid was not the size of Mars, but she wondered what would happen if both Plan A and Plan B failed. It would be a pretty hard hit for mankind. All the coasts of the Northern Atlantic would be hit. That implied, of course, her Morocco, but also France, Ireland, England, and the East coast of the States. She had to remain focused, though.

"Still impressive, the Moon Base," Glover commented. "Think that we are refilling our ship with liquid hydrogen and liquid oxygen extracted from ice at the bottom of the Shackleton crater."

"Yes," Alice admitted. "Mankind is full of ingeniousness when its future is at stake."

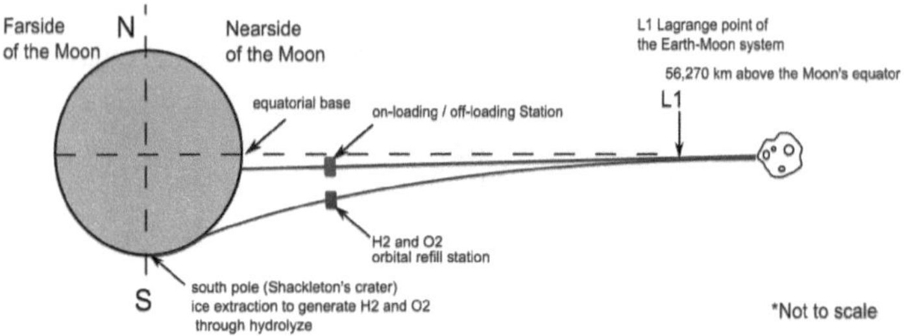

Figure 10: drawing of the lunar base and elevator with the refill station. Based on the work by Wikipedia user Bryan Derksen, but adapted to the story of this book.

When their tanks were full, they undocked from the station and navigated away from the Moon.

"We have a bit less than six hours left, before the success odds of the unproven warpedo technique tends toward zero," Glover informed.

"I have the warp coordinates ready," Alice said. "But we are still a bit too close to the Moon, from a space regulatory perspective."

"Let's break the rules," Glover decided.

Alice looked at her screen and simply said: "Very well, let's initiate the warp checklist."

They all three verified the warp coordinates and program settings, checked the nuclear reactor states and finally, together, pushed their warp handles simultaneously. The warp trip took less than a second and Aisha felt a bit disappointed.

"OK, where is the asteroid?" Alice wondered.

"I have activated the scanners," Glover said. "We also have to find the warpedoes."

"I have spotted four beacon signals," Aisha announced. "Between 5,000 and 20,000 km away".

"Not very precise, these warpedoes," Glover commented. "I see them as well. I will remote control them toward us. Keep looking for the asteroid."

"It has no beacon," Alice complained. "Our anti-collision radars are effective at 10,000 km [6,250 miles] only."

Aisha looked quickly at her tablet.

"We may have overwarped it," she said. "An asteroid leaves traces of water and dust. Our radar will be able to spot its trace within a range of 2,000 kilometers [1,250 miles]. We fly in a zigzag from our current position around the calculated trajectory to the Earth. We will find the trace and follow it."

"We'll do as you say," Alice said. "Please engage in the maneuver, and I'll follow the navigation."

"Copy that."

One hour and twenty minutes later they finally found the traces left by the asteroid, and Aisha directed the *Alcubierre* to follow them. The four warpedoes intercepted and controlled by

Glover were now flying in formation with the *Alcubierre*.

"Celestial body 6,000 km away," Aisha said, pointing out a dot on her screen.

"I see it," Alice said. "Good call, Aisha."

"We will be on it in thirty minutes," Aisha informed them.

"Good," said Glover. "It will leave us a bit less than four hours to warp four warpedoes into it. That should be fine."

Half an hour later, they were flying five kilometers behind and above the asteroid. It was about 900 m long, 500 m wide, and 450 meters high (3,000 ft x 1,600 ft, x 1,500 ft). Aisha had never seen such a large asteroid, and the *Alcubierre*, with its length of only 49 meters (160 ft), must have looked like a pilot fish stalking a great white shark.

"Orbit control. This is the *Alcubierre*," Alice said on the radio. "Target in sight. Commencing the physical experiments."

Nerds on Earth listening to space radio communication were not supposed to understand what they were talking about.

While Aisha was flying the *Alcubierre* steadily behind the asteroid, Glover directed one of the warpedoes to its front left side.

"It's now 50 meters from the asteroid," Glover said. "Damn it, gravitation is pulling it. I'm telling it to warp now."

There was a green flash, and the warpedo disappeared.

Glover raised the eyes from his screen and said: "The warping worked, but it did not come out of warp inside the meteorite. Where is the warpedo?"

"Weird, we should run a scan for it," Alice said.

While Alice was running the scanner, Aisha remained focused on flying the spaceship. Glover was maneuvering a second warpedo toward the front left side of the asteroid.

"I will launch the second warpedo," Glover notified. "Alice, can you check I'm doing it right?"

Alice scanned through the settings and confirmed: "The distance and coordinates are correct. Shoot it."

Glover pressed a button, and they saw the second warpedo disappear in flash of green.

"There seems to have been zero impact again!" Glover lamented. "Alice, can you check?"

"I will need five minutes to run the calculation," Alice answered. "Perhaps there was an impact, but we missed it."

It felt like an eternity, flying behind the meteorite while waiting for Alice's program to return the result. Finally, she broke the silence.

"Zero impact. The two first warpedoes have not caused any seismic quake within the meteorite. They just disappeared."

"Damn it," Glover said. "If only Anatoli or Tintin were here. Or even Mikko and Valeriya! I should not have let all the warp experts leave at the same time…"

"Are they regular communication warpedoes?" Aisha wondered.

"Yes," Glover admitted. "We have never developed meteorite-diverting warpedoes. I guess it will be our next priority, but we need to handle this asteroid first."

"It won't work," Aisha said. "The communication warpedo cannot warp out from within the meteorite if shot at such close range."

"How can you be so sure?", Glover replied.

"They are drones. They have a safety mechanism. If their radar tells them they are being asked to warp on a collision course, they will just extend their warp journey by an extra five hundred thousand kilometers. It's standard safety procedure, even for the Forward class ship. I just read it two nights ago."

"Damn it," Alice cursed. "Aisha is right. I had forgotten it. For our plan to work, we would need to have the warpedo warp into the meteorite from Earth. Their radar would not detect it and not trigger the escape maneuver."

"But we can't do that," Glover objected. "Our warp drive is not precise enough."

"No, unfortunately, we can't," Alice admitted. "I'm afraid we've reached an impasse."

"Let's move to plan A-b", Aisha suddenly suggested. "We just land the remaining torpedoes gently on the meteorite and use their EM-drive at max speed to try and divert it."

"It won't be enough, I'm afraid," Alice said, "But we have run out of options."

"Agreed," Glover said. "Let's proceed. I'll steer warpedo number three, and you steer warpedo number four."

While Aisha was flying the *Alcubierre*, Alice and Glover steered their respective warpedoes toward the front left of the asteroid and landed gently on it. Both warpedoes tried to divert the asteroid as hard as they could, but the celestial body's gravity eventually pulled them out of balance. Aisha saw on the screen how both warpedoes just broke into pieces on the meteorite.

"We must have had at least an impact," Glover said.

"Let me run a calculation of the new trajectory," Alice said. "I will need fifteen minutes."

Aisha put the *Alcubierre* in autopilot mode and drank some water from her bottle. Both Glover and Alice remained focused on their screens, silent.

"We definitely had an effect," Alice said. "The asteroid has slightly deviated its course. It will hit Svalbard, on the Barents Sea, instead. It will still be a nasty collision."

"Shit," Glover said. "We have three hours left to attempt a minimal deviation, and no ¿warpedoes left. Alice, inform Orbit Control."

"Orbit control. This is the *Alcubierre*," Alice called. "The theory is still unproven. Experimentation was a failure."

"What's next?" Aisha wondered. "We wait for the bomb?"

"There is something else we can do," Glover said. "We just need to deviate the asteroid slightly more and have it go over the North Pole. I first want your approval. And we will need to put our space suits on, since the risk for collision will be high."

Glover explained his idea and both Alice and Aisha accepted it, despite the risks involved. Fifteen minutes later, they had all dressed in their space suits and come back to their control stations.

"Orbit Control. This is the *Alcubierre*," Alice notified. "We are testing Newton's law of physics to divert a celestial body. High risks involved. Aware of the commitment."

"Alcubierre, *copy that*," Orbit Control replied. "*Plan B still elusive.*"

"Aisha," Alice said, "Your ship."

"My ship," she acknowledged.

Aisha steered the *Alcubierre* to the left of the asteroid. Once they were flying parallel, three kilometers (9,800 ft) to the left of it, Aisha suddenly turned to go straight toward the front of the meteorite. She rolled the *Alcubierre*, to have the asteroid above the ship. They were flying less than a hundred meters (328 ft) away, and Aisha suddenly pulled the side-stick to do a loop-turn around it. As they were as close as seventy meters (230 ft) from the Asteroid, all the possible alarms on board went off:

"*Terrain! Terrain! Bank Angle! Bank Angle!*"

Once they had closed the loop, they were now back to the left of the asteroid and navigating away. Ralf asked Aisha to repeat the maneuver three more times before Alice could analyze the impact.

"We are back in business," Alice said after a long calculation. "There has been a tiny effect. We managed to apply a force of 700 kilonewtons on the asteroid."

"We will need much more if we are to divert it," Glover said. "Aisha. When you close your looping around the asteroid, can you try to be as close as twenty meters (66 ft)?"

"I can," Aisha replied, "But we will be exposed to a force of 12G. Can the ship take it?"

"Alice?" Glover asked.

"Yes. The *Alcubierre* can handle 30G," Alice replied. "Glover, you may be the first to pass out, though. Our G-suits are rather inefficient when submitted to a force greater than 7G ."

Through his space suit, Glover smiled and commented: "Again, another thing we will have to think of for next time. It's incredible what we learn in times of crisis."

He turned serious and added: "Aisha, do what you have to do. Don't worry about me."

Aisha repeated the maneuvers, looping around the front of the asteroid, trying to be as close as possible on the left side and far away on the right side. After the seventh looping, Glover had passed out. Aisha continued flying the *Alcubierre*, using both the chemical propulsion and the EM-drive to maneuver the ship. Several times, she realized she was only a couple of meters away from collision, and every time she promised herself that she would be more careful with the next pass. After making at least fifty loops, she wondered what the status was.

"Alice, have we had a significant impact on the course?"

Alice did not answer, she had also passed out. Aisha reflected briefly it was quite an advantage to have lost one's legs. Blood could not flow into her feet and she could endure much more G-force than normal people.

She engaged the autopilot and grabbed Alice's tablet to look at it. It was difficult to use with a space suit, but Aisha found the instructions to plot the course of a celestial body using the radar. She skipped the theory and went directly to the practice. Fifteen minutes later, she determined that she had to do between thirty and fifty more loops to complete the diversion of the asteroid. Alice and Glover were still unconscious.

"Let's get it over with," she said, and steered the *Alcubierre* one more time toward the asteroid.

"One loop…" she counted, "two loops…"

Every time she looped around the asteroid, the closer she flew. The closer the better, after all. That was Newton's law. The closer to the gravity center, the higher the exerted force.

It was only physical.

As she was making her forty-second loop, she felt a sudden shock and realized that she had lost control over the *Alcubierre*.

She immediately switched the EM-drive off and activated only the chemical propulsion to try to stabilize the spaceship. In her headset, she could hear all the ship's alarms going at the same time: "*Collision, collision, damaged structure, leaking atmosphere…*"

When she finally understood that the ship had bounced on the front of the asteroid and was now about to crash further back, she used all the available chemical thrusts to brake the impact. Despite that, the shock was incredibly violent. The whole starboard side of the *Alcubierre* was torn apart, and a large section of the habitable ring flew away.

Aisha saw Glover's seat just break away with its occupant on it.

"*Glover, wake up!*" Aisha screamed.

She looked around. The ship had now crash-landed on the asteroid, but Glover had been catapulted away.

She unstrapped herself and jumped into the broken air lock. It was a strange feeling to be moving on the surface of an asteroid as the gravity was hardly noticeable.

She opened the air lock outward, attached the air lock's safety line to her space suit, grabbed two extinguishers, put one under her arm and used the other one to propel herself into space after Glover. It was chemical propulsion all right, she thought.

She understood that the debris from the ship were falling back, though very slowly, toward the asteroid. When she was able to anticipate Glover's trajectory, she used her second extinguisher as a thruster to close on him. At last, she had him.

"Glover, Glover!" she called. "Do you hear me?"

Glover did not answer, but his space suit did not look damaged. Aisha had no propellant left in any of her extinguishers.

"Alice," she called on the radio. "Are you all right?"

No answer. Could it be that they had glided too much to the side and the asteroid was now hindering the radio waves? Aisha decided to wait until they landed on the asteroid. There was nothing else to do anyway.

There were still floating, attached to the cable but very slowly falling toward the asteroid. It took a few minutes before both Aisha and Glover landed softly on the rocky cruiser.

They weighed a ten thousand billionth of what they would weigh on Earth. As a result, it was easy for Aisha to put Glover over her shoulder and head back to the shipwreck, holding the safety line with one hand. She called Alice at regular intervals.

She finally got a reply: *"Aisha, this is Alice. I'm all right. How are you, where are you?"*

"I am with Glover," Aisha replied. "He is unconscious but fine. We are further down on the meteorite. About 200 m (656 ft) away from the shipwreck."

"Do you need help?"

"No, try to salvage what you can on the ship. I'm carrying Glover. Will be there in five or ten minutes. Not easy to walk in this low gravity."

It actually took fifteen minutes for Aisha to bring Glover back to the *Alcubierre.*

"I have some good news and bad news," Alice announced. "First of all, we have succeeded in diverting the asteroid enough from its course. It will pass 1,000 km (621 miles) above the North Pole."

"Then it was not all for nothing", Aisha commented.

"I have informed Orbit Control of our situation. They still have no news from the *Eleonore Roosevelt*, but the *Orion* from NASA is on their way, and they will be picking us up in twenty-two hours."

"Not too bad," Aisha replied. "What about our atmosphere compartments? Are they all broken?"

"That's the bad news," Alice replied. "The *Alcubierre* was never built for interstellar expeditions, only to test the warp drive. Not enough redundancy on it. We will have to wait in our suits, which means we cannot check on Glover's status."

"Glover's status what?" a voice said.

It was Glover.

"You passed out during the loop maneuvers," Aisha explained. "We crashed, and you were ejected out. We got you back, though."

"Good for me," he said. "What about the Earth?"

"The Earth is fine," Aisha replied, irritated. "Apart from that earthquake in Rome killing 15,000 last week, the Earth is fine."

They spent the next twenty-two hours waiting in the shipwreck, chatting and, barely, sleeping. Glover told the two women of his experience in Finnish saunas. As an American, he was still uncomfortable being surrounded by so many naked men. There was always the old Finn showing his gear to his sauna companions. It made them laugh.

Finally, the *Orion* arrived. It was a conventional spaceship equipped with both chemical propulsion and EM-drive. It had a large gravity ring revolving around its 0-G core. The crew of the NASA spaceship dispatched a White Parrot to land on the asteroid close to the crash site. Half an hour later, all three were onboard the *Orion*.

"Welcome onboard, space people," the NASA commander said. "You're lucky the *Orion* has not been decommissioned yet. We are still waiting for WARSEC Ventures to deliver us our first Forward class ship."

"What a day," Glover replied. "First, I am saved by a pilot from the EU Air Force, and now by NASA. That must be a first for someone from the US Navy."

"Hm," replied the commander. "I can smell that you have used your diapers. But I guess that's not a first. For none of us, unfortunately. The changing room is over there."

"Thank you, commander."

"By the way, guys," The NASA commander added. "Nice work. We have still not made contact with the *UNSS Eleonore Roosevelt*. So, I am not sure the Plan B was possible at all, especially since they had still not agreed to let nuclear bombs go into space. The European president, this leftist idealist, opposed it."

Aisha was too tired to have an opinion on the matter.

10: Rail Guns to Orbit (January 2102)

January 6th was a holiday in Finland. They, or at least the few who still did, celebrated the epiphany when Jesus had been presented to the wise kings. On that first Friday of the year 2102, Ralf Åhman believed he ought to celebrate the day when heads of states had been brought back to reason.

In Vaasa, night had already fallen at half past three. In his office at the WARSEC headquarters, Ralf contemplated the artificial light cast on his two cactuses. When he thought about it, he had had them since his time as a student in Uppsala and they were still alive. They had followed him to Cambridge, for his PhD, to New York City, for his debut at the UN Secretariat, to Cyprus, where he had mediated the reunification of the island, to Vienna, where he had been appointed as the director of UNOOSA, and now to Vaasa. Cactuses were quite resistant and could be abandoned for longer periods. The perfect plant for busy diplomats.

He looked through the window. From his office, he could see the lights of Vaasa Airport, and the giant arena behind it. There was no snow. Even in Vaasa, snow would not come before the end of January, these days. Global warming was a real bitch.

January 6th was the day when Finns were said to be the most depressed. The New Year celebrations were over, the Christmas decorations removed, and people's wallets almost empty. He had read the suicide rate in Finland was the highest in the week following that very day.

Ralf was not depressed, though. He was quite happy.

Finally, heads of state had been brought to reason. They had only needed an asteroid.

It had been a hectic three weeks after the meteorite incident. Ralf had been summoned to New York, to explain himself before the UN 4th Committee and also before the UN Security Council.

Why had not WARSEC spotted the asteroid sooner? Because they did not have equipment as good as NASA's. The cost of a proper detection system around the Earth amounted to the cost of three Ambassador class ships. Perhaps was it worth delaying all interstellar missions and building a meteorite detection system instead? The US president had insisted on pushing the current interstellar mission, against the advice of WARSEC. However, with the coming sales of Forward class ships to the NASA, ESA, CNSA, and Vahlroos Travel, WARSEC would soon have the resources to build a decent meteorite detection infrastructure.

Otherwise, UN member states were more than welcome to increase their contribution to the WARSEC budget, but they had reduced it lately. In fact, they had all been lucky that NASA had detected the asteroid in time.

Detection was one thing. Diverting an incoming asteroid was another thing. The method used was not to be attempted again, Ralf agreed. It was a pity, however, that the UN Security Council could not agree on the deployment of nuclear bombs in space.

The US was willing as long as they remained under the control of the US Air Force. An unacceptable proposition, the EU would reply. There should be no nuclear bombs in space. At least not in the control of a sovereign state.

What if WARSEC was to keep the custody of these nuclear weapons? The secretary-general's proposition met firm opposition from the US, China, and Russia: Handing over nuclear weapons to the UN was unacceptable. One could not create such precedent. Hira Dorjee-Sherpa tried another approach: What if the US nuclear bombs deployed in space were under the custody of NASA, rather than the Air Force, would it be acceptable? It would not.

As the representative of the EU to the 4th Committee, Esko Punainen had been quite embarrassed. He had wanted to side with Ralf but he had to defend the position of his president, and

EU president Guido Niedling was firmly opposed to putting nuclear bombs in space, unless they were under the control of the United Nations.

The only time of relaxation in New York had been when Glover Johnson, Alice Fù, and Aisha Barjaoui had all been awarded the *Silver Moon*, a newly created UN award for astronauts. It had had no impact on the tensions between the US and EU presidents regarding the deployment of nuclear weapons in space. In fact, Ralf suspected their confrontation was hiding something else: the EU president wanted to introduce a global tax on capital under UN coordination, while the new US president was firmly opposed to the idea.

The negotiations in New York had been so tense and long-lasting that for the first time in years, Ralf had been unable to spend Christmas in Scotland, at his mother's. Luckily, he had managed to have her come to New York and bring his two kids, Dag and Eleonore, with her. Glover had also been in New York, with his daughter Rika. Christmas in New York was not that bad.

He might have enjoyed it if Dr. Sheldon Cooper had not also checked in at the Radisson hotel and stalked them all the time.

The renowned Texan geologist from Cambridge University had made some new calculations, using one of the seismic models Amina Dörflinger had developed as part of her master's thesis. If the meteorite had crashed on the Italian peninsula, simulation showed that there would have been a 3.7% probability of triggering the eruption of the *Campi Flegrei*, the super-volcano under Naples. It had to be taken seriously: 65 million years ago, the majority of dinosaurs had not gone extinct from the impact of a giant asteroid, but from the subsequent chain eruption of super-volcanoes.

And Dr. Cooper would keep harassing the WARSEC director. By the way, Ralf was partly Swedish, wasn't he? Did he happen to know scientists working at the Swedish Academy of Science? It would be great if he could intercede a little bit. It was about time geologists be rewarded with a Nobel Prize in Physics.

Dr. Sheldon Cooper had been a pain in the brain, all along. Ralf Åhman had, however, found a way of using him before the 4th Committee of the UN General Assembly. After Dr. Cooper's exposé, a first consensus had emerged: *they had to do something!*

Eventually, Tatjana Aydemir had come to the rescue. The Lunar Coordination Center director had been on the test mission of the *UNSS Eleonore Roosevelt* and had missed most of the crisis. She had come to New York only after spending Christmas with her family in Germany. She would never put her professional career ahead of her personal life, and she was certainly right.

Before the 4th Committee, she put forward an interesting reasoning. According to her, there was no need to put nuclear weapons into orbit. Instead, they would have to design new warpedoes specially meant to divert asteroids, and that could be achieved in less than two years with their current technology. The probability of being targeted again by an asteroid of that magnitude within two years was asymptotic to zero anyway. She had been applauded for a long time.

She had taken advantage of the opportunity to put forward the danger of smaller asteroids. It was not an issue for people on Earth, since smaller meteorites usually burned up during their atmosphere entry. But it was for the orbital station. So far, the orbital station had been zigzagging to avoid incoming smaller meteorites. As it was being expanded, escape maneuvers had become more and more complicated. Not to mention the Lunar Base, which was under regular bombardment from smaller asteroids.

What had she had in mind? There came her suggestion: They should equip both the lunar orbital base and the orbital station with rail guns.

Rail guns? Guns with magnetic rails able to launch projectiles a few hundred kilometers away with terrible kinetic energy. They were in use in most of the navies of this world and, most importantly, were recoilless, a must when handled in space.

Ralf had never previously taken Tatjana's concerns seriously, though she had a point. Her exposé had triggered a new negotiation race, facilitated by the UN secretary-general.

Finally, on January 4th, the Security Council and the 4th Committee had agreed to let the UN's space agency deploy rail guns on the orbital station. Within two years, both the Earth and its orbital installations would be fully protected from incoming celestial bodies.

A diplomatic feat Ralf had never dreamt of being possible. However, the fact that even US President Barry Silverbane had sided with the UN resolution was not the mere result of the random functions of the universe. Ralf knew whom he had to thank. He took out his laptop and started drafting an email.

Dear Mr. Vahlroos,

I thank you for your best wishes for the New Year and wish you likewise. I have heard what you did to inform your president, Mr. Barry Silverbane, of the true benefits of letting WARSEC deploy rail guns in space.

Vahlroos Travel and V-Space are, after all, stakeholders of the orbital station and the lunar hotel and will benefit from the deployment of the new rail guns. I am forever grateful for your duly informing the US President

.

It seems, after all, that in space, cooperation truly shows its superiority over competition. If the Earth was spared by a meteorite last month, it was only thanks to international cooperation: NASA radars detected the incoming asteroid. WARSEC used a spaceship manufactured by the Russian, Chinese, and Japanese space agencies. The pilot handling the maneuver was from the EU Air Force.

Cooperation is in the air, and I sincerely hope that our future partnership will flourish. WARSEC Ventures will deliver the first Forward class ship to Vahlroos Travel in March this year (apologies for the four-week delay), and I wish you all the best for your new touristic lines to Mars and Venus.

Best regards,

Ralf Åhman
General Director
World's Agency for the Regulation of Space Exploration and Colonization
WARSEC Headquarters
FI- 65380 Vaasa
Finland – European Union

Informing was the politically correct word for *lobbying*. Ralf had absolutely no idea how much money Michael Vahlroos had spent on lobbying President Silverbane to side with the other UN member states about the rail guns, but he was happy about it.

As a UN diplomat, though, he could not just openly thank a CEO for lobbying a US president. That was against the code of conduct of UN personnel. Hence, the neutral wording.

11: CYLINDRICAL YEAR
(SEPT 2101 – SEPT 2102)

The first two months on board the *UNSS Ernest Shackleton* had not been as calm as both Amina Dörflinger and Samir Benyamina had imagined a space cruise would be. The captain, Anatoli Govorov, had insisted on having an incident simulation every second day. It did not stop the two former Cambridge climbers having a good time, though.

A ship of the Forward class was meant to transport up to 120 passengers and crew, and there were in total thirty-eight rooms. This was more than enough for the 29 crew of the *Shackleton*, and it had taken only one night for Samir to move into Amina's room.

Both had decided not to grow fat as was often the case when people were on longer expeditions, be it an interstellar journey or a submarine cruise with the US Navy. Each member of the crew was required to spend at least one hour daily in the gym, but Amina and Samir would spend at least four hours working out and bouldering every day. It had taken them only two weeks to build up a quite decent climbing gym in the greenhouse, where vegetables and fruits were grown.

The climbing gym had been much appreciated by the rest of the crew, and Anatoli, the captain, often trained there, as his kokoni dog, Calypso, could use the artificial garden for her personal needs.

Often, Rebecka Levi, the farming engineer, would be working in the room while they were climbing. She was not, however, technically an engineer and she wore a suit of the same light blue color as Amina, the color of the scientists. Both Samir and Amina witnessed how a romance developed between Rebecka and Anatoli. Good for them, Amina thought.

When she was not working out, Amina was working together with Rebecka on modelling a system to optimally force an oxygenation event on a planet with a carbon dioxide-based atmosphere and the presence of liquid water.

Amina was reasonable enough *not* to believe that an exploration mission might find a planet with such conditions in her lifetime. As far as she was concerned, humanity was more or less doomed to go extinct, and it really did not bother her at all. It would not be the end of the world, only the end of mankind. And so what? The Tyrannosaurus Rex had ruled on the Earth for about two million years. Mankind would for less than a quarter of million years. Geologically speaking, we, *Homo sapiens*, were losers. We just had to accept it.

However, Rebecka seemed much more idealistic. Though she had quite a cynical view of mankind and religion, she did believe that the only goal of mankind was the same as any other species: survival. If it meant traveling around the galaxy in the search for a suitable planet, she would do it, whatever the odds of success.

While Amina was on a scientific space cruise mostly to have fun while getting paid, Rebecka was genuinely there to try and save mankind. She would spend hours in front of her computer, reviewing the models Amina had proposed in her PhD.

Amina was not really willing to help and waste time reviewing data models, but she did it nonetheless. After all, Rebecka was a sarcastic atheist like her, and if sarcastic atheists stopped helping each other, it would be the end of civilization, which she did not really mind, as long as it was after her own death.

While Amina was spending too much time in front of her computer for Samir's taste, he engaged in more productive activities. As a robot engineer, his main duties would start after their arrival in the Epsilon Eridani system. Meanwhile, he was only tasked with keeping the 0-G core clean (one hour's work a day with robots helping) and spending a six-hour watch every second day in the operation room. He also had to revise for a few hours a week the procedures he would be needing after their arrival at their destination. But he could dispose of the rest of his time as he liked, and he did.

By the fourth week of the journey, he had transformed his now unoccupied room into a home brewery, and he had manufactured all the components he needed to distil his own vodka and ferment his own wine.

Wine was the easiest to make. From the grapes he collected in the greenhouses, he would make juice, pour it into a sanitized large bottle with sugar and yeast, shake it and add some more sugar again. In the greenhouses, they were growing both red grapes and white grapes and Samir made some attempts to produce white wine, red wine, and even rosé, by pressing the red grapes more delicately.

By the middle of November, he had produced two hundred liters of red wine (53 US gallons), a hundred litter of white wine (21 US gallons), and twenty liters of rosé wine (5 US Gallons). He had expanded his workspace to two other empty rooms where he stored all his bottles.

He decided to take it more slowly as more and more in the crew were wondering what was happening to the red grapes, though he had noted they all preferred to eat the green grapes instead. Both Amina and Rebecka were aware of his activities, but Rebecka would not report it to Anatoli.

From November and onward, Anatoli had stopped organizing frequent incident simulations, and Samir had more time to experiment distilling his own vodka. Nobody missed the potatoes, and he could continue with his experiments without being worried. By the end of December, he had five liters of vodka at his disposal.

Overall the first four months of the journey went rather well, and there was a very good ambience onboard. Dr Eamon Windsor noted that sexual relationships were more stable on this journey than on his previous expedition. Engineers, however, complained they had all too often to clean inside the White Parrots, which were regularly stained.

As a trained cook, Samir had got used to preparing meals for Rebecka and Amina, who were constantly working, as well as for his engineer colleague Adodoola, who was now having an affair with the doctor. Eamon and Anatoli soon became aware of Samir's cooking skills and wanted him to cook a real meal for the whole crew at least twice a week.

Samir did not mind, and Eamon noted that having good socializing dinners made of fresh food onboard was excellent for the morale of the crew. It was definitely better than dry food.

The crew had time to watch some old space movies, like the 1968 movie *2001: a Space Odyssey* by Stanley Kubrick, or the 1972 picture *Solaris* by Andrei Tarkovsky.

Before the start of each of movie, they were shown an information notice meant to make them aware of the untenable population growth, as decided by a UNESCO treaty: *This movie was made in 1968. Back then, the world population was about 3.7 billion. In 2101, the world population is about 10.5 billion.*

Of course, the astronauts were well aware of that and would

instead discuss the true content of the movies at dinner.

As he was putting risotto into his plate, Anatoli said: "You have in front of you one of the men who invented warp travel. You're welcome. Without him, we would all become crazy like in *Solaris.*"

As he poured some water into his glass, the MD, Eamon Windsor, said: "To come back to *a Space Odyssey*. I'm happy we don't have artificial intelligence computers onboard like this Hal. It's a creepy machine."

"It's never gonna happen," Samir said. "Artificial intelligence cannot end up with a robot computer like Hal. Look, in 1968, they thought it would be the case in 2001. In 2016, scientists believed it would happen around 2078. We are still waiting."

"If things go wrong in these movies," Adodoola said, "It's mostly because of the composition of crews. They are all straight white males. Impossible to have a happy ending."

They all laughed. Astronauts used indeed to have a deep male supremacist culture, back in the 1960s. Fortunately, the situation had evolved.

On December 31st, as they were celebrating New Year 2102, they rapidly ran out of the four bottles of Prosecco that had been saved for the occasion. Samir surprised everybody by bringing forth a couple of bottles of red wine.

Anatoli wondered where they were from, and Rebecka explained that they were part of a homebrewing experiment, that she, as an agronomist, had sponsored.

The WARSEC director had indeed asked for wine production in space, to sell it to rich tourists at the orbital station. Rebecka believed that wine produced onboard the *Shackleton* and having been in the Epsilon Eridani star system could certainly be sold at an even higher price on Earth.

Anatoli and Eamon asked to see the stock, which Samir unwillingly showed them.

Anatoli laughed: "We will need to produce much more of it if we want some bottles to make it back to Earth."

By February 2102, Amina had much more free time, as Rebecka was now fully satisfied with their final developed model. She and Samir spent more time at the gym and started to watch more movies.

One week, they decided to watch only old mountaineering movies. First, they watched *Nordwand*, a German movie from 2008. At the start of the movie, they were informed, in accordance with the UNESCO convention, that the story was set in 1936, and that, back then, the world population was 2.2 billion. They were now in 2102, and the world population was 10.5 billion. The movie was very good and extremely realistic, for both Samir and Amina.

"Well, I don't want to climb the North Face of the Eiger," Samir concluded at the end.

They then watched *Touching the Void*, a 2003 movie based

on the book by Joe Simpson (the story was set in 1985 when the world population was 4.8 billion, they were told).

"We should go climbing in South America when we are back," Amina suggested.

Next on the list was a 2000 film called *Vertical Limit*, set at a time when the world population was 6 billion. It was so bad that they decided not to waste their time watching it to the end.

"What bullshit," Samir said. "They are supposedly at an altitude of 7,000 m, and they run like crazy with explosives. Even when I was smoking cannabis, I could not have thought of something that stupid."

"They don't follow proper safety procedures, and just cut ropes here and there," Amina complained. "How could the producers find the money to fund their crap movie?"

Another movie they watched was the 1961 war film *The Guns of Navarone*, with a story set in 1943, when the world population was only 2.3 billion, the UNESCO label informed them. This was not a mountaineering movie in itself, but there were some climbing sequences. Both Samir and Amina thought it was hilarious.

"Incredible," Samir said. "The main character, Keith Mallory, is supposedly the best mountaineer of New Zealand, and have you seen how he climbs the cliff? He puts some bolts in, but use them as handles, instead of clipping the rope into them. He never belays himself a single time. No wonder they had an accident. I will think twice before I take a kiwi on my rope team."

"The best part is at the end," Amina added, "after they have booby-trapped the blockhouse and escape with the rope. Instead of abseiling down elegantly like any self-respecting alpinist, they just climb down the rope like constipated kids."

Time went by onboard the *Shackleton*, and Samir spent more time working on alcohol production. The doctor had, however, rationed the alcohol consumption to one liter of wine per person per month, so that they would have some left after their return. Samir had been promised sixty percent of the profit, provided they managed to make any.

Eamon and Anatoli thought that he should use the money to open a restaurant on the WARSEC campus when they were back in Vaasa. They both would be happy to invest in it.

On that day of July 2102, while doing his watch in the operation room, Samir was dreaming of what his life could be, back in Vaasa, after he had been granted a two-room apartment and owned a restaurant of his own. He would be like a king. He would have come up from being a little drug dealer in Beaudottes to being a legitimate restaurant owner in Vaasa. That would be too good to be true.

"*Too hot! Reactor 3 too hot!*" an alarm warned.

Samir looked at the control panel, and at Gabor Horvath, the pilot he was doing his watch with.

"The coolant in Reactor 3 has stopped working," Samir

said calmly.

"OK. Calm. The reactor should shut itself down," Gabor replied. "We are fine on eight reactors for a while. Ava and Zhinia will fix that one.

"It has not shut down," Samir said softly." For some reason, the deuterium is still being supplied to the reactor. I will shut it down manually."

Samir pressed four buttons.

"Weird," he noted. "The manual shut down does not seem to have worked. Deuterium keeps pouring in. We have an explosion risk. We should abort the warp journey and eject the compromised reactor."

"Calm down, Samir," Gabor replied. "This might be an error on the control display. I will wake up our nuclear engineers. Ava and Zhinia will know."

"I don't think we have the time," Samir objected.

Samir watched Gabor stand up from his seat and go to the stairs taking him to the room deck. This was not supposed to happen, Samir thought. The probability of having a CFR failure during their journey was assessed to be less than one in a million. The fusion reactors had been ignited for more than twelve months. Were they on the wrong side of the statistics?

He looked at the clock. The alert had started twenty seconds ago.

He peeked at the navigation map. The probability of having a celestial body in this area was said to be close to null.

He glanced at the secured handle to stop the warping and again at the warning indicators and the clock.

Now twenty-seven seconds since the start of the incident.

Was it really a failure of the instruments, giving wrong information? When he was climbing, he was always extra careful. Why would he gamble now? Because a pilot, allegedly more experienced, was telling him everything was fine.

Thirty-two seconds had gone.

Fuck it.

Samir pressed the master alarm button, and its strident sound filled the whole ship. He opened the box protecting the warp handle. He grabbed it and called on the intercom:

"CFR malfunction. Risk for explosion within twenty seconds. Coming out of warp. Full emergency."

He pulled the warp handle. They were still alive. They had come out of warp and not crashed into an asteroid. He pressed quickly on a few buttons to turn on the auxiliary power unit and opened the box with the button to eject compact fusion reactor 3, and turned the safety key.

"About to eject reactor 3," he announced in the intercom. "Power disjunction expected. Brace for impact. Three… two… now…."

He pushed the button. The failing reactor was ejected. It had worked! They were safe.

Except that the sudden shortage of power supply affected the electricity dispatcher. The ejection had caused a sudden power failure.

To Samir's relief, the auxiliary power unit started normally, but it was only meant to supply the strictly necessary systems.

As a result, the magnetic rail powered gravitational decks slowed down until they came to a halt. The habitable rings were now in weightlessness.

As he had had time to strap himself to his seat, Samir had managed the transition pretty well but, hearing the cursing and screaming, he understood that some in the crew had had no time to prepare. He was the only one in the operation room, and he had to fly the ship. He activated all the radars to scan for incoming objects and hoped a pilot would soon turn up, to do an escape maneuver if necessary. He had done two hours of simulator and was in no way able to avoid a collision with a meteorite.

"Fuck, Samir. What have you done?"

It was Gabor, who was now floating back into the control room, now in weightlessness. He was bleeding slightly from a cut on his forehead.

"You caught me when I was on the stairs," he said. "Why have you ejected the reactor?"

"It was compromised," Samir explained. "It was too high a risk."

"We don't know that," Gabor said. "Look at the screen. Has the reactor exploded?"

A second later, they saw it explode in a huge flash of white.

"Sorry, Samir," Gabor apologized. "You obviously did the right thing."

"Reactor 3 has exploded ten kilometers from the ship," Samir said on the intercom, "Reactors 1 and 2 and 4 to 9 are still operational. The transformers have been damaged."

They soon heard the captain giving instructions over the intercom. "*Ava, Adodoola, Aaron, and James, you fix the transformers,*" Anatoli was saying. "*The others, let's regroup in the 0-G operation room. Samir and Gabor, you join us, while Lucy, Natalia, and Zhinia fly the ship from here, in the secondary control room.*"

A moment later, Samir and Gabor joined the others in the 0-G operation room, just behind the main oxygen recycling unit and the nuclear reactor compartments. Lucy Li, the first pilot, was sitting on the captain's chair, while Natalia Bielski, the second pilot, sat in the pilot's chair. Zhinia Bhullar, one of the nuclear engineers, sat on the engineer's seat.

"Iman," Anatoli said. "You inspect the ship with Pedro and Ivo, while I check on the transformers with Samir. Gabor, you look bad. Let Eamon check you."

Iman Nassirbakli, the chief engineering officer and XO, gathered the two structural engineers, Pedro Simoes and Ivo Hübler:

"Ivo, you inspect the gravitational deck. Pedro, the green

matter generator and the front. I'll inspect the core and the cargo bay."

While the structural engineers set to their respective tasks, Samir and Anatoli went into the nuclear reactor compartment, at the front, where the other engineers were working on the transformers.

"It was quite a powerful electric shock," said Ava Pearson, the other nuclear engineer. "The transformers completely burnt out. Aaron is getting the spare parts."

A moment later, the Israeli-Palestinian system engineer, Aaron Mizrahi, was back with all the kit to replace the transformers.

"It should take maximum an hour to change them."

"Good," Anatoli said. "Samir, you help them. James, you come with me. I now want the safety specialists to inspect the outside of the ship."

While Samir, Adodoola, Ava, and Aaron were working on the transformers, the chief security officer Hans Doer and his two safety specialists, James Young and André Dumouteil, did a space sortie to inspect the fuselage of the ship.

It took a whole two hours to restore the main power supply, and another hour and a half before the structural engineers gave their green light for the restarting of the gravitational decks. Four hours after the start of the incident, they all had a debriefing session in the main control room, on the now working again inner gravity deck.

"The ship is fine," Iman announced. "No detected structural damage inside or outside. The main power has been restored, and the electricity infrastructure has been rechecked."

"We have four lightly injured crew," Eamon informed.

"Good," Anatoli said. "Do we know why the deuterium kept filling the reactor after the coolant stopped working?"

One of the nuclear engineers, Ava, said: "Since the reactor has exploded, we will never know for sure. Was it the automatic valve that was broken, or was it the electronic signal to it?"

The XO, Iman Nassirbakli asked her: "Have you checked the other reactors?"

"After we fixed the transformers, I tried manually switching on and off the valves on all remaining reactors, and it worked.

"OK," Anatoli said. "From now on, I want you to design a routine to test the shut-down of one reactor every third of fourth day. Each reactor should be tested monthly, instead of yearly. I'm becoming paranoid."

"Sure, Anatoli," Ava acknowledged.

"Samir," Anatoli went on. "You did well, but next time it happens, press the master alarm button at the first alert."

"Yes, Anatoli," Samir replied.

"The question that remains is: what we do next?" Anatoli asked the crew. "With eight reactors, we can still continue to Epsilon Eridani. Or we may abort the mission. Who wants to return to Earth?"

Samir raised his hand. Samir was surprised to see that he was the only one in the crew who wanted to turn back to Earth.

"Samir, you want to abort the mission?" Anatoli asked.

"Remember Glover Johnson?" Samir answered. "I'd rather be a living Shackleton than a dead Scott."

"I understand your position, Samir," Anatoli said. "If a single one of us wants to abort the mission and return to Earth, then we will do it. However, I can understand that we are now all emotionally charged. So, we shall have this discussion again in three days. In the meantime, I want a standard orbital watch. We never know, there might be some asteroids or comets, and we should avoid them."

Later that day, Synøve Solberg, the head scientist, tried to convince Samir to continue.

"You know, Samir," she said. "That thing with Shackleton. That's bullshit. Yes, he rescued his crew from the *Endurance*. But then he perished anyway during another expedition."

"Of what?" Samir asked.

"Of heart failure," Synøve answered. "He was overdoing things, took no rest, was too stressed. It did not pay off in the end. It's not because our ship is called the *Shackleton* that we have to overdo things. We live in much easier times anyway. I'm only an astrophysicist. Do you really think I would have joined if it was dangerous?"

"You have no idea how close to a catastrophe we were,"

Samir replied.

That night, as he was lying in bed with Amina, she said:

"In mountaineering, when one guy falls into a crevasse and is being held by the rope team, he often wants to abort the whole climb. And that's fine. If you are emotionally shocked, you can't attempt a climb the same day without putting lives at risk. Now it's different. It's a two-and-a-half-year mission. We cannot attempt a new climb in three days. This is our life's expedition. We will probably never do another one after this."

"You don't understand," Samir retorted. "I am the one who pulled you all out of the crevasse, and you have not even realized it. Gabor performed poorly. He did not want to abort the warp and eject the CFR. I kind of disobeyed him. He was over self-confident."

"You have not told us about it," Amina said.

"Of course not," Samir said. "There is no reason to tell everyone and increase the stress level of the crew. We should not bully him either. I gave him my feedback directly, and I told Eamon and Anatoli, that's all. But still, I don't want to continue. Or I may die of heart failure like that poor Shackleton."

"You are tense, Samir," Amina said. "Let me help you relax. I will give you a massage. Think of the wine you have produced. It is not worth anything unless it has been in another stellar system. If we turn around now, you will not be able to start a restaurant."

The next day, Samir said that he was in favor of continuing the expedition, and the *UNSS Shackleton* resumed her warp journey toward Epsilon Eridani

12: 10.52 LIGHT YEARS AWAY (SEPT 2102 – DEC 2102)

The *UNSS Ernest Shackleton* came out of warp on Saturday 27 September 2102, one year and four weeks after their departure from the orbital station. All were a bit nervous before the warp-out, but the arrival position was located 100 Astronomical Units from Epsilon Eridani, and there were no comets.

They spent four days looking for the warpedoes sent from Earth while scanning the surrounding space with their deployable telescope. When they finally retrieved the two warpedoes, they were delighted to have some news from Earth that was only two months old. There was no Italian onboard the Shackleton, but they were all shocked to learn that Rome had been devastated by a terrible earthquake in December the previous year. 16,587 dead. The Colosseum had collapsed.

They were also quite surprised to learn about the meteorite incident.

"Damn it," Anatoli exclaimed. "They crashed the *Alcubierre.*

I liked that ship. I built it."

"You should be happy they stopped that asteroid," Eamon corrected.

"It was not a reason to crash the *Alcubierre*. It was not even the property of WARSEC."

Apart from the Rome earthquake, the meteorite incident, and the coming deployment of rail guns in space, not much worth noting had happened on Earth. Synøve Solberg noted that Denmark had won a gold medal in ice skating at the 2102 Winter Olympics in Interlaken, Switzerland. It was the second time the Danes had ever won a Winter Olympics medal. Their first one had been a silver medal in women's curling, obtained in 1998, in Nagano. The Swedes had performed very poorly while the Norwegians had won most medals. Synøve was satisfied.

They had also received some recent movies, and most were eager to watch the latest James Bond, especially Eamon Windsor, the doctor.

"The new James Bond has some south Asian origins like me."

"He's a real chameleon, that James Bond," Amina replied. "Always changing color. First, he was white and dark-haired. Then he suddenly became blond, then dark again, then black, then red-haired. And now, half-Asian"

"What's funny," Samir said, "is that he is now changing employer for the third time. OK, three times in 150 years, it's reasonable, but still. He used to work for the UK and MI6. Then he moved to the Military Intelligence Service and the EU. Now, he works for a special crisis headquarters of the United Nations I am not even aware of."

"It's because it does not exist," Anatoli said. "The UN does not have spies in service with the right to kill. But it sells more globally if any nation on Earth can identify with James Bond."

"When shall we watch the movie?" Eamon asked.

"Not now," Synøve said. "We have just analyzed the data collected by the telescope, and we got some interesting findings. We should continue the mission, and we will have one year and three weeks to watch it as many times as we want on the way back."

"I agree with Synøve," Anatoli said. "Let's go through the plan of the mission."

A moment later, in the control room of deck one, Synøve revealed the results of the collected data.

"Epsilon Eridani," she said, "is a K2 class star, hence its orange color. It has a mass 20% lower than that of the Sun, but its luminosity is still a third of it. Though on Earth, we believed this star to be only 700 million years old, it seems that it is in fact 2.4 billion years old. Still, much younger than our Earth."

"Any trace of the expected planets Epsilon Eridani b and c?" Anatoli wondered.

"So far, no," Synøve replied. "As you know, their presence has been controversial, since the asteroid belts cause a lot of background noise for the Earth-based radars. But it could be that they are on the other side of the star. From here, we can see the outer asteroid belt, and we receive an echo of the inner belt."

"What course of action do you propose?" Anatoli asked the chief scientist.

Over the next two weeks, they followed Synøve's advice. They first sent a warpedo back to Earth to inform them of their safe arrival and their losing reactor number three. Then, they warped to four different locations above the outer asteroid belt, deploying a large communication satellite to orbit around the star with the flow of meteorites.

From there, they located a planet. They warped to its orbit where they deployed four observation satellites.

It was a super-Earth, a telluric planet five times the mass of the Earth.

Its larger mass had enabled it to retain a thick atmosphere consisting of mostly hydrogen, helium, and methane. Its surface consisted of barren rocks, and its temperature was measured to be on average minus 150 oC. The planet was dismissed as non-colonizable, and the probability of finding life on it was assessed to be very remote. Nonetheless, they launched a probe into its atmosphere, which was damaged on landing. They were, however, able to collect some data.

Synøve dismissed this planet as a waste of time and

proposed to move to the inner asteroid belt.

Once again, they deployed four communication satellites on four different locations on top of the asteroid belt. For every satellite deployment, they could now admire the orange light of Epsilon Eridani, and Samir thought it was more pleasant to work in space, the closer to a star one was.

When they had deployed the fourth satellite, Synøve called for a new briefing in the concave-floored operation room of deck one.

They had found two smaller planets orbiting closer to the star. It was 17 October 2102.

"While we were deploying the satellites over the inner asteroid belt," Synøve said, "Our telescope spotted two smaller planets, about the size of the Earth. Let's call them Epsilon Eridani b and c, to follow the astronomical nomenclature. The giant Earth can be Epsilon d."

Some more satellite deployment, Samir thought. Never any time for a break.

Standing in front of a large screen, Synøve went on;

"Epsilon Eridani b has a mass 12% larger than Earth, but a radius only 8% bigger. Obviously, a higher density. It orbits between 0.76 and 0.78 Astronomical Units around the star. We have calculated it orbits the Epsilon Eridani star in 286 Earth days. It has a revolution period of 21 hours."

Hm, Samir thought. It would mean that he would weigh twelve percent more on that planet. If he lived there, he could gain muscles without even having to work out.

Synøve then introduced the other detected planet: "Epsilon Eridani c has both a mass and a radius 6% lower than Earth. It orbits around the star at a distance between 0.86 and 0.89 AU. It takes this planet 324 days to orbit around the star, and it has a revolution period of 19 hours."

Anatoli, who was sitting on a chair close to the large screen, asked the chief science officer:

"What is the surface temperature measured?"

"We could not measure exactly," Synøve replied. "But the average temperature is most likely between 10 and 60 °C, which means that the presence of liquid water is more than likely."

"Liquid water?" Anatoli asked.

Samir saw how everybody's face suddenly lit up.

Synøve smiled and said: "We all know what it means. We scientists will all have at least a couple of scientific articles published in *Science* each."

All the scientists, including Amina, started cheering: "Publication in *Science*! Publication in *Science*! *Science*! *Science*!"

When they had calmed down, Eamon Windsor, the doctor, commented for himself: "Unbelievable. We may have discovered two colonizable planets and all these scientists think about is how many articles they are going to publish and in what journal."

They first warped to Epsilon Eridani b, which was the closest to the star. There, their first surprise was to see three moons were orbiting around it. The second surprise was to see how blue the planet was.

There *was liquid water on it*. And much more than on Earth!

They started by deploying a dozen communication, geo-positioning, and observation satellites around the planet, which took a whole day, and then navigated to the respective moons, where they put a pair of observation satellites in orbit of each. Two of the moons were rather small, being a tenth and an eighteenth of our moon's size respectively.

The biggest moon, however, was only twenty percent smaller than Earth's Moon, and Anatoli let the *Shackleton* orbit it to study it more carefully, while the scientific team were analyzing the data collected by the satellites about the nearby planet.

In the control room on deck one, as pilot Lucy Li was flying the ship, Anatoli said to Gabor and Samir: "I have calculated we have enough liquid hydrogen and oxygen to land on the moon with a White Parrot and take off again. I would like to go and explore that deep crater on the north pole of this moon. Shall we make a go of it?"

Eamon thought it was a very bad idea, and so did Samir. They were already at risk with one missing nuclear reactor. They could not just go on a landing party on the moon and burn more liquid oxygen and hydrogen. Furthermore, landing parties were strictly forbidden by their instructions.

To Samir's dismay, Amina said she was interested in some lunar geology. Besides, she had never been on the Moon, unlike most of the engineers and pilots onboard, so if she were given the opportunity to walk on *a* moon, she would gladly do it. Samir joined the group unwillingly. They needed him to steer two insect-like robots that could be sent into the crater.

They put their space suits on and boarded one of the White Parrots in the cargo bay. The large cargo door opened and the small white double-decker space-only vehicle set course toward the north pole of the largest moon of Epsilon Eridani b.

Gabor first flew the White Parrot a few times above the north pole's crater to take low-altitude photographs. The deep, dark crater looked menacing to Samir, as if it could swallow their little shuttle. Amina speculated it must have been caused by a mighty asteroid collision. Anatoli ordered Gabor to land the shuttle a few hundred meters away from the edge of the crater.

They already had their space suits on and they walked out of the White Parrot as soon as they had landed.

Amina laughed: she was walking on *a* moon.

"We are really light, here," she said.

She squatted and jumped with her two feet. She landed on the roof of the White Parrot, but bumped off and fell on the other side. She was laughing.

"Careful, Amina," Samir said, irritated. "If you damage your suit, you're in deep shit."

"I know the Armstrong limit. But I always wanted to try that anyway."

Anatoli interrupted them.

"Samir, take the robots. We're going to check that crater out."

When they were on the edge of the crater, Samir directed his two insect-like robots into it. The two robots moved quickly on their eight legs down the crater. Soon, they were out of sight.

Samir was steering them with his control pad, while Anatoli and Gabor watched him. Amina was walking further away.

Suddenly they all felt a violent quake on the ground.

"What the hell was that?" Samir asked.

They were soon covered in a huge cloud of dust.

"A meteorite just crashed nearby," Amina announced over the wireless. "This is a young star system. There are loads of meteorites here."

"Shouldn't we leave?" Samir wondered.

"Relax, I guess the meteorite fell at least a kilometer away," Amina replied "The dust cloud is caused by the low gravity. The probability of getting killed is still less than when doing mountaineering."

Anatoli decided to call the *Shackleton*.

"*Parrot One* to *Shackleton*," he said. "We just got a meteorite crashing nearby."

"Yes, we saw it.," Lucy's voice replied on the radio.

"Why didn't you warn us?" Anatoli asked.

"We calculated it was safe for you," Lucy replied. "The doctor wanted to scare you."

Next, they heard Eamon laugh on the radio.

"It's not funny," Anatoli said. "Please, from now on keep us informed of any incoming object."

"I found ice!" Samir suddenly exclaimed. "The robots are now at the bottom of the crater, and there seems to be a lot of ice."

Amina hugged Samir, though they felt it was awkward because of their space suits.

"You see," Anatoli said, "It was not a waste of our time."

Samir managed to bring only one robot back up, though. The other one had slid on the ice and broken two legs. It was an acceptable loss, given the valuable information they had obtained.

If there was ice on that moon, it could be used to produce liquid hydrogen and oxygen, which could be used to fill the tanks of chemically propelled aerospace shuttles. That was a must if one wanted to later conduct a full exploration of the planet nearby. It was theoretical, though. It would need the approval of the United Nations and require a crew to come back with a ship of the *Eleonore Roosevelt* class, capable of carrying Space Bear shuttles.

When they were back onboard the *Shackleton*, Synøve suggested that they should navigate back to the planet's orbit, since the satellites deployed around the moon would collect enough information on their own.

The chief scientist now had additional information concerning this planet, Epsilon Eridani b. The planet was tectonically active, and there was a magnetic field protecting the atmosphere from solar radiation. The atmosphere consisted mostly of nitrogen and carbon dioxide, and of a very tiny quantity of oxygen. All the crew, especially Amina and Rebecka, were excited at this information.

It meant that the planet was terraformable and colonizable. In theory.

In fact, the planet was not that hospitable. Oceans covered 90% of its surface. The surface temperature was between thirty and sixty degrees Celsius, which was too hot. According to Amina, it was due to the greenhouse effect induced by the high concentration of carbon dioxide in the atmosphere. If they could force an oxygenation event, the average temperature would automatically decrease. That was only physical.

There were, however, objective threats to any hypothetical colonization of this planet, Synøve explained. The tectonic activity was higher than on Earth, and currently, two major underwater volcanic eruptions were occurring. Besides, more meteorites were falling on that planet than on Earth.

They launched three probes onto Epsilon Eridani b. The

first one was destroyed on landing, but the second one did a successful sea landing, while the third one landed close to a mountain range close to the equator.

Next, they managed to release two high altitude solar-driven drones in the stratosphere. These drones were meant to fly indefinitely at very low speed to take pictures and map the surface.

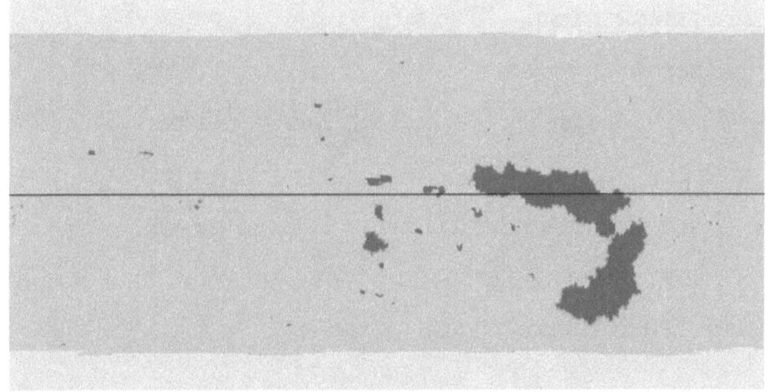

Figure 11: Map of Epsilon Eridani b

After that last deployment, Samir was happy to get some rest, but Amina was so excited by the data collected that she would spend hardly any time with him.

When he was sleeping, she would just wake him up and ask him to have a quickie, so that she could be more relaxed for the night. Samir realized he had just become a relaxing sex object, but he did not mind. He spent more time with the dog Calypso and Anatoli, who also complained that Rebecka was too much absorbed in her work.

Finally, on Monday 27 November 2102, Synøve suggested that they should warp to Epsilon Eridani c, as they were to leave the star system on December 31st, at the very latest.

They came out of warp just behind the second planet's moon, which was about the size of the Earth's Moon. As they navigated sideways, Epsilon Eridani c progressively revealed itself to their cameras, displaying itself on the large screen of the operation room.

They were *shocked.*

"It's a green planet," Rebecka whispered. "There is vegetation on it."

"Holy shit," Eamon exclaimed. "There is life on it."

Synøve jumped in excitation: "Oh yeah! We will not only be published in *Science* but also in *Nature!*"

Anatoli decided to dispatch Gabor Horvath, Samir Benyamina, and safety specialist André Dumonteil in a White Parrot with a modular EM-drive to put two observation satellites in orbit around the moon, while the *UNSS Ernest Shackleton would* set course directly to the planet's orbit.

Samir did not know if he should be excited or scared at the prospect of finding life on another planet. As they were deploying the two observation satellites around the moon, he secretly hoped they would not come across some aggressive aliens. André was not helping either.

"*Pacific exploration, my ass,*" André said with his heavy

French accent. "*What a bullshit! We should bear arms. What if there are intelligent and hostile creatures here?*"

"You should not have watched *Alien* on the way here," Gabor retorted.

They did not come across any alien, though.

After they had successfully deployed their satellites around the moon, Gabor steered the White Parrot so as to orbit the moon several times while gaining momentum. Finally, he pulled the side-stick, and the White Parrot was catapulted toward the planet's orbit, where the *Shackleton* was already deploying satellites.

SX-White Parrot docked into a modular EM-drive

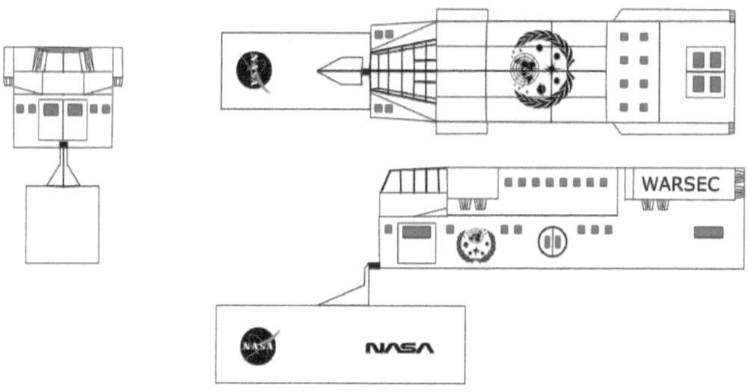

Figure 12: SX-White Parrot docked into a modular EM-drive. The EM-module enables the White-Parrot to be propelled using electromagnetic impulse powered by the module's onboard Compact Fusion Reactor. Here, the EM-drive is leased by the NASA to WARSEC.

The EM-drive the White Parrot was docked into enabled them to be propelled by magnetic impulse, which was more efficient than chemical propulsion. They still needed seven hours to link up with the starship and André would constantly suggest they may come under attack from an ET creature.

"*Ta gueule, André,*" Samir said eventually ('Shut up, André.').

When they were back onboard the *UNSS Ernest Shackleton*, Anatoli informed them that Adodoola, Hans, and Natalia had already deployed the remaining observation and communication satellites. They had none left, but also no other planets to explore.

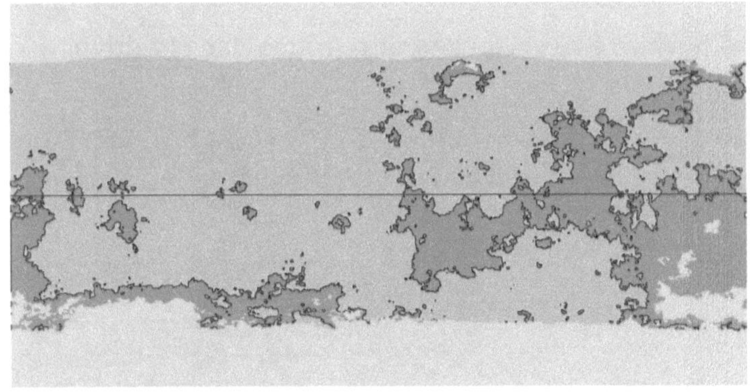

Figure 13: Map of the planet Epsilon Eridani c.

Later that evening, Synøve Solberg held another meeting in the operation room. As she was standing in front of the large screens, she gave a brief exposé:

"Epsilon Eridani c's surface consists of 55% land and 45% oceans. The planet is tectonically active with a magnetic field protecting it from solar radiation. Its atmosphere consists of 62% nitrogen, 3% carbon dioxide and 35% oxygen. And yes, we can confirm there is life on the surface."

Scientists looked both excited and irritated. Synøve was soon to disclose why:

"According to the Vienna Treaties from 8 December 2094, any exploration of a planet with the obvious presence of life cannot be conducted without the prior joint authorization of the United Nation's General Assembly and Security Council."

The ship's commander, Anatoli, was sitting on a chair not far from the Norwegian astrophysicist. He asked her: "What does it mean?"

She was straightforward in her answer: "We are not permitted to land any probe on its surface, without approval from New York."

Anatoli Govorov looked thoughtful and finally said: "What do they really mean by exploration, in the Treaties?"

Synøve shrugged and conceded: "We would need to double check to be sure."

Over the following week, Anatoli, Synøve, and Samir read the Vienna Treaties again and again. As far as Samir was concerned, it was the first time he had read an international treaty. It was not as complicated to understand as he had first thought.

"I hate to say it," Anatoli said, "but it's the first time I wish I had a legal expert onboard."

"I think we have to take into account the intent of the treaty," Samir said. "The intent is that mankind shall not come into direct contact with an advanced form of life. By 'advanced form of life' is meant a multi-cellular organism. A trilobite is an advanced form of life according to the Vienna Treaties."

"The intent is stated clearly," Synøve said. "We do not want to bring diseases to them, and we do not want to bring diseases from them. Then also, hypothetically, in the case of the presence of an advanced alien civilization, we, of course, do not want to start an interstellar war."

"When it comes to advanced civilization," said Amina, who was eavesdropping, "I really think you can take it easy. *Homo sapiens* did not appear on Earth until 4.5 billion years after its creation. I am surprised we found life at all in the Epsilon Eridani system, though the star is only 2.5 billion years. I guess it is because it is far less powerful than the Sun."

"Do you exclude the presence of any civilization on this planet, Amina?" Anatoli asked.

"I do," Amina replied. "As a geologist, I would not expect more than some kind of trilobites."

After long discussions, they decided that deploying high altitude drones in the Atmosphere would not violate the Vienna Treaties, as long as they were correctly sanitized. They would not bring any disease to the planet and would not be detectable from the surface of the planet.

They succeeded with the operation in the second week of December.

Equipped with solar panels and helium-filled fuselage and wings, the large stratospheric drones had an unlimited autonomy.

As the four drones were now cruising in the planet's stratosphere, the crew of the *Shackleton* was provided with new high-quality images of the planet's surface. As well as large trees, they believed they had captured some images of middle-sized reptile-like animals.

Each of the large high-altitude drones was equipped with a smaller electric powered drone which could undock from it, fly closer to the ground and dock back into the mother drone in the stratosphere to recharge its batteries. The low altitude flight had, however, to be guided by a remote drone pilot.

On 24 December, Anatoli decided they would make an attempt to fly the mini-drones at a low altitude to try to capture some more images of the life forms on that planet. Both Samir and Adodoola were to pilot a drone each.

For the occasion, the *Shackleton* came into low orbit, only 150 km (500,000 ft) above the planet's sea level. All the southern hemisphere of Epsilon Eridani c was covered with land, with the exception of a gigantic bay. Samir was to fly his drone low over the water by the coast, while Adodoola was to fly her drone over the land close to a mountain range.

With the exception of the two pilots and the engineer on duty in the control room, the rest of the crew had assembled in the concave-floored operation room, where both robot engineers were to steer the drones. The images were broadcasted on the large screens.

Adodoola's drone was first to go. It soon arrived at its intended destination, and flew by a little mountain range. The cameras showed some gigantic trees, down in the valley. Higher up were some hilly ridges naked of trees, where the drone could hope to more easily capture images of any wildlife activity.

Adodoola steered the drone in their direction. And, then, on a small, sunny, rocky ridge, she spotted five green-grey animals resembling some kind of large lizards or iguanas. They were gazing unintelligently at the drone.

Adodoola flew by a few times and then steered her drone upward to the stratosphere. An hour later, she managed to safely dock her mini-drone back onto the high-altitude mother drone.

It was now Samir's turn to fly at low altitude by the coast of the giant bay. The descent from the mother drone to the sea level went fast.

"Some animals are jumping out of the water," Amina pointed out, looking at the screen.

Samir decided to do a fly-by at about 500 meters (1,600 ft)

of altitude to take a closer look at the water.

"You see, under the water?" Rebecka pointed at the screen. "They are quite large. Like fifteen meters [49 ft] long, probably some kind of whales."

"Samir," Anatoli said, "Try to fly very low, close to these jumping creatures. Those will be nice images to take back to Earth."

Samir obeyed and brought the mini-drone closer to the water, where the whale-sized creatures were jumping.

"Perfect," Anatoli commented. "Ten meters [33 ft] altitude is safe enough".

At the same moment, they all saw on the screen how a whale-sized animal with open jaws and huge teeth jumped toward the camera. The next second the camera and drone signals were lost.

13: QUARANTINE
(JAN 2103 – FEB 2104)

The *Shackleton*'s warp-out above the Sun's comet belt was planned for 20 January 2104, and they were expected in the Earth's orbit the following day. The journey back from Epsilon Eridani had not been particularly glorious for Samir.

After the peculiar filming of land and sea animals living on Epsilon Eridani c, the *Shackleton* had collected the last batch of data from that planet and warped to Epsilon Eridani d, to collect another batch of data. They had sent a warpedo 65 to Earth with the already collected data and the announcement of their expected arrival date.

Before warping out of the Epsilon Eridani system, Iman Nassirbakli, the XO, had been inspired: he had led the *Shackleton* to the inner asteroid belt. There, Samir had once again been dispatched in a White Parrot with Gabor and André. They had installed their two EM modules on two small sized asteroids to steer them towards Epsilon Eridani b's far orbit. They had also been asked to steer a third meteorite toward Epsilon Eridani c's far orbit.

It had not been uneventful. Their White Parrot had eventually collided with a small asteroid, and they would certainly all have perished if it had not been for Iman's and Adodoola's intervention with the second White Parrot.

They had finally warped out of the Epsilon Eridani star system on December 31st, 2102. They had only one White Parrot left, and no rescue modular EM-drive. However, should the UN decide to colonize these planets, asteroids would already be orbiting them on their return, making it easy to deploy space elevators.

Synøve Solberg had promised they would be able to watch the more recent movies on their way back, but it did not apply to everybody. With the data collected, the planetologists, geologists and biologists had a lot to do. The Chief Science Officer had asked geophysicist Amina Dörflinger, planetologists Akira Nakano and Geologist Chen Wang to work together with agronomist Rebecka Levi to propose a workable solution to force an oxygenation event on Epsilon Eridani b, the planet that had no life on it.

Because it required advanced programming skills and geologists were not the best programmers, she had obtained permission from Iman Nassirbakli to borrow his system and robot engineers to assist the scientists.

Samir had nothing personal against Chinese and Japanese people, but Akira and Chen were really working too much, and created social pressure, as they expected everybody else to do the same. They worked so hard that they barely spent one or two hours at the gym a week.

In the evenings, Amina would just look like a zombie. They had way too little sex.

Samir asked why there was so much focus on forcing an oxygenation event on Epsilon Eridani b, since there was oxygen on Epsilon Eridani c.

"WARSEC would never authorize the colonization of a planet with obvious forms of life on it," Rebecka explained.

"Why is that?" Samir wondered. "Is that for some ideological reason? The UN rights and blah?"

"For very practical reasons," Amina replied. "You remember the Vienna Treaties? They are dead scared of any possible virus, bacteria, or nasty parasite coming from outer space. And even if they were to change their minds, your filming of the sea monster would make them think twice before they decide to colonize Epsilon Eridani c."

In June 2103, when Samir casually asked Amina if she was pregnant, they suddenly realized it had gone too far. Amina had gained twelve kilos (26 lbs), and it was not pregnancy, just fat. Samir had gained fifteen kilos (33 lbs).

In the end, Samir complained to Dr Eamon Windsor: just

because Ernest Shackleton had died of heart failure, half of the crew of the *UNSS Ernest Shackleton* should not undergo a similar fate.

The doctor asked the scientific team to calm down. His own dear Adodoola had also gained some weight. Bizarrely, both Chen and Akira had remained as thin as ever.

By September 2103, the scientific team had come up with a fully workable solution to force an oxygenation event on Epsilon Eridani b in fifteen years with conservative assumptions. However, in the best case, it could take only eight years, Amina explained.

When the work pressure finally eased, Samir and Amina decided to work out hard to get back their climber weights.

It was impossible. However hard they tried, they were still five or six kilos too heavy. Amina decided to give up as she was not competing in climbing anymore. Samir soon imitated her and contented himself with having a for-his-height normal weight.

The *Shackleton* came out of warp at about 100 AU from the Sun on Sunday 20 January 2104. Ten hours later, they were warping toward the orbit of the Moon and from there navigated to the orbital station, where they arrived on Monday 21 January.

As they approached the orbital station, they could see how it had changed from the screens in the operation room. It now had six gravity rings, instead of four. One of the rings was a dedicated greenhouse to grow fresh fruits and vegetables, mostly for the now eight hotels and many more restaurants onboard the station. The station was also equipped with four twin rail guns at its corners, to deflect any incoming meteorite.

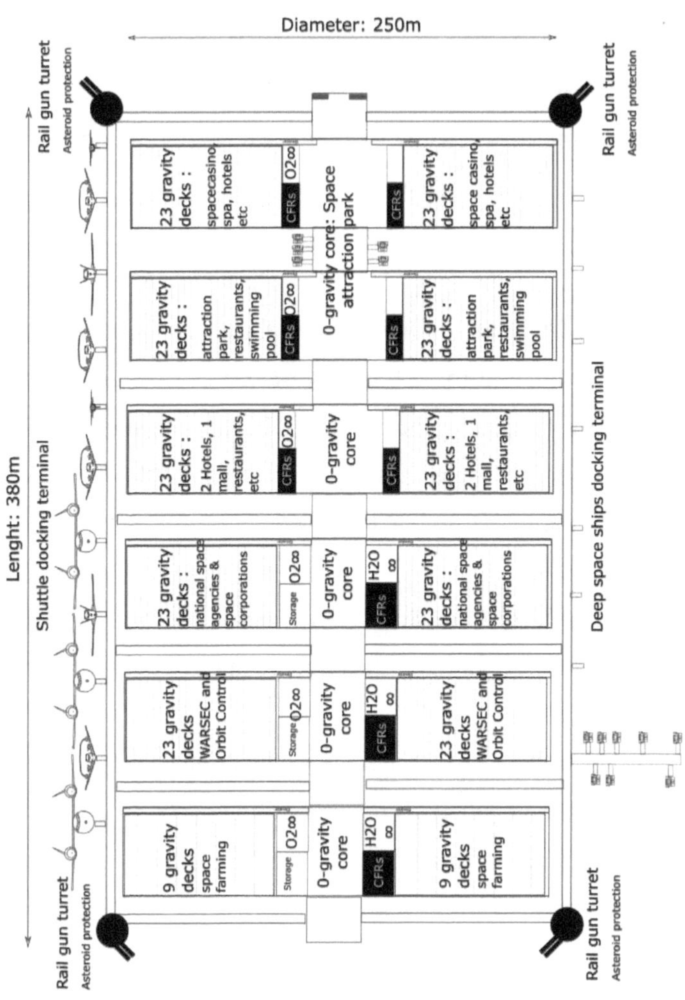

Figure 14: The orbital station in 2104, equipped with rail guns for asteroid protection.

Around the station, they could see on their screens six large spaceships, each about a quarter of a kilometer long and with a diameter twice as long as a handball court. They were the ships of the Ambassador class, Anatoli announced.

As he was checking the smaller radar screen, he pointed at ships on the large screen and said:

"Over there, this is the *UNSS Eleonore Roosevelt*. There, you have the *UNSS Trygve Lie*, the *UNSS Dag Hammarskjöld* and the *UNSS Ralph Bunche*. On this side, you have the *UNSS U Than*, and the *UNSS Javier Pérez de Cuéllar*. The one docked at the orbital station is the *UNSS Kofi Annan*; it will be commissioned in three days. As I can see, the *Ban Ki-Moon* is still being manufactured on the Moon."

At the orbital station, the *UNSS Ernest Shackleton* was not allowed to dock, though. They had to stay in quarantine for four weeks.

Orbit Control was all the more serious since Anatoli, Gabor, Amina, and Samir had been on a landing party on one of the moons of Epsilon Eridani b.

Samir thought it was stupid. Their journey back had taken one year and three weeks and no one had contracted any disease.

In fact, Samir realized he had not even contracted a single flu since he had left the Earth in August 2101. The bright side of confinement in space, he thought.

For four weeks, space safety specialists would examine the hull of the *Shackleton*, while doctors in the orbital station were analyzing medical samples sent from the spaceship.

As the crew of the *Shackleton* were waiting in orbit, they were greeted on the wireless by Mikko Andersson, the commander of the *UNSS Forward*, who was at the orbital station. He had come back from Sirius, which was only 8.58 light years from Earth, in July, seven months earlier. His quarantine was long over, and he had had wonderful holidays, he told the crew of the *Shackleton*.

How had the Sirius system been? Well, there was a star twice the mass of the Sun, and a white dwarf. There had been no planets to find, but a lot of asteroids and comets. They nearly collided with one. After the boring Alpha Centauri system, the *Forward* had had the opportunity to travel to boring Sirius, Mikko concluded.

To the consolation of the crew of the *Shackleton*, they could see on the screens that both the *Nansen* and the *Amundsen* were still in quarantine.

The *Nansen*, under Valeriya Limonov's command, had come back from 61 Cygni on 28 December, and they were at the end of their quarantine. 61 Cygni was a binary star system, 11.4 light years away. Its two stars had masses thirty to forty percent less than that of the Sun, but with a very weak luminosity. There had been no planets to be found. It had been a rather disappointing journey for Valeriya. In a way, Alpha Centauri, and mostly Proxima Centauri, had been more interesting.

The *Amundsen*, led by Tintin Mutumbo, had returned from Tau Ceti, a star system located 11.9 light years away, on 5 January 2104. They still had two weeks left of quarantine. Tau Ceti was 30% smaller than the Sun and shone half as much, but it proved to have five planets. Unfortunately, they had had not much time to linger, but four of the five planets with a size comparable to Earth were too close to the star. Traces of water vapor had been detected in their atmospheres, but these planets had to be excluded as potential colony candidates. The fifth planet was in the so-called habitable zone, and liquid water had been detected on its surface.

However, it had a mass 3.5 times that of the Earth, which caused its atmosphere to retain a huge concentration of hydrogen, helium and methane. The scientists onboard the *Amundsen* believed that this planet should not be considered the first choice for further interstellar colonization projects.

Over the wireless, Tintin also complained to Anatoli how bored he had been during the expedition. He was not willing to go on more interstellar expeditions. In the first months of the interstellar journey, he had kept himself busy by drawing a comic strip. He had done a new album of Tintin, called *Tintin back in Congo*, or *Tintin de Retour au Congo* in French. He had uploaded it to WARSEC's intranet, and the Samir had a good time reading it.

The story was set this time in 1960 and 1961, after the independence of the country, rather than under its colonization period. Captain Haddock was depicted as the anti-hero, fraternizing with French and Belgian white mercenaries, while Tintin failed to hinder some plots against the Congolese prime minister and later against the UN secretary-general. It was quite cynical and sarcastic. *Tintin by Tintin*, as Tintin Mutumbo would call it.

Tintin also explained to Anatoli that he had done some new calculations about warp techniques. When they were back on Earth, he would like to spend some time with Anatoli and the other warp experts to go through his more recent findings. According to him, it was possible to have a spaceship warp spacetime at 250 times the speed of light while using only twice as much energy, provided they got their hands on the purple matter.

"250 times the speed of light?" Anatoli exclaimed over the radio. "That means that traveling to Epsilon Eridani would take only fifteen days!"

"Yes," Tintin replied. "With this same technique, we might also be able to develop warpedoes going at warp 550. They could travel between Earth and Epsilon Eridani in only 7 days. Believe me, Anatoli. I am not going on a new interstellar mission before we have faster spaceships."

On Earth, they had known about Epsilon Eridani b and Epsilon Eridani c since March 2103, when they had received the warpedo 65 with the batches of data.

There was little interest in the returning of starships in general. What was more boring than a quarantined ship orbiting around the Earth? That was the paradox of warp technology. Now that displacement faster than the speed of light was feasible, it had opened new horizons, that could not be followed in real-time. For most people on Earth, though, what could not be told in the instant was not worth telling at all.

To the crew of the *Shackleton*, it seemed as if Earth's population did not appreciate what their discovery meant. First, they were not alone in the universe. There was proof of life in a system only ten light years away. No proof of intelligent life, but proof of life nonetheless. Second, interstellar migrations would probably become possible in a dozen years or so. Perhaps this piece of information was too big to swallow.

Samir was happy anyway that there were not stalked by journalists when they landed in Vaasa on Wednesday 20 February 2104.

The return to Earth turned out to be more difficult than he thought, though. Amina had decided that they should terminate their sexual relationship. What happened on the *Shackleton* was to stay on the *Shackleton*.

But once in Vaasa, they realized that their friend Sanne van der Maas was now in a relationship with Thierry Diakité, the lead robot engineer from Burkina Faso.

Aisha Barjaoui had left the EU Air Force and was now a level 5 pilot for WARSEC. She was sharing a flat with her boyfriend from the legion, Torbjørn Eriksen, who had just been accepted as a space rescuer in the UN agency. He had only worked a couple of years as a para-rescuer in the EU Air Force before being subject to a downsizing program, which he had welcomed with open arms.

Seeing that his friends were all in relationships was not easy for Samir, all the more as he got to know that his ex-girlfriend from Cambridge, Emily Chapman, was now married to a male midwife, and they had a kid.

While Amina decided to spend a few weeks in Switzerland to visit her mother, Samir remained in Vaasa.

It was still winter. There was snow and nights were still long. He decided to go to the climbing gym to try and meet some new Finnish girls.

14: DEBRIEFINGS
(MAY 2104)

On Wednesday 7 May 2104, it seemed that the spring had only just started in Vaasa. Most of the trees and plants were burgeoning, but only a few of them had flowers and leaves. The WARSEC director, Ralf Åhman, had called for an informal meeting and the UN secretary-general was to attend.

It had taken only forty-five minutes for Hira Dorjee-Sherpa to come from New York on board an Albaspace Neo put at her disposal by WARSEC. She arrived at two in the afternoon Finnish time, and they started their meeting an hour later.

Ralf had booked a smaller conference room for the occasion, as they were no more than ten. The secretary-general had brought two of her assistants, while WARSEC's senior management was represented by Ralf Åhman, the director, Glover Johnson, the Space Coordination Centre director and Tatjana Aydemir, the Lunar Coordination Centre director. The WARSEC experts consisted of Synøve Solberg, the senior scientist who had been to Epsilon Eridani, and Sanne van der Maas, a junior space economist.

They all sat around the rectangular table. Since the secretary-general was blind and she didn't have her earGlasses with her, Ralf decided not to display any slides on the canvas screen.

He started: "As you know, the *Shackleton* has discovered two habitable planets within the inner asteroid belt of Epsilon Eridani, 10.5 light years away. These two planets, Epsilon Eridani b and Epsilon Eridani c, have a size similar to the Earth and the presence of liquid water. On Epsilon Eridani c, life has been detected."

"Are there any more convenient names for these two twin planets?" the secretary-general asked.

"Names have to be given by the International Astronomical Union or IAU," Ralf replied. "This is not our prerogative, though the crew of the *Shackleton* proposed some names to the IAU."

"What names have been proposed?" Hira asked.

"Well," Ralf replied, "They have proposed *Titanic* for the giant Earth, and *Remus* and *Romulus* for the two Earth-sized twin planets, though I am almost certain that these names will be rejected."

"Why?" The secretary-general asked.

"Partly because Remus and Romulus are a reference to some Roman mythology and Europeans are in the minority at the IAU," Glover explained. "Also because there is also a planet called Romulus in *Star Trek*. We don't want the colonizers to be called *Romulans*, or to have any trouble with the *Star Trek* franchise."

"OK," Hira said. "Let's keep calling these planets Epsilon Eridani b and c."

"We now have seven and, soon, eight starships of the Ambassador class, and eight starships of the Forward class," Ralf said. "Now that we have found two potentially habitable planets, we can be sure that we will be pressured at the next General Assembly to start interstellar colonization as soon as next year."

"Is that reasonable?" Hira wondered "Can we embark on a colonization mission next year?"

"Yes, we can," Ralf affirmed. "And we should. As you know, WARSEC's economy is a kind of bubble. We are economically viable only if there are enough private activities in space. Vahlroos Travel has increased space tourism within the solar system, but this is not enough. The best thing for us would naturally be to have a full-scale migration to another planet underway. Synøve, please give your view on the colonization of the two planets."

"Two twin planets," Synøve started. "One with life, and one with probably no life, and with only a very tiny concentration of oxygen in its atmosphere. Any colonization project on Epsilon Eridani c, which has life, should be rejected. We can't get into close contact with unstudied life forms, lest we may contaminate them and they us."

"Agreed," the secretary-general said. "And it is also in accordance with the Vienna Treaties. Besides, there seem to be some nasty predators on this planet. However, would it be possible to explore it?"

"Well," Synøve conceded, "All the scientists at WARSEC would love that. But it is for the United Nations 4th Committee to decide, together with the UN Security Council."

"It should not be given any priority," Glover pointed out. "From a safety standpoint, we cannot allocate resources to the exploration of this planet while colonizing another planet."

"You are correct, Glover," Synøve admitted. "However, the moon orbiting this planet is similar to ours, and could be colonized with a moon factory. We could deploy an orbital station around the planet, and in many years, when the time is appropriate, we could send some exploration landing parties."

"What about the other planet?" Hira asked, "Epsilon Eridani b?"

"This planet should be the target of our first colonization attempt," Synøve asserted. "It has three moons. The largest one has a great quantity of ice located in a crater at its north pole. This means a supply of hydrogen and oxygen for our aerospace shuttles. Ninety percent of its surface consists of oceans, and therefore we believe we could force an oxygenation event in less than fifteen years."

"Fifteen years?" Hira wondered.

"From a geological standpoint," Synøve replied, "It's a

million times faster than the speed of light."

"We have analyzed the geological data from the moons," Tatjana went on, "both at Epsilon Eridani b and c. We are confident we could build some efficient moon factories. There will be enough resources to build up and extend the orbital stations we would deploy around the planets. We could also manufacture new aerospace shuttles on the spot."

"What about meteorites?" Glover asked. "I have understood there are more of them falling on these moons than on ours."

"This is correct," Tatjana replied. "Though the majority of these meteorites are of moderate size. We should deploy some further rail guns and, of course, dig. Not only should the habitable huts be buried, as on the moon, but also most of the workshops. Then, of course, radars will constantly be monitoring incoming objects, and workers will have to be evacuated to shelters when a bigger meteorite is spotted than can be deflected by the rail guns. Nothing that is not manageable."

The secretary-general remained silent for a while, while she digested the information, and finally asked: "What would be the steps of the colonization?"

Ralf looked at Sanne van der Maas.

The tall junior economist looked at Hira Dorjee-Sherpa and said:

"Currently, we have planned a colonization program in four waves. Each wave will consist of at least two Ambassador class ships and perhaps one or two Forward class ships. The first wave will install the local moon base and deploy an orbital station. That way, there will be orbital hydrogen and oxygen supply when the second wave arrives six weeks later. The second wave will start the land exploration of Epsilon Eridani b while deploying a space elevator so that we can more easily bring heavy equipment down to the planet, especially fusion compact reactors. We believe that the colonization management team should be in wave two. The second wave will select and install the first settlement on Epsilon Eridani b. When the third wave arrives, four weeks later, they will expand the settlement with production units, more power units and, more importantly, farming units."

"When will we start the oxygenation forcing?" the secretary-general asked.

"That will be part of wave four," Sanne replied. "They will bring photosynthesis organisms a whole five months after wave one. By then, the geologists and geophysicists of wave two will have marked the key oxygenation positions. Then will start the long commuting. While the ships of wave two, carrying the colony management team, are meant to stay in the Epsilon Eridani system, the ships of the other waves will be commuting between Epsilon Eridani b and the Earth to bring more plants, vegetables and, progressively, animals. Proper interstellar migration will not be able to start before the oxygenation event has been sufficiently advanced."

"How many people are required for your plan?" Hira asked.

"Almost 5,000 people," Sanne replied. "To that, we have to add the thousand astronauts needed on Earth to man the orbital station and moon factory. Not to mention the now two thousand personnel that will be required here in Vaasa."

"How are we gonna pay for all these people?" Hira asked.

Sanne hesitated a short while, looked a Ralf, and then back at the secretary-general, and finally said:

"Well, we don't pay them. We only promise to pay them. That's why Ralf talks about a bubble, but I would disagree with him."

"I don't understand," the secretary-general said.

"We still need to hire three thousand people," Sanne replied. "In total, we will have four thousand people gone for ten years on a colonization mission, cut off from the Earth currency system. We won't need to pay them for the time of the mission, as long as we provide them with housing and food. However, we need to be able to pay them at the end of the mission."

"How will that work?" the secretary-general asked.

Sanne looked at Hira Dorjee-Sherpa and explained: "The colonization will be operated by a private cooperation owned by WARSEC, and of which each participant in the operation will be a shareholder. Progressively, we will create a new kind of monetary system in the colonized planet, and we will be able to pay the first colonists in non-convertible money, that it is to say, not with real Earth money, but with money we have created ourselves."

"Then it is a bubble, isn't it?" Hira said.

"Not exactly," Sanne replied. "The non-convertible money created will still reflect the value of the assets and resources on the colonized planet. Then, when interstellar trade becomes possible, the colony's currency will gradually become convertible. As a result, the shares of the colony operating company should be worth quite a decent amount of money to pay the colonization team with."

"Do you mean, Sanne, that we can colonize a whole other planet at minimal cost?" the secretary-general.

"Provided we can have a working and regulated interstellar trade and migration within ten years," Sanne replied. "Should the colonization fail, however, we won't be able to pay the employees, and it may be a bubble."

"This won't happen," Tatjana replied. "Interstellar travel will become easier and faster. We will be able to do what it takes to succeed. Tintin Mutombo has come up with a new method of warping spacetime. Within six years, we should have spaceships able to travel the distance between Earth and Epsilon Eridani in two months for the biggest of them and two weeks for the smallest of them."

"Two weeks?" The secretary-general looked surprised. "If indeed we colonize Epsilon Eridani b, I may pay them a visit."

"A successful colonization of Epsilon Eridani is the only way out of bankruptcy, anyway," Ralf said. "I have at least one slide I would like to show you."

One of Hira's aides promptly went out of the conference room while Ralf touched the control screens on the table a few times. When the aide was back in the room with Hira's earGlasses, a slide was projected on the canvas screen.

Once Hira had put her glasses on, Ralf said:

"As you see on that graph, the contribution of the member states is ridiculous, when compared to a full NASA budget. It is even decreasing. We have only managed to accomplish all we have so far thanks to the increased revenue from commercial activities. There is the fee on commercial satellites and orbital flights and the tax on space profits. However, this, together with the member states' contributions, accounts for only about one-third of our total budget. The majority of our income is coming from the sales of aerospace shuttles, through WARSEC Ventures. This source of revenue is expected to decrease over the next decade as the market matures."

"But if we could colonize a planet," Sanne jumped in, "Not only we will be able to sell or lease starships to commercial space transportation companies, but also we will boost private commercial activities to a critical level. Taxing these will progressively be sufficient to cover WARSEC's budget entirely, and our UN agency will be financially safe."

"I see," Hira Dorjee-Sherpa said. "That, then, will be the goal of my last General Assembly as a secretary-general, this September: to obtain the consent for the colonization of Epsilon Eridani b,"

Later that evening, they went out to have dinner at the *Eridani Charlie*, a newly opened restaurant just outside the WARSEC campus. It was owned by Samir Benyamina, who had been a robot engineer onboard the *Shackleton*.

"He obtained the start-up capital by selling interstellar-produced wine," Glover explained to the secretary-general. "Anatoli Govorov and Eamon Windsor are both minority shareholders in the restaurant."

They had booked a table, and they were taken care of by young waiters.

"Initially, Samir tried having robot waiters," said Sanne, "But they bugged constantly. Even Thierry could not fix them, so it was simpler to hire some students from Vaasa University."

"The bugburgers with melted French blue cheese are not bad," Ralf told the secretary-general. "Personally, I prefer the bugburger with mozzarella cheese, sun-dried tomatoes and pesto."

Samir greeted them and took their orders. At a table nearby were Aisha Barjaoui, Torbjørn Eriksen and Antoine Léger, also eating some bugburgers, burgers made of insect paste.

"Finnish Food is good," Antoine said to Aisha and Torbjørn, while eating his blue cheese burger. "But I need my weekly dose of French cheese."

"Then you will never make it on a colonization mission," Torbjørn replied. "I don't think they will bring with them an unlimited cheese supply."

"I've heard rumors they plan to bring up a few cows and ewes with the third wave," Aisha mentioned. "If you can find some cheesemongers willing to be part of wave three, the problem may be solved."

They were interrupted by Samir, who had stepped out of the kitchen.

"Listen up, space folks," he said. "You may want to watch this."

He switched on the restaurant's TV screens. One of Hira's aides helped her put on her earGlasses.

The screens were displaying images of a large cylindrical ship standing vertically on a launch pad, in what looked like a desert. It was suddenly surrounded by a white mushroom of water vapor and started moving upward, propelled by its rocket engines. As the camera followed the cylindrical spaceship climb upward like a rocket, it suddenly disappeared in a flash of purple.

Samir said: "Breaking news. Two hours ago, V-Space and the Vahlroos Corporation succeeded in sending a starship into orbit from the surface of the Earth. It's called the V-liner. It uses the purple matter and can travel at warp 80, eight times faster than our ships."

15: THE V-LINER
(MAY 2104)

Sophie Couillard looked at herself in the mirror in her room in the orbital station's Sheraton hotel. Her black jeans, white T-shirt and her navy blue blazer suited perfectly. She was neither too overdressed for the orbital station, nor too underdressed for Michael Vahlroos.

In the background, the TV went on in her windowless room.

"I have let the UN settle the situation in Western Sahara, our relationship with Morocco has normalized, I have stopped nuclear bombs from being deployed in space. We are at peace..."

"You want to raise taxes."

"Only if we manage to do it on a coordinated global level. President Silverbane, in the US, will not be re-elected this November, believe me."

"Who will be the next US President?"

"I assume Nancy Littlewolf will win the Democrat primaries."

"Silverbane calls her Pocahontas."

"You're condescending. When she's elected US president, together with China and the South Asian Union, we will have a golden opportunity to introduce a global tax on capital, under UN patronage. Then, and only then, we will we increase taxes. It will be coordinated. That's why you should re-elect me."

It was Friday 23 May and the EU elections were scheduled for the second Sunday of June. As a Canadian, Sophie had no real interest in whether or not Guido Niedling would be re-elected as European president … she switched to Fox News:

"Wolf Welsh, the famous South British explorer, is dead. He had swum across the melted glacial Arctic Ocean and climbed to the top of Everest. He showed us what it takes to survive in the most difficult environments. Not anymore. This morning, in Bhutan, he attempted to jump off a very dangerous waterfall. Despite repeated warnings from the local authorities, he insisted on going ahead with his jump. Sadly, he has perished. Our special envoy is now in Cornwell to interview Wolf Welsh's thirteen-year-old son, now an orphan."

There was a knock on her door. She switched off the TV and opened it. It was Michael.

"Shall we go to dinner?" he said.

She followed him to the elevator.

It had been worth waiting for with the development of the V-liner. Thierry Diakité had claimed that it would be able to reach warp 40 with the purple matter. In fact, her new engineers had made it go to warp 80.

There was a high probability that WARSEC would start the colonization of the Epsilon Eridani within two years. Their starships needed a year and three weeks to get there. The V-liner would take only a month and a half. Of course, it could not transport as much, but still, they would be able to sell it to WARSEC. Even better, they could be licensed by WARSEC to help with the transportation of merchandise there.

Besides, when they had fixed the warp atmosphere entry, it would be able to travel to any position within the Earth's orbit in less than fifteen minutes. With it, it would take only fifteen minutes to commute from New York to the Moon. This would also be beneficial for Vahlroos Travel. They were living in exciting times.

In the Sheraton's restaurant, they were shown a table. Michael ordered a bottle of Epsilon Eridani Red. It tasted OK.

"Good work, Sof," he said. "The testing of the V-liner has gone beyond expectations."

"It was wise to keep a conventional atmosphere entry mode," Sophie remarked. "OK, it takes two hours for it to land but it is workable, and it has enabled us to test four warp take-offs over the last two weeks."

Michael took a few sips of his Epsilon Eridani Red and said: "What would really please me, Sof', would be to test the warp re-entry."

"Our engineers do not recommend it," Sophie noted. "They think we should stick to a conventional atmosphere entry for the time being. The fragmental entry should work in theory, but they believe the risk of failure is still around 20%. Way too high. They think we should try it first on Mars, where the gravity is lower and the atmosphere thinner. That way, it will give our AI the possibility of finding out the best re-entry procedure in safer conditions."

Michael smiled and said: "What do our engineers know? Look at this bottle of Epsilon Eridani Red. It costs six months' salary for a senior engineer in Bobo-Dioulasso. When you earn as little as them, what do you really know about anything?"

"I think we have very good engineers," Sophie retorted.

"They lack vision. They think only about safety and regulations. Imagine being able to travel to anywhere on Earth within fifteen minutes. Fifteen minutes from New York to New Zealand, fifteen minutes from the orbital station to New York. Fifteen minutes from the Moon, or even from Mars to New York. That's what I call a vision."

"WARSEC has so far agreed to let us use the ship's conventional atmosphere entry," Sophie replied. "They are opposed to any warp entry."

"I know," Michael admitted. "However, earlier this week, I took the liberty of contacting them and informing them we plan to go ahead with the testing next Monday anyway."

"You contacted them without telling me?" Sophie asked

angrily. "I am the general manager of V-Space."

"And I am the CEO of Betalpha," Michael reminded her. "I played open. I sent them the protocol for the fragmented entry so that they can make an assessment. I had a conversation with Ralf Åhman this morning. He is at the station. They are becoming more open to us. They need us."

"As we need them," Sophie reminded Michael.

Suddenly, two black men showed up and sat down at their table. One was athletic, dark-skinned, and wore the regulatory orange suit of WARSEC engineers. The other one was very tall, but with a lighter skin complexion, and wore jeans and a T-shirt reading: "*With great brains come great possibilities.*"

He just grabbed Michael's glass and took a few sips.

"Hmm", he said. "Château Eridani, very pleasant, *très… délicieux.*"

"Show some respect, Tintin," Michael replied.

"I'm kidding," Tintin added. "This wine is awful. It costs six months of an engineer's salary, and I always wondered what kind of people would pay that much for something that average. Now, I know the answer."

Michael gazed at his two former employees and finally turned to the tallest one:

"Tintin Mutumbo," he said. "You haven't changed a bit over the last nine years. I assume one stops growing after receiving a Nobel Prize in Physics."

He turned to the other visitor:

"Thierry Diakité, I am pleased to see that at least you can behave."

"Ralf sent us," Thierry explained. "You ruined our Ascension week, hence the bad mood. We had to review all your protocols in an emergency."

"And?" Sophie asked.

"We're impressed," Tintin replied. "Your new engineers are pretty good. Neither of us had thought about that fragmented approach, when we used to work for V-Space."

Michael had a quirky smile and said: "You see, you are not the best. Burkina is full of talented engineers."

"I'm pleased to hear that," Tintin went on. "Talented African engineers are good for Africa. However, nine years ago, we proposed a workable concept, with horizontal atmosphere warp-entry, and you rejected it."

"Our concept was fail-proof," Thierry went on. "The V-liner's fragmented vertical entry is impressive, but it still has a 20% probability of failure. Your engineers calculated right. And I have no idea how this risk can be decreased."

"Your concept had no gravitational rings. It was not suited for interstellar travel," Michael replied.

"Did it have to be?" Tintin exclaimed. "Interstellar travel is so far the prerogative of WARSEC, not of V-Space. When the time has come for commercial interstellar travel, I will send you an email, I guarantee."

"Please calm down," Sophie said. "I have noted your

comments. I assume you give us the red light and we are not allowed to test that warp entry."

She was relieved. She did not want to go ahead with a stupid decision.

"Not just that," Thierry replied calmly. "You seem to have pissed off all of the WARSEC senior management. That's why they did not even bother to come and see you."

"What do you mean?" Sophie asked.

"We informed Ralf and Glover of the 20% probability of failure," Tintin explained. "They asked us what the consequences would be in case of failure."

"Your new CFR's safety standards are impressive," Thierry went on. "That's why they were certified by the FAA in the first place. In case of a crash, there won't be any nuclear apocalypse."

Tintin looked at both Sophie Couillard and Michael Vahlroos and said: "In short, you get the green light for your test on Monday."

He then shrugged and added: "But I shall warn you. Glover just hopes you land on the wrong side of the statistics. And it will happen eventually. It's a Bernoulli law, I'm sure you're familiar with probabilities. The probability of a crash in five warp-entries is asymptotic to 100%. So, when you do land on the wrong side of the statistics, be sure to expect hell."

"What do you mean?" Michael asked.

"I know Burkina's president," Thierry said, "She was my schoolteacher when I was a kid, in Kodala."

"That is so sweet," Michael said ironically.

"She told me she is ready to take retaliatory steps against V-Space with retroactive taxes," Thierry informed. "Besides, in case of failure, be assured that the Betalpha board will let you down. This time you will not be able to blame it on an excess of regulation, as you usually do."

"You are delusional," Michael said. "Do you know how much more I earn than you do? How could you know these things better than I do?"

Tintin stood up, looked down at the Vahlroos Corporation CEO and said:

"Do you know how many more Nobel Prizes I've got than you? An infinity. We physicists can divide by 0, by the way. We are not stubborn mathematicians."

Thierry stood up as well, before giving a last piece of advice:

"If, despite everything, you decide to go ahead with the test on Monday, please, do it unmanned. The crew will not stand a chance in case of failure. If you decide not to go ahead with the test, WARSEC will be willing to cooperate with you for the colonization of Epsilon Eridani b. Ralf told me to tell you that."

Both Tintin and Thierry left.

A waiter brought them some green mussels with melted garlic butter and bread.

"I think we should pick the reasonable approach," Sophie said eventually. "Our ship is good enough. Let's cooperate with WARSEC instead. Perhaps we should reactivate the old V-craft project if we really want a ship with atmosphere warp-entry."

"Blackmail," Michael retorted. "They are blackmailing us."

"They are stating a fact. It's a Bernoulli law, as Tintin stated. If the probability of each atmosphere warp entry is 20%, then the more entries you do, the greater the overall probability of failure. That's math."

"I don't believe in that," Michael replied. "I've been blessed with success so far. You don't scare me."

"It's not a question of beliefs," Sophie objected, "It's a question of science. For science's sake, call off the test!"

Michael stood up and said: "Can you hear yourself?"

Some guests in the restaurant started looking at them, and Sophie felt embarrassed.

"Can you hear yourself?" Michael repeated. "Stop going the competition's way and be brave. The test shall go as planned and it shall be manned. I trust human pilots more than computers."

Michael stormed out of the restaurant, leaving Sophie on her own at the table. Damn it, she would have to pay for the unnecessarily expensive average wine.

The test warp atmosphere entry was scheduled for Monday 26 May 2104 at 13:00 UTC. Ralf, Glover, Tintin, and Thierry watched the TV broadcast from the WARSEC cafeteria in the orbital station. V-Space had deployed three dozen camera drones along the planned landing trajectory.

At 13:05, they saw the V-liner come out of warp at an altitude of 30 kilometers (98,000 ft) in a giant purple flash. Instead of stabilizing vertically, the V-craft tilted westward.

"It's falling horizontally," Thierry said. "Turbulences not accounted for…"

"What are the pilots doing?" Glover asked. "They should warp away back into space."

"They must first stabilize the V-liner, even horizontally," Tintin explained. "You can't start the Alcubierre drive if you are too unsteady."

"Shit…" Glover said. "They are now 7,000 m [23,000 ft] above the ground, completely disoriented, and falling like a bomb".

Progressively, however, the V-craft managed to stabilize. It was almost vertical, and it started all its rocket thrusters to brake.

"Too low," Glover said. "They won't brake. They should warp now!"

"Warp up, stupid! Warp up!" Thierry screamed.

There was an explosion, and black smoke came out of the ground. The V-liner had crashed in the Sahara.

"Poor pilots," Ralf whispered.

16: PROMOTION AND EVICTION (JUNE 2104)

The sleek windowless Albaspace Neo was shooting through the sky, propelled by its scramjet. V-Space's executive jet had taken off from New York LaGuardia at 13:47 East Coast time and would land in Bobo-Dioulasso, Burkina Faso, at 18:28 local time. The flight was only forty-one minutes long, but Sophie Couillard had already adjusted her watch. She was trying not to pay attention to the ex-CEO of the Vahlroos Corporation, who was in a terrible mood.

"The bastards! They fired me! I'm the minority owner of Betalpha, and they fired me!"

She finally gazed at him. Michael Vahlroos was sitting opposite her, in the executive suite of the aerospace shuttle.

"They promoted me," Sophie noted calmly. "I'm now the CEO of both V-Space and Vahlroos Travel".

"Which they will rebrand V-Travel."

"You could congratulate me," Sophie remarked, irritated.

"They did not sack you for the failure of the test, but for your arrogance."

"They had no right!"

"You sacrificed the crew. Three fine pilots died, Michael! Do you realize this? You barely seem to care about it… It's like when your son was kidnapped and murdered, years ago."

"Please, Sof, that's not the point."

"You don't listen to legitimate warnings from, sure, competitors, but also partners. You organize a test without conferring with me. You were so sure of your success you put camera drones all along the entry trajectory and broadcast it live on the Fox Channels!"

"I thought it would succeed."

"Despite all the warnings? The crash has been terrible PR for all of the Vahlroos Corporations. The stocks have plummeted. Jim Pattisson is an investment banker. Of course, he's fired you!"

"You don't seem sorry for me," Michael reproached.

"You still own 25% of Betalpha, meaning a quarter of the Vahlroos Corporations. You have your yacht and your Vahlroos Tower, so no, I don't feel sorry for you. Why are you on this plane in the first place?"

"I put us in this mess, I will get us out."

Sophie looked at Michael and said: "Thank you. But I think I will be just fine."

"Burkina Faso has announced their intent to increase taxes

on our corporation. I can have a chat with the president and convince her otherwise."

"What will you tell her?" Sophie asked.

"That if she goes ahead with the tax increase, we move out of Burkina."

"We are not moving out of Burkina," Sophie replied.

"Why not?"

"First of all, I am in charge now, so this is my call," Sophie answered. "Second of all, Burkina remains the best manufacturing site in the world. No earthquakes, no hurricanes, good railroad connection to the sea, very educated workforce, good infrastructure. The Bukinabé state is fully reliable and provides good public service. They are entitled to increase their taxes. I believe we owe them well enough."

"You crazy Canadian," Michael said in distaste. "You seem to blow with the wind. That Guido Niedling will be re-elected president of the EU next Sunday, and Pocahontas will most likely be the new US president."

"Don't call her Pocahontas," Sophie corrected firmly. "Nancy Littlewolf is her name. Regardless of your political opinions, you should respect her."

Michael unstrapped himself from his seat and went to the minibar. He took a little bottle of champagne and opened it. He poured one glass for Sophie.

"You deserve it for your promotion."

He poured a glass for himself.

"I need it to get over my sacking."

He handed over Sophie's glass, took his and sat back in his seat.

"I was out of line," Michael apologized. "Over the last few days, I have re-read *Atlas Shrugged*."

"Never heard of it."

"By Ayn Rand," Michael added. "It's just… I think we are living in dangerous times. In the end, they will manage to introduce a global tax on capital. This could be very, very dangerous. That would mean be the end of freedom for mankind."

"Rising sea levels, increasing amount of not only tropical storms and tornadoes but also earthquakes and volcanic eruptions…" Sophie enumerated. "In the end, we are all happy with working public services. When you see what's happening to our planet, our civilization won't make it without working public services… Working public services in a more committed environment will necessarily require more taxes."

"Taxes, yes. But not a global tax on capital, targeting only the wealthy!"

"As long as this tax is voted democratically and not excessive, I don't see the problem," Sophie replied. "Inequalities have also reached new records worldwide. You live in your tower in New York, I live in Burkina Faso. I have really nothing against the rich contributing a bit more."

Michael smiled.

"You say that because you have no yacht, not yet. But now you're a CEO. One day, you will understand."

Sophie rolled her eyes.

"I'm an engineer," she replied, "I have a quite scientific mind. Despite that, I cannot understand how one person can produce, in one hour, six hundred times more wealth than another. Twenty times… thirty times…. forty times… I would understand. But six hundred times? And yet some CEOs earn six hundred times the minimum wage! You earned three hundred times the minimum wage."

"And so what? Are you gonna decrease your new CEO wage?"

"Already have. I shall earn only thirty-five times the minimum wages. It was part of the deal of my take-over. But quite frankly, I'm happy with that."

"No wonder, women CEOs earn less than men," Michael said condescendingly. "You don't know what you are truly worth."

"Or perhaps you men hugely overprice yourselves," Sophie retorted. "You are just bubbles, with your egos as inflated as your reproduction organs… But it lasts like…? Thirteen seconds…perhaps? Like in your case."

A stewardess, who had just come into the executive suite, giggled at Sophie's comment.

"We're gonna land in ten minutes, please fasten your seatbelts."

Michael looked embarrassed and changed the subject.

"So, my dear CEO, how do you plan to save the company of which I still own 25%, if I may ask?"

"The fundamentals are still good. The market size is still growing, and we have a ten-year window before it starts contracting. If the colonization of Epsilon Eridani is a success, then it won't contract anyway."

"You plan to keep pushing on the Albaspace Neo?" Michael asked.

Sophie took a few sips from her glass of champagne and said: "It's a winning product. But of course, I plan a lot on the leasing of Forward class ships for Vahlroos Travel, sorry V-Travel. Currently, we are only organizing orbit flights around Mars and Venus. WARSEC will build a large base on Mars, as part of a colonization exercise and deploy an orbital station around it. I have the approval of the board to co-finance it. That way we will be the first to open a hotel on Mars and organize touristic landing parties on the red planet."

"What about the V-liner?"

"I will scrap it," Sophie said determinedly. "As I should have done nine and a half years ago when we had that meeting with Tintin and Thierry. We should have invested in their concept, the V-craft, instead. If the board had been willing, I would have had that program re-activated. It's a winning concept, and WARSEC is not smart enough to understand it."

"Too bad the board does not want it either," Michael noted

sarcastically. "Investment bankers are sometimes way too risk-avert."

"Whose fault is that?"

"Sophie!" Michael exclaimed suddenly. "I have a brilliant idea! I have such a brilliant idea! I'm so good!"

"What's your idea?"

"I'm gonna buy V-Space."

"You what?"

"I'm gonna buy V-Space, V-Travel and V-Fusion. They are my key companies. I just need 60% in V-Space and V-Travel and 51% in V-Fusion to do whatever I want. I just need to sell all my other shares in Vahlroos Investment, Vahlroos Property, Vahlroos Energy, and V-lab. It will suffice."

"No, it won't," Sophie replied calmly. "The board won't let you. If you do a hostile take-over, the stock will skyrocket. You will need more money."

"I will find a reliable partner," Michael said, looking thoughtful. "I shall found a new company, let's call it V-Equity. I will found it tonight, and prepare my take-over. I promise you, Sof', by the end of the year, I will be your new owner, and I will let you pursue your dream of re-activating the V-craft."

"You won't have enough," Sophie assured. "Perhaps, if you sold your ranch, holiday mansions, and yacht, you may have a chance, but even that's not certain."

On the screens of the windowless executive suite, they could see that the Albaspace Neo was now on its final approach to Bobo-Dioulasso Airport. The sun was now touching the horizon in the west.

"Sophie, Sophie, Sophie," Michael said slowly. "I promise I will regain control. I've been blessed. I feel it. My purpose in life is to bring freedom back to entrepreneurs, to individuals. Whatever UN idealists do, I shall promote free capitalism on Earth and in space. That's my purpose, and I can feel Jesus."

"Really?" Sophie asked as the Albaspace touched the runway.

"I'm blessed, I feel it, and I shall prevail in my enterprise. For mankind and for God."

The plane braked and started taxing toward the V-Space offices.

"You are a true evangelist," Sophie said with a tone of reproach.

"I am, Sophie," Michael admitted. "I am, and it has kept me going."

"I mean, I am a Catholic atheist. But you are a true evangelist."

"A Catholic atheist?"

"All I care about Catholicism is that Pope Francis II does not get killed by Catholic extremists. The resurrection, the Virgin Mary, Jesus, God, all that is bullshit to me. But you, you are a true evangelist."

"I am, Sof, and proud of it, a true evangelist and Calvinist."

The Albaspace stopped. Sophie Couillard unbuckled her seat belt and stood up.

"Well, you should not be," she said.

"Why not?" Michael asked. "Calvinism brought democracy to the Netherlands and Switzerland. It was half a millennium ago. Calvinist ethics have made capitalism thrive. I'm a proud Calvinist."

"Well, you should not be," she repeated very slowly. "Calvinism is the most despicable theological doctrine that I know of."

"How dare you?"

"You call yourself blessed and all that bullshit. What you mean is that people are, in fact, from their birth, not born equal, not only in terms of physical or intellectual ability but also in the eyes of God. Calvinism stands in the way of the very declaration of human rights. Calvinism is the reason slavery has endured for so long in the United States. Calvinism is what justified the apartheid in South-Africa for forty-five years. Calvinism is what has caused the American nation to deny global warming for seventy-five years. I shall reiterate it here and now: Calvinism is the most despicable theological doctrine that I know of."

Michael remained seated, speechless, as Sophie headed for the plane's exit.

He eventually followed her to the tarmac. There, he walked at quite some distance behind her, as she headed for the entrance of the V-Space building. The sky was now turning yellow and red as the sun was disappearing behind the horizon. Beyond the tarmac, the Earth was red.

There was a call. It was the muezzin calling to the evening prayer: "*Allah-wa-akbar.*" When he was done, there was a concert of psalms played by the clocks of a nearby catholic church. Eventually, some loudspeakers yelled some "*Jesus loves you*" kind of songs. It came from one of the nearby evangelist churches.

Sophie raised her arm and pointed her middle finger toward the sky. She turned to Michael and smiled:

"You see? Nothing happens! Why don't you swap your blind and reasonless faith for science? It's a far surer investment, these days."

17: KUSHA AND LAWA
(AUG 2104)

One Saturday morning in August 2104, a group of WARSEC employees were having breakfast on the terrace in front of Samir's building, on the Vaasa Campus in Finland.

Around a rectangular outdoor table sat Aisha Barjaoui, Torbjørn Eriksen, Samir Benyamina, Amina Dörflinger, Rebecka Levi, and Antoine Léger.

Next to the table was a large TV and they were watching the 2104 Summer Olympics.

"I can't believe the Olympic Games are taking place in Riyadh," Rebecka commented. "Who would have thought they would one day be respectful enough of human rights to host them?"

The ex-legionnaire captain shrugged: "History has shown that human rights standards are no requirement to host the Olympic Games."

Aisha looked at Antoine, whose face was still disfigured

by the severe burns he had incurred in Khouribga, during the European-Moroccan war. She said:

"Human rights or not, it's completely stupid to host the Olympic Games in Riyadh. Look, everything is done indoors with air conditioning."

They were watching the climbing competition.

"When I see that," Amina said, "I realize I'm too old for this shit".

"You got the bronze medal at the Riga Olympics, didn't you?" asked Torbjørn.

Amina nodded. She had indeed come third in lead-climbing at the 2096 Summer Olympics.

As they were watching the competition, a small half-Hispanic, half-Afro girl ran to their table and asked if she could taste their food. It was Rika Johnson, Glover's daughter. She would turn seven in October.

Samir looked at her and asked: "Do you want some *karjalanpiirakka*? They are home-baked."

The girl nodded, took one Karelian pasty and put some scrambled eggs on it and, as she did, was joined by her father, Glover. The director of the Space Coordination Center greeted the whole table with a hand gesture, and he was invited to join them to watch the climbing competition.

Shortly after, a small brown kokoni dog jumped at Rika and begged for her Karelian pasty. It was Calypso, Anatoli's bitch.

The Russian astronaut was soon there and said:

"I just met Ralf. He will call for an information meeting in the Aula at 13:00. The International Astronomical Union has given its verdict on the naming of the celestial bodies of the Epsilon Eridani system. He wants to inform the WARSEC personnel before the IAU informs the public later today."

At 13:10, the large auditorium in the Vaasa headquarters was overcrowded when WARSEC's director took the floor. It was some time before IT support confirmed that the staff onboard the orbital station, and on the Moon, could see the broadcast on the intranet.

Then, Ralf Åhman started:

"Dear all of you, the International Astronomical Union, based in Paris, France, has finally given their verdict on the names of the newly discovered celestial bodies in the Epsilon Eridani system."

There was some cheering in the room.

"Let's first talk about the star," he continued. "Epsilon Eridani has now been given a second name. It will be called Ëarandil. I don't know who suggested that. It sounds a bit as though it comes from the *Lord of the Rings*.

There was some laughter in the room.

"Ëarandil… Ëar like in Eridani. Ends with L, and there is an L in Epsilon. I think it makes sense.

"Next," Ralf went on, "let's talk about Epsilon Eridani d, that giant telluric planet which has five times the mass of the Earth. It orbits the star between the inner and outer asteroid belts. The crew of the *Shackleton* had proposed the name *Titanic*. And the IOU has decided to call it…."

"Titanic! Titanic! Titanic!" screamed Anatoli supported by some former members of his crew.

"And no…," Ralf replied. "They decided to call it *Macronus*. I think it comes from a French president once believing he was as great as Jupiter."

Some laughed, but most looked at each other wondering who this French president could have been.

 Ralf went on with his show:

"And now the twin planets, Epsilon Eridani b and c," Ralf added. "The crew of the *Shackleton* had suggested calling them Remus and Romulus. I received complaint calls from the *Star Trek* franchise as soon as their proposals were known. Romulans are indeed supposed to be bad guys, not human settlers."

There was some more new laughter in the room.

"As you can imagine, the proposal was not accepted, and not even seriously considered by the IAU. Instead, they have decided to call them *Kusha* and *Lawa*. These are two twins, children of a certain Rama and Sita, whose tale is known to all of you who are familiar with the Hindu epic Ramayana. As for me, it was completely new."

There were some whispers in the auditorium.

"Epsilon Eridani b", Ralf added. "the closest planet to the star, will from now on be referred to as *Lawa*. There is no life on *Lawa*, and the 10% of emerged and vegetation-free rock gives a golden complexion to this planet. The same complexion as *Lawa*'s. So, *Lawa*, like no-life. This is a bit counter-intuitive, but we will get used to it."

"Meanwhile, Epsilon Eridani c," Ralf went on, "which is covered with vegetation and oceans and has a greenish-bluish color, will be called *Kusha*. *Kusha* with a K like in "killing sea monsters. That one will be easier to remember."

There was long and loud laughter, and Ralf gestured them to stop with the palms of his hands.

When the Aula was listening again, Ralf added:

"In about two months. The General Assembly will decide if we will launch a colonization program to *Lawa* next year. That may be very exciting, and I hope to be part of it. As you all know, my mandate as the director of WARSEC ends in April 2105. I have clearly stated I did not wish to have my mandate renewed for a third term. However, I would be more than happy to be part of the colonization program. Logically, the 4th Committee of the United Nations General Assembly should ask the UN Trusteeship Council to send an envoy to observe the colonization process. If they do, I intend to apply for that position. That will be all."

After he had said these words, there was thunderous applause in the auditorium.

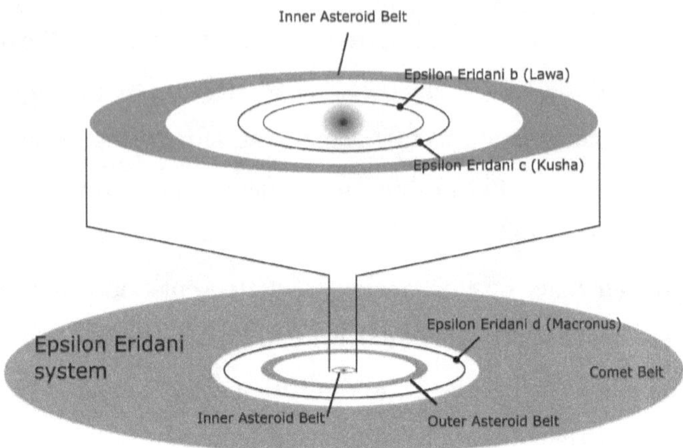

Figure 15: the Epsilon Eridani system with the three planets, as named by the International Astronomical Union.

18: THE 159ᵀᴴ SESSION OF THE GENERAL ASSEMBLY (SEPT 2104)

On Friday 10 October 2104, Sanne van der Maas was in the small WARSEC room on the 35th floor of the United Nations Building, in New York.

On one wall were pictures of Henry Kissinger, Dwight Eisenhower, Charles de Gaulle, George W Bush, Han Solo, Chewbacca, Count Dooku, and Emperor Palpatine, as well as many posters from the *Star Wars* franchise: they were the realists.

On the other wall were pictures of Woodrow Wilson, Eleonore Roosevelt, Dag Hammarskjöld, Jean-Luc Picard, and Mr. Spock, as well as many posters from the *Star Trek* franchise: there were the idealists.

It was the same room that had served as the room for the United Nations Office for Outer Space Affairs, back in 2094.

Sanne sat on an office chair and was watching a videocast on her laptop. The famous geologist Dr. Sheldon Cooper was one of the guests invited to the panel.

"*Nobody on Earth seems to be really surprised by the fact that life has been found on an exoplanet. Dr. Cooper, how do you explain that phenomenon?*"

"*Over the last fifty years, astrophysicists have mentally prepared us with the probability of finding life somewhere else in the universe. For each star system, it's only a question of probability. If you take an infinite number of star systems, then, the probability of finding life in at least one of them becomes quite significant.*"

"*But still, is that not extraordinary?*"

"*I would not call it extraordinary. Images of life captured on Epsilon Eridani c, sorry, on Kusha, seem to show some Devonian-like creatures. What would be extraordinary would be to find an intelligent form of life… When it comes to that, I would say the odds are pretty thin.*"

"*But, Dr Cooper, aren't you surprised that there has not been any bigger hype around it? People do not seem to be bothered at all that another star system is about to be colonized.*"

"*People don't seem to believe that geologists should be rewarded the Nobel Prize in Physics either. What shall I say? I think this is just the translation of what mankind has become: 58% of the world population now consider themselves as either atheist or agnostic. Only 22% of the world population remain deeply religious. Of course, Tox news has laid the emphasis*" *on them, when showing the reaction to the discovery of life on Epsilon Eridani c, but they are not representative. Bollox news did not even mention them."*

"Pardon me, Dr Cooper. One does not say Tox news, but Fox news. And one does not say Bollox news, but the Bolloré media group."

"Apologies, it was just a slip of the tongue."

"That Dr Sheldon Cooper cannot take a rest from the media, it seems."

It was Ralf Åhman who had just entered the room. He added: "Come on, Sanne. The SG will meet us in five minutes. Let's not make her wait. It's three floors up."

A moment later, Sanne and Ralf entered the secretary-general's office, on the 38th floor of the United Nations Building.

Half of her office was occupied by a large bureau and a few chairs, the other half by a set of black leather sofas. Hira Dorjee-Sherpa gestured them to sit on the couch in front of the window and sat herself on the one opposite them. She was not wearing her earGlasses.

Sanne looked around. On the wall on her right was a large painting with Nepalese motifs. It was her first time in the secretary-general's office. She felt thrilled. Ten years earlier, she had been eighteen and just arrived on Earth after being rescued from Mars by the *Alcubierre*. Now, she was sitting in the secretary-general's office discussing the first interstellar colonization project by mankind.

Hira started:

"My second term at the head of the Secretariat will end on 31 December. This 159th session is my very last session of the General Assembly as a secretary-general. Where do we stand with the 4th Committee?"

"We have agreed on a resolution draft to submit to both the General Assembly and the Security Council," Ralf replied. "It retakes the four main orientations we wanted."

Hira showed her left little finger and said: "First of all, increase of our interstellar exploration efforts."

"Precisely," Ralf confirmed. "The 4th Committee wants us to start a program to explore all the stars within a range of two hundred light years. It was more than what our scientific team recommended, but it will just take more time."

"The exploration will be fully automatic?" the secretary-general asked.

"Correct," Ralf replied. "Thanks to the five interstellar explorations we have done, we have devised a routine to have the exploration process automated. We will use specially designed exploration warpedoes, which are seven times faster than our Forward class ships. They arrive in a system, scan for celestial bodies. If some are found, they deploy observation satellites around them as well as some communication satellites. Up to a dozen per system. The warpedoes then warp back to Earth when the data has been collected."

"What if a warpedo comes across an intelligent alien species? What is the procedure?" Hira asked, in the most serious manner.

"Pretty straightforward," Sanne explained "If, against all odds, a warpedo detected any unexplained radio signal within a system, it would record it briefly and warp back to Earth. The exploration mission would be automatically aborted."

"Good. What was our second main orientation?"

Hira now showed both her left little finger and her left ring finger. She hesitated: "The building of new, faster starships?"

"Exactly," Ralf affirmed. "Our engineers have just started to work on the design of three new classes of starships, using the purple matter instead of the green matter. We shall build on the progress made by V-Space. The Forward Neo class should be able to cover the distance between the solar system and Epsilon Eridani in about two weeks. The Ambassador Neo class should take about four weeks. They are also working on a Quantum class, which would take about two months to travel the distance, but be able to carry ten times as much as the Ambassador class. According to our team, the first Forward Neo should be operational within five or six years."

"And for the financing?" Hira wondered.

"In terms of cash flow," Sanne answered, "some partner space agencies, such as NASA, ESA, and the Chinese Space Agency are willing to contribute significantly. In exchange, they will be entitled to free-of-charge starships, so that they can conduct their own exploration, within WARSEC's regulation."

"Excellent," The secretary-general said as she now showed her left little finger, ring finger and middle finger. "The third orientation was the colonization of *Lawa*."

Ralf confirmed and explained: "We stick to the initial plan of colonizing the planet in four waves. Together with the 4th Committee, we agreed on a departure date of the first wave around July 2105. The colonization will have to be formally under the supervision of the United Nations Trusteeship Council, who will have to send a representative there."

"I wonder if we can find somebody at the UN Secretariat to fill that role," Hira said. "Concerning the financing of the colonization program: is it as you previously proposed?"

"This is what we drafted in the resolution draft," Sanne confirmed. "The 4th Committee was favorable to this solution."

"Of course they were," Hira said. "It does not cost them anything. Do we have enough personnel for the colonization program?"

Ralf looked quickly and enquiringly at Sanne, who showed him two fingers, and said:

"We are currently still two thousand people short. Mostly for the Colony administration teams, and the construction and mining teams, as well as parts of the medical team.

"These roles do not require intensive space training since they will be deployed directly on *Lawa* upon arrival," Sanne assured. "On *Lawa*, the environment is not as exposed as in space as the atmospheric pressure is similar to that on Earth."

"These new employees will only need to pass the *Basic Safety Course 1*," Ralf said. "Even I managed it. However, they are expected to have genuine experience in the construction field or in the mining or farming fields. So far, we have had difficulties in attracting volunteers. As soon as the resolution is voted, we will launch some massive advertising campaigns."

"That sounds good," Hira said, now showing four fingers of her right hand. "Lastly, the fourth orientation for the next five years is the exploration of *Kusha*, am I right?"

"Yes, you are," Ralf answered. "The 4th Committee was more aggressive on it than we had expected. I suspect some of our scientists have talked to them. They almost wanted us to rush an expedition to *Kusha*. But we can't with our currently available resources. Not without running huge risks in terms of safety, which is out of the question."

"I understand," Hira said.

"We somehow managed to find a compromise," Ralf added. "In a first step, we will only deploy an orbital station around *Kusha*, for scientific observations. After the colonization process has stabilized on *Lawa*, we open negotiations for a land expedition on *Kusha*. However, it will certainly not happen in the next five years."

"Thank you for the summary," the secretary-general said. "At the 4th Committee, was there any noteworthy opposition from any country?"

"Surprisingly, no," Ralf said. "No country opposed the colonization program, since it will not cost them anything. They supported the development of the new starships as they may benefit from it."

"Good," Hira said. "Anything else?"

"Well," Ralf mentioned, "if I had been willing to jeopardize these four formal orientations, I could have added a fifth proposition."

"What for?" The secretary-general asked.

"To ask for the creation of a UN space police force or space guards to enforce space regulations when more and more private actors come to space. The incident with the V-liner showed that space could rapidly turn into a kind of 'Wild West.'"

"You have a good point, Ralf," Hira conceded. "However, as you said, the time is not appropriate for such propositions."

Ralf looked at Hira and said: "That will be for the next WARSEC director and the next UN secretary-general."

"Yes. That will be for them," The secretary-general acquiesced. "The vote on the resolution is scheduled for next week."

19: THE CHURCH OF QUANTOLOGY (OCT 2104)

The New York headquarters of the Church of Quantology were located on 34th Street, in an ancient twenty-story-high building. The office of the chairman of the Religious Quantic Center was located on the top floor.

An aide introduced Michael Vahlroos and Sophie Couillard into the large office, and they were greeted by a short but athletic man with black hair and blue eyes. He was wearing a navy blue suit.

"Welcome," he said. "I am Gerry Cruiser, founder of this marvelous Church and chairman of the Religious Quantic Center. Please have a seat."

Gerry Cruiser sat down on a comfortable chair behind his immense desk, while Michael and Sophie had to make do with kitchen-style chairs.

"Nice office," Michael began. "Congratulations on your

enterprise."

Gerry shook his index finger in disapproval and said:

"The Church of Quantology is not an enterprise. It's an odyssey. And it's only the beginning. You may want to convert to it."

"No thanks," Michael replied. "I'm already a true evangelist, and I don't need a second religion."

Gerry raised his eyebrows and said: "Are you sure? Taking our lessons for reasonable fees, you will master the quantum states of physics and learn how to be in several states at the same time. It may give you plenty of practical, useful applications, like curing yourself of cancer with just your own thoughts, or like—"

"Like gambling or trading with a 90% chance of winning?" Sophie interrupted. "Please, Mr. Cruiser. I'm an aeronautic engineer, and Mike once studied nuclear physics."

Gerry Cruiser shrugged and said: "Very well. I was a fighter pilot in the EU Navy. I know physics and mathematics. It did not hinder me from founding…this."

"Mathematics certainly helped you," Sophie retorted. "Helped you manipulate people. Have them pay for expensive bullshit courses. Make them believe they will be able to cure themselves, or gamble or trade online with a 90% winning probability. You furthermore steer their bets and win with an edge on all sides. That's very clever. But not very religious."

Sophie turned to the ex-CEO of Vahlroos Corporation,

who was looking at his feet, and asked: "Mike: why have you brought me here?"

"Oh, I will answer you," Gerry replied. "You are here mainly because physics is not a religion. And if it were, you'd have a much easier time raising money. I believe it was a certain Leon Lederman who said something like that. The 1988 Nobel Prize in Physics. He was so right."

Michael raised his eyes from the floor, looked at the guru of the Church of Quantology and said: "Gerry Cruiser, you know Vahlroos Corporation."

"I know the *ex*-Vahlroos Corporation," Gerry replied. "I know, of course, V-Space and V-Travel, of which Sophie Couillard is the CEO. I know you crashed a starship. The V-liner, wasn't it called?"

"Unfortunate event…" Michael said.

Gerry's blue eyes seemed to pop out of their orbits as he exclaimed: "Unfortunate event? Three pilots died. As a former fighter pilot, I don't like rich businessmen and incompetent engineers who put pilots' lives at risk, especially when they have been warned before."

"It's—" tried Michael.

"Tut, tut," Gerry interrupted as he placed a paper on his bureau. "It's here, in *The Chained Palmiped*. WARSEC asked you to have an unmanned test. Did you listen? No."

"The design was flawed," Michael admitted. "Our mistake. We have another design, a better design, which is flawless. The ship will be smaller, but flawless."

"Well, why don't you go ahead with that?"

"Betalpha Corporations won't let us invest a single dollar more into warp-ships," Sophie explained.

"I have founded V-Equity," Michael went on. "I've used all the capital I have withdrawn from Betalpha and the other daughter companies of Vahlroos Corporation. I am launching a hostile take-over. I want to take control of V-Space and V-Travel, as well as 50% of V-Fusion to secure the supply of compact fusion reactors. When I do, I intend to keep Sophie, here, as the CEO of V-Space and V-Travel."

"Good for you," Gerry replied. "What do you want from me?"

"My hostile take-over has jacked up the stocks of V-Space and V-Travel. Betalpha will do everything not to let them be cheaply acquired. I need 40% more capital to succeed."

"Sell your yacht, your ranch, your holiday mansions," Gerry replied, "Do it now, before they put a global tax on capital. The market is good, you should be able to complete your acquisition."

"Don't tell me what to do," Michael commended. "I'm here to make you an offer: be my partner to increase V-Equity's capital by 50% and help me complete my acquisition plan."

"What's in it for me?"

"With your help," Michael said, "V-space could launch a starship with atmosphere entry capacity in five years. There will be no competition. It will enable travel from anywhere to anywhere on Earth in less than fifteen minutes. And when interstellar travel and trade open for private companies, we can offer a better service than WARSEC. We believe in an 8000% return on investment within twenty years."

"Multiplying my investment by nine in two decades?" Gerry said. "With such a business case, why do you come to me, and not to any other major private investor?"

"Because we can't launch a starship within five years without your help," admitted Michael.

"Why? Explain?"

"The design of the ship we want to build," Sophie started, "was conceived by two of our former engineers who now work for WARSEC."

"Hire them back!" Gerry exclaimed. "Triple their salary and hire them back!"

"I'm afraid," Sophie said, "That these two engineers are so loyal to the idea of the United Nations that they would not even consider our offers. When they left us for WARSEC, they accepted lower salaries."

"Loyal to the idea of the UN?" Gerry wondered. "What a stupid idea! But how can I help you?"

"We believe," Michael replied, "that these engineers have kept working on what was called the minority project, even after they left V-Space. Especially that Thierry Diakité. He is constantly obsessed with solving problems. It's in his nature."

"Everybody needs a hobby," Gerry commented.

"If one could peek into his computer," Michael began, "one would probably find information saving us three or four years of research."

"I see," Gerry said. He looked thoughtful.

Michael hesitated but went on: "How to say this delicately? It has been rumored that the Church of Quantology has been used on several occasions to help the intelligence services of major powers to retrieve some key information."

"Interesting rumors," Gerry commented to himself.

"We therefore assume," Michael went on," that, with your help, we may retrieve information that will help us complete a new class of starship within five years."

The Quantologist cast a malicious glance at both Michael and Sophie and asked:

"Do you want us to help you steal information?"

"It's not stealing," Michael objected. "It's only taking back something that was stolen. We believe that Thierry Diakité completed more research that he claimed to have done while he was still employed at V-Space. Usage logs of our quantum computers points in that direction. We want back what belongs to us."

Gerry's face lit up and he said: "Then, if it is ethical, I think we may be able to help you."

But he added: "However, it will cost you."

Michael did not flinch. "How much?" he asked.

Gerry Cruiser took out his smartphone and tapped a few times on its screen. A huge flat TV appeared from behind some closed panels, on the wall behind Sophie and Michael. He somehow switched it on.

"*My position on a global tax on capital? If I'm elected president, I will be willing to cooperate with the EU and Chinese presidents on that topic with the UN. But—*"

Gerry muted the TV and commented: "Not that channel."

"When I think that Nancy Littlewolf may be our next president, I almost want to puke," Michael commented to himself.

Gerry tapped a few more times on his smartphone and said: "This channel, the United Nations web channel. As we speak, the UN Security Council is giving their green light for the colonization of *Lawa* and the later exploration of *Kusha*."

"Yes," Michael said. "This was expected."

The Quantologist looked intensely at both Gerry and Sophie and added: "Life does exist on *Kusha*. Its atmospheric composition means that a human being could breathe normally on it. Yet, the UN has decided never to colonize it."

"Of course," Sophie said. "Life implies diseases. We don't want to bring back unknown diseases to Earth."

Gerry Cruiser went on: "Your new starship, you said, will be able to enter the atmosphere of *Kusha* at warp, and land on it without being detected by any scientific station orbiting around it."

"In theory, yes," Sophie said irritated. "What do you want?"

Gerry Cruiser switched off the TV with his smartphone, looked both Sophie Couillard and Michael Vahlroos in their eyes and said:

"I want a planet."

20: ANNOUNCEMENTS (JAN 2105)

On the evening of January 2105, Sanne van der Maas, Thierry Diakité, Tintin Mutumbo, and Tatjana Aydemir went out for dinner at the *Eridani Charlie*. They were shown to their table by Samir Benyamina.

"How was your three-month's rotation in space?" Thierry asked Samir after they had sat down.

"Boring," Samir replied. "I was mostly manufacturing warpedoes. Not as challenging as a starship".

"Come on," Tintin replied. "First of all, that means you have become an expert in the integration of an Alcubierre-drive. Second of all, we need these warpedoes to automatically explore star systems."

"Shouldn't you take a holiday?" Tatjana asked Samir.

"I visited my sister in Umeå recently," Samir replied. "Not a chance I am visiting my father in Paris, though. Anyway, I am trying to sell the place."

"You're gonna sell the *Eridani Charlie*?" Sanne wondered.

"Well," Samir replied. "I have been accepted into the colonization program. That means I will be away from Earth for at least six years, perhaps even ten. How could I run the place from *Lawa*?"

"Any luck so far?" Thierry replied.

"A few restaurateurs have shown interest," Samir answered. "With what they are offering, it would mean a profit of barely 1% for a year in business. Eamon and Anatoli want me to try to find better bidders, since they also own shares."

"Are they helping you at least?" Sanne asked.

"Barely."

"Screw them, then," Tintin said. "Eamon is a former king and not poor. Anatoli is as rich as I am. We shared a Nobel Prize in Physics. Don't let them pressure you. You don't need to make a large profit, you just want your capital back. You can just invest it, and in ten years, you may have a nice surprise."

"We'll see," Samir replied. "I'll let you look at the menu. Tell me when you are ready to order."

As Samir went to wait on other customers, Sanne looked at the TV in front of their table. On it were some clips of the swearing-in ceremony of the new US president: Nancy Littlewolf.

"The new UN secretary-general does not attract as much attention," Sanne commented. "We will see if he is as good as Hira."

"Ramòn Bergoglio?" Thierry said. "Well, he is from Argentina, and I have understood he is quite religious. I would have preferred an atheist SG."

"As long as his faith does not interfere with his work," Sanne replied. "I'm dying to see who he is going to appoint as the director of WARSEC."

Tatjana poured some water into her glass as she said: "So am I. I've heard that many politicians from many countries would like to get the position. Former US president, Shannon Fang and Former EU president Eugénie Bonavita have shown strong interest."

"Bonavita?" Thierry said. "That would be hell. All the more reason to leave for *Lawa*."

"Good for you," Tatjana said, and as she pointed at both herself and Tintin, added: "How about the rest of us who stay behind?"

Thierry shrugged and said: "Why don't you join us?"

Tintin, who was reading his menu, looked at Thierry and said: "I've told you. I will not take part in an interstellar journey before it has become possible to travel between Epsilon Eridani and Earth in less than a month. I still think WARSEC is rushing into the colonization program. Had we waited another five or six years, we would be able to make the journey in about a month, perhaps even two weeks for the starships of the Forward class."

Sanne turned to him and said: "We are not having this conversation again. You know, it's for financial reasons. The sooner the colonization is started, the better for WARSEC's finance. Otherwise, there is a risk the whole organization goes bankrupt."

Tintin looked unimpressed. He added: "Besides, I still have my family living in Congo. I want to be able to visit them not too infrequently."

"Same here," Tatjana replied. "I have two kids. My husband has followed me to Toulouse and ESA, then to Vienna and UNOOSA, and now to Vaasa and WARSEC. I can't just leave them for five or six years. I will wait until the new warp drive technology is operational."

"I've heard that Ralf is planning to leave his ex-girlfriend and his two kids to join the program," Sanne said. "Not to mention Glover who plans to take with him his daughter and leave his ex-wife."

"Well," Tatjana objected. "I don't necessarily approve of what all the senior leadership are doing with their private lives."

"Some of the miners and construction workers arriving in the third and fourth waves will also have their families with them," Thierry said.

"That's true," Sanne confirmed. "We needed to hire workers with experience, and many of them already had stable relationships and kids. There will be a couple of hundred housewives, house-husbands and kids in the colonization program."

Samir came back, and they ordered the usual.

Before he left for the kitchen, Thierry asked him: "Samir, you are probably better than me with this kind of issue. Since November, it seems that the batteries on my smartphone and on my tablet are emptying faster than they should. I have switched the batteries and it still happens."

Samir thought a while and replied: "Have you checked the power consumption of each of your apps?"

"I have, actually," Thierry said. "It doesn't add up. There must be a defect in the power transfer from the batteries."

"Or you have a hidden virus program using power in the background," Samir said.

"The IT department has not found anything," Thierry objected.

"If I were you," Samir said. "I would check with Alice: she was a hacker in her youth. She may be able to help you."

The new UN secretary-general, Ramòn Bergoglio, arrived in Vaasa on Monday 26 January 2105. He was on his world tour to introduce himself to all the UN agencies. After being in Paris, Geneva, and Vienna, he was closing his European tour with Finland, where the WARSEC headquarters was located.

It had been a depressing day in Vaasa, with thick cloud cover, and a mixture of snow and rain falling. The sun was to set by a quarter to four, but only a hopeless optimist would have seen any daylight that day.

Samir Benyamina had been at the climbing center with

Amina Dörflinger and the former legionnaires: Aisha Barjaoui, Torbjørn Eriksen, and Antoine Léger.

"Shall we go back to the campus and see the new SG?" he asked his climbing partners.

"*Pas envie*," Aisha replied ('Not in the mood'). "It's crappy out there. The presentation is in half an hour anyway. Why don't we watch it online?"

"I have my tablet with me," Antoine replied. "Let's watch the SG's introduction on the intranet. That leaves us thirty minutes for some more climbing."

Half an hour later, they sat on some crash pads arranged as improvised sofas in a corner of the climbing center. Antoine was tapping frenetically on the screen of his tablet, which he inadvertently covered with chalk.

They had trouble logging onto the intranet, and when they finally were on the broadcasting channel, the meeting had already started.

On the stage of the great Aula auditorium were Ramòn Bergoglio, the new secretary-general, Hira Dorjee-Sherpa, the former SG, and Ralf Åhman, the current WARSEC director. Behind them, a slide was projected on the wall.

"What have they said?" Samir asked

"Wait," Amina said browsing through the screen. "Here, there is a text outline of the main announcements so far."

"I see," Antoine said. "So…The new SG is proud of working

with WARSEC and blah. Ah, here. The new WARSEC director will be Hira Dorjee-Sherpa. She will succeed Ralf Åhman on 1 April 2105. Ralf will be the representative of the United Nations Trusteeship Council at the Lawa committee. He got the job he wanted. Unless there was simply no other diplomat willing to—"

"Sshh," Aisha interrupted. "Listen to what Hira is saying. No, she' giving the floor to Ralf now."

"*Thank you, Hira, thank you, Ramòn,*" Ralf said on the video broadcast. "*I am greatly honored to be appointed as the representative of the UN Trusteeship Council in Lawa. However, I still have two months as the director of WARSEC and I would like to make a few announcements, concerning some reorganizations. The decisions were taken jointly with Hira.*"

Ralf clicked his pointer device, and a new slide was displayed on the canvas screen behind him.

"*Tatjana Aydemir has been appointed director of the Space Coordination Center, and is now level 9. She will be replacing Glover Johnson. Tatjana had been working at WARSEC since its foundation almost ten years ago. She previously worked for the European Space Agency. Next.*"

"*Synøve Solberg has been appointed director of the Exploration Fleet, and also promoted to level 9. She has been on both the Alpha Centauri and Epsilon Eridani expeditions. With her fleet of mostly drones, she will be tasked with exploring star systems within 200 light years from our Sun.*"

"I'm happy she isn't coming with us," Amina commented. "With her, life is all about writing scientific articles and publishing them. It's exhausting in the end."

Ralf clicked and displayed another slide, with Tintin's picture this time.

"Tintin Mutombo is now director of R&D and promoted to level 8. He will continue to work with the development of faster starships. Hopefully, in five to six years, it will take only two weeks for us to come back to Earth. Well, you all know Tintin. He shared the 2095 Nobel Prize in Physics with Anatoli Govorov for their unified gravitation theory, which gave us the Alcubierre drive. Next.

"Finally, Glover Johnson has been appointed as the director of the colonization fleet and stays at level 9. Former rear admiral in the US Navy and specialist in nuclear propulsion, Glover has worked for WARSEC since its beginning. He will direct the colonization operations on Lawa. He will also be taking his seven-year-old daughter with him.

"Before I give him the floor, I would like to give you some more updates on the colonization: We have now finally recruited all the personnel required for the program. We are talking about 4,643 WARSEC employees, spread across our pilot teams, engineering teams, medical and safety teams, construction and mining teams, farming and oxygenation teams, not to forget the scientific and administration teams. Volunteers for this program are allowed to bring their families along with them, and we will have 387 wives,

husbands, and kids on-board. In total, we are talking about more than 5,000 souls embarking on this great colonization program. Glover, the floor is yours."

"I hope they accepted my application to be on the first wave," Amina said. "I hate kids."

Glover took the pointing device from Ralf and clicked on it. A slide showed an artist's representation of *Lawa* and its three moons, with the Epsilon Eridani star in the background.

"As you have heard already, we will depart in four waves," Glover started. *"On July 7th, the first wave, consisting of the* UNSS Eleonore Roosevelt *and the* UNSS Trygve Lie *will depart from Earth's orbit. The journey will take one year and three weeks, and when they arrive, they will regroup around Lawa. The crew of the* Shackleton *has sent two asteroids to the planet's orbit. One will be used by the* Roosevelt *to install a moon elevator. A moon landing party will build a hydrolyzing station in the north pole's crater, while another will start installing a Moon Base around it. Two Forward class ships will bring parts to start the manufacturing of Space Bear Neos locally. Meanwhile, the* Trygve Lie *will deploy a small orbital station around Lawa. When done, they will go to Kusha, and deploy another orbital station around it."*

On the slide, an animation showed how the lunar base, moon elevator and orbital station were to be deployed as Glover talked.

"The second wave will depart from Earth on August 12th. It will consist of the UNSS Dag Hammarskjöld *and the* UNSS

Ralph Bunche, *and will arrive at Lawa five weeks after the first wave. By then, hydrogen supply should be available on the moon. The second wave will send the first landing parties and install a base camp. They will bring a space elevator that will be deployed at ground zero, to make it possible to bring down heavy payloads to the surface of Lawa."*

On the slide, the two new ships were displayed, and the deployment of the space elevator was illustrated with a short animation. Glover went on.

"The third wave will consist of the UNSS U Than *and the* UNSS Javier Pérez de Cuéllar. *They will depart Earth on 12th September. Upon arrival at Lawa, they will build up the base camp by deploying farming installations, factories, and mining complexes."*

"The fourth wave, or oxygenation wave, will consist of the UNSS Kofi Annan *and the* UNSS Ban Ki-Moon. *They will depart the Earth on 12th December so that they arrive when everything is ready to start the oxygenation event."*

"The colonization's senior leadership will be posted with the second wave. Both the Dag Hammarskjöld *and the* Ralf Bunche *will remain in the Epsilon Eridani system, while the other ships will return to Earth and come back to Lawa with more seeds, to continue the oxygenation process. The* António Guterres *and most of the Forward ships will stay in reserve, in case one of the starships requires assistance. I myself will be onboard the* Ralf Bunche, *together with our new UN Trusteeship representative,*

Ralf Åhman. Details of the assignments will be posted on the intranet this evening."

"What about training?" the new UN secretary-general asked.

"Thank you, Mr. Bergoglio for asking this question," Ralf said. *"Most members of the farming and construction waves, as well as those of the oxygenation waves, are new to WARSEC. They will only be required to pass a* Basic Safety Course 1. *The exposition to danger on a planet with that kind of atmosphere is less than on a moon. They will train at deploying farming and factory units in Antarctica and in the Sahara."*

"For the first two waves, however, a full-scale exercise is scheduled from March to May," Ralf added. *"The first wave will practice deploying a lunar base and a moon elevator on our Moon, as well as an orbital station, in March and April. The second wave will practice deploying a space elevator on Mars in that same period. Preparations will start in February."*

"Shit," Samir said. "Impossible to get any holiday here."

"You never take any holiday, anyway," Amina replied.

Later that evening, Samir, Aisha, Amina, and Antoine went to the *Eridani Charlie*. Samir led them to a table and sat down with them: "It's on me."

They ordered, and Antoine took out his tablet and started peeking at it.

"So, what wave are we in?"

"I'm in wave 2," Antoine said. "I will be on board the *Dag*

Hammarskjöld, under the command of Mikko Andersson. I will be together with Sanne and her boyfriend, Thierry."

"What waves are we on?" Amina asked.

"You, Amina," Antoine replied, "You will be onboard the *Eleonore Roosevelt* to *Lawa*. Alice Fù will be the commander. As soon as the orbital station has been deployed, you will transfer there, and study the satellite data to prepare the landing."

"That was what I expected," Amina replied.

"You will be on the same starship as Samir," Antoine went on. "Samir, you will be with the team installing the lunar base on Lawa's largest moon."

"What about me?" Aisha asked.

"You, Aisha," Antoine continued, "you will be with your beloved Torbjørn Eriksen on board the *Trygve Lie*, under the command of Anatoli Govorov. You will assist with the deployment of the orbital stations, first around Lawa and then around Kusha."

"Well," Samir said. "We three are lucky to be in the first wave. Too bad for you, Antoine."

"Why do you say that?" Antoine replied.

"Well," Samir replied, "in the first wave, we are only 436 passengers and crew per starship, for 350 rooms. Meaning, I will have a room of my own, given my seniority. In the second wave, you are almost 700 onboard per starship. Sharing a room with someone for so long, it's OK when you do your European Civil Service, it's not for an interstellar journey."

Suddenly someone irrupted at the table. It was Torbjørn Eriksen.

"Sorry for being late."

"You could have wiped your boots," Samir reproached him, looking at the now dirty floor of his restaurant.

"You will never believe it," Torbjørn added.

"What?" Aisha said.

"Jean-Claude Rheinfeldt, he has been working at WARSEC for four months now."

"I know," Antoine replied, "I recommended him. We had to massively expand our team of safety specialists. He was on an intensive course between September and December."

"But he is on the first wave!" Torbjørn complained. "As a space rescuer, I may have to cooperate with him. You don't want him in your team!"

"Why not?" Amina wondered.

"You know these Ridley Scott space movies where they make stupid decisions, and everybody dies?" said Torbjørn, "It's because they have a Jean-Claude Rheinfeldt onboard!"

21: FULL-SCALE EXERCISE (MARCH – APRIL 2105)

After one month of preparation briefings, the astronauts of the first wave arrived at the orbital station on Monday 3 March 2105. The exercise started on Wednesday 10 March. The crews of the *UNSS Eleonore Roosevelt* and the *UNSS Trygve Lie* first spent a week practicing fire drill and space evacuation in the near interstellar space.

The two starships warped back to Earth's far orbit on Thursday 18 March. There, Samir Benyamina boarded one of the eight White Parrots of the *Roosevelt*. His White Parrot docked into a modular EM-drive and started to navigate away in order to capture an asteroid passing by and put it into the Moon's geostationary orbit.

They were twelve astronauts packed into the small White Parrot, and Samir did not like it. They were in weightlessness all the time, and the toilets were inconvenient to use. There was no shower, and it might have been bearable if their mission had been shorter. It would, however, require a whole week to capture the asteroid and bring it into the Moon's orbit.

Iman Nassirbakli had been really inspired to decide to capture the three asteroids already when the *Shackleton* was in the *Epsilon Eridani*'s system. They would need no more than three days to fine tune their orbits.

Samir had to fly a robot to land an EM-drive on the asteroid. Back in Epsilon Eridani, he had done it in a much more dangerous environment, as they were right inside the asteroid belt. This time it was easy.

They finally captured the asteroid and steered it toward what was called the Earth-Moon Lagrange point L2 or the Earth-Moon System. It was located 67,000 km (42,000 miles) from the Moon's center on its far side and basically meant that the asteroid would orbit around the Earth at the same rotation speed as the Moon.

Five days later, the asteroid was indeed in a lunar-synchronous position and was now usable as a counterweight for a lunar elevator.

Their White Parrot was met by both the *UNSS Eleonore Roosevelt* and the *UNSS Trygve Lie*. The commander of the *Trygve Lie*, Anatoli Govorov, informed them that the orbital station had been successfully deployed. They were now to proceed with the next step of the exercise, the deployment of a second lunar space elevator on the Moon.

With the help of three other White Parrots, they landed

huge coils of carbon fiber cable on the asteroid. Meanwhile, two White Parrots landed on the Moon a few hundred kilometers away from its south pole and the Shackleton Crater, where they unloaded a thousand kilometers of carbon-fiber cables as well as a smaller rocket to be fired into orbit.

When they were ready. Samir's White Parrot started dragging the carbon fiber cables from the asteroid down toward the Moon's south pole. They had to descend 64,000 kilometers (40,000 miles), and the maneuver was both long and dangerous. Samir hated it, all the more since he had very little control over it. The pilot flew the White Parrot directly toward the moon and strove to cancel the orbiting effects.

It took them eight hours to reach the target altitude and, as they stabilized, the moon-based team informed them that they had fired the rocket with the lunar section of the cable attached to it.

The challenge was now to have the two ends of the two cable sections meet and connect. Samir was steering the two robot-driven modules. He managed the interception, but happened to break one of the connecting modules, as the shock was so violent. The safety specialists cursed him, as they had to spacewalk to fix the cable connection.

The operation was, nonetheless, a success, and on Saturday 28 March, they were unloading heavy payloads to the Moon's south pole, using that second moon elevator. Other parties of the Eleonore Roosevelt had already started to assembler a lunar base around it, wielding tunnel boring machines to dig underground galleries where they would install not only habitation modules, but also an assembly hangar.

A week later, the new lunar base at the south pole was operational, and liquid hydrogen and oxygen supply was available for orbiting spaceships. Samir was not unhappy to be granted a few days rest onboard the *Eleonore Roosevelt*. He had spent seventeen days in either 0-gravity or lunar gravity, and was quite content to enjoy artificial Earth-gravity again. They had done the hardest part of the exercise.

Alice Fù was quite satisfied with the results of the exercise as they had only taken two and a half weeks to complete their objectives. At Lawa, they would have five weeks at their disposal, but if they could start manufacturing Space Bears before the arrival of the second wave, it would be a bonus.

Over the next two weeks, they had to dismantle the lunar elevator while the team on-board the *Trygve Lie* was dismantling their orbital station. They were to be re-used once in the Epsilon Eridani system.

On Sunday 19 April, Alice Fù declared that the exercise was over, and a success. They would now warp together with the *Trygve Lie* to Mars, where the *Dag Hammarskjöld* and the *Ralf Bunche* had deployed a space elevator and a base camp close to the now abandoned Martian colony.

When they arrived in Mars's orbit, they found out that the Martian base camp installed at the foot of the Martian Space Elevator was now bigger than the forsaken Martian colony nearby.

They also noted that some of the Forward class ships had the logo of *V-Travel* and they saw some Albaspace Neos flying around in Mars' orbit.

"V-Travel opened their Martian hotel earlier this month," Alice explained to her crew. "It's located close to the WARSEC base camp. I have heard it's currently fully booked. Many tourists wanted to see the exercise."

"Can we land on Mars?" Amina asked Alice.

"As a matter of fact, yes," Alice replied. "Glover Johnson wants to test having as many people as possible in the base camp, so we are even required to do some sightseeing on the red planet."

22: MOUNT ELYSIUM
(MAY 2105)

While the *Dag Hammarskjöld* and the *Ralf Bunche* were each carrying a Space Hound with atmosphere entry capabilities, the *Eleonore Roosevelt* and the *Trygve Lie* were only transporting White Parrots and two AF5 Dachshund S each.

That meant that their crew had to queue for the Martian space elevator to play the tourists on Mars. Aisha Barjaoui, however, obtained the authorization to fly an AF5 Dachshund to the Martian colony. It had never been attempted before but the Dachshund was supposed to manage it.

Both Anatoli Govorov and Alice Fù thought that it was a good idea, since their starships would be the first in the Epsilon Eridani system, and the AF5 Dachshunds would be their only atmosphere entry vehicles until the arrival of the second wave. It could not hurt to test it in Martian conditions.

Aisha invited Samir Benyamina, Torbjørn Eriksen, and Amina Dörflinger to accompany her: They could be up to six passengers and crew onboard the AF5 Dachshund. They all gladly accepted, to skip the elevator queue. Alice Fù also volunteered to be Aisha's co-pilot, though she had no previous atmosphere flying experience. This was the paradox of being a spaceship commander. Alice could fly both a starship and a White Parrot but she could not fly regular planes.

Aisha, who had been part of the *Trygve Lie* crew with Torbjørn, first docked her Dachshund on the side air lock of the *Eleonore Roosevelt* and Alice, Amina, and Samir boarded the little aerospace shuttle. Alice took the copilot seat, while Amina and Samir sat with Torbjørn in the tiny passenger cabin.

Half an hour later, the Dachshund undocked from the *Eleonore Roosevelt* and started orbiting Mars.

"To land at the base camp, we need to plan for atmosphere entry 3,000 kilometers west of it," Alice said to Aisha.

"Yes," Aisha acknowledged. "We will just do a few orbits and let the computer calculate the best entry point."

It was silent in the cockpit and the cabin as they all gazed at the red planet. They were all wearing a space escape suit. The Dachshund was certified safe for atmosphere entry, and even had an escape pod, but one could never be too careful when attempting something new.

"It's hard to believe that Sanne grew up there," Samir said finally.

"Yes," Amina conceded. "I've heard she is down there. We will ask her to show us around the old colony."

As they were orbiting the red planet, their eyes were drawn by a huge volcano popping out of the ground, north of the Martian equator. Torbjørn pointed at it, and said:

"You know what we should do? We should climb Mount Elysium. It's the highest mountain in the solar system. It's not even technical. Easier than Everest."

"It's slightly more difficult, though," Amina objected. "You have to wear a Martian suit all the time. You get the slightest trouble, and you die."

"It could be attempted with the proper support team," Samir replied. "However, it would be surprising if the WARSEC leadership agreed to it."

"Why not?" Amina asked. "Sanne always wanted to climb on it when she was a kid. She can perhaps convince Glover and Hira."

"*Flat angle! Flat angle! Flat angle!*" an alarm suddenly announced in the cockpit.

"What's that?" Samir asked.

"*Steep angle! Steep angle! Atmosphere! Atmosphere!*" another alarm beeped.

"Nothing," Aisha replied. "The Dachshund is always nervous when it comes to atmosphere entry."

A moment later, Samir could see through the window a rain of heated particles, and the thin air around the shuttle had turned yellow. They were entering the Martian atmosphere. They all remained silent for a while.

"OK," Aisha eventually said. "We are now safe. We will land in thirty minutes."

Aisha landed the AF5 Dachshund S vertically on the launch pad the astronauts had built. She taxied the space shuttle to the hydrogen and oxygen station to refill the tanks. As they stepped out of the Dachshund, they realized how light they were on Mars. It was not as disorientating as walking on the moon, but one felt definitively lighter than on Earth.

"We are now almost three times stronger than on Earth," Aisha said. "We should be able to climb Mount Elysium even if we carry oxygen bottles twice our weight."

She looked confident indeed in her thick white space suit, despite her two artificial legs.

The Martian base camp had grown into a large settlement. There were numerous habitable compounds, greenhouse units, water generating units, smaller factories, and mining installations. From a certain distance, they all looked like orange sand dunes, as they had been covered with multiple layers of water tanks and Martian gravel to protect against the solar radiation.

V-Travel's hotel stood at the edge of the settlement and looked like two red domes with a tower in between. The tower was equipped with a panoramic restaurant at its top. Guests in it were not protected from solar radiation during the day, but could enjoy an evening dinner in safety, gazing at the stars.

Alice pointed at it and said: "Now that Michael Vahlroos has re-taken control of V-Space and V-Travel, things are moving faster. Good that he left Sophie Couillard in charge, though; she is a much better leader than he is."

Alice had planned to visit the V-Travel hotel, and took leave from the group. Meanwhile, the four friends tried to orient themselves on the base camp. One of the habitable compounds had been labelled as the camp's headquarters, and they found Sanne van der Maas and Thierry Diakité in it. They had directed the deployment of the Martian Base Camp.

They were told that Ralf Åhman, Glover Johnson, his daughter Rika, and even Hira Dorjee-Sherpa and her husband would soon land on Mars.

"Interesting," Amina noted sarcastically. "If you are in the leadership, you can just take your plus one on a Martian excursion."

Sanne shrugged: "Perhaps. On the other hand, Hira's husband is a Himalayan mountain guide. I have talked him into organizing an expedition to Mount Elysium. If he convinces Hira, we may have a chance to climb it."

"Is there any good reason to climb on Mount Elysium?" Thierry asked.

Sanne turned to him, touched him on the cheek, and said: "Absolutely none. Expect that it is there. If we climb it, then it's good PR. Some millionaires on Earth may be willing to pay a fortune to climb it as well, and it means more funding to WARSEC."

"Everything is about money, isn't it?" Aisha said.

Sanne looked at her: "It always is, whether you like it or not. The Martian colony was a failure because of a lack of funding. Without money, no interstellar colonization. Talking about the abandoned Martian colony, it's only ninety kilometers (56 miles) away; would you like to drive there?"

"Sure," Amina said. "We were about to ask you."

They changed to lighter green Martian suits and boarded an MX3-Crawler, which was a white, pressurized, tracked vehicle.

As he drove, Thierry said: "We have to prefer tracked vehicles over wheeled vehicles on Lawa. Tires get worn quite fast, and we will not be able to grow rubber trees in the first five years of the colonization. But we will be able to exploit metallic ores to manufacture caterpillars. The average speed, however, is only thirty kilometers an hour [19 mph]."

"In the Army, tanks are twice as fast," Aisha remarked.

"We could go faster," Sanne admitted, "but it would not be safe. And we can't expect quick assistance anywhere on this planet."

It took them three hours to reach the colony, which looked like a small desert of orange Martian dunes. As in the base camp, all the buildings were buried under layers of ice crates and Martian gravel.

There were four habitable compounds at the center of the colony, and around it were several greenhouses, mining units, and hydrogen and oxygen tanks. On the ground, numerous cables and pipes linked the different units.

"Quite impressive," Amina commented. "When was it built, again?"

"Thirty years ago, in 2075," Sanne replied.

"Where did you live?" Thierry asked.

Sanne pointed to one of the buildings: "That compound. The Amsterdam compound."

She led them into the air lock.

A moment later they were inside the compound, and the oxygen and power supply was still working.

"Amazing that it still works" Samir marveled.

"It was built to last," Sanne explained.

"And you grew up here on your own?" Aisha wondered.

"Both my parents died of cancer when I was a child. But I was the only child to live past ten.

The other parents let their children accompany them on Martian sorties in daylight and expose themselves to sun radiation. My parents, at least, forced me to stay inside. I could go out only at night. Then, when the other adults became smarter with their other kids, we got a shortage of vitamin D and bone reinforcement medicines, and the younger kids could not make it without those. The last adult died of cancer when I was sixteen. I spent two years on my own here."

They checked around the forsaken colony and took quite a few pictures. Sanne was sorry to discover that all the plants in the greenhouses were dead, while Samir showed a keen interest in the Martian bikes. He wanted to take one for himself.

"Why not?" Sanne said. "But I'm not sure how you will be able to get it back to your starship."

"I'll find a way," Samir replied.

They were back at the Martian Base Camp after night had fallen. In the headquarters compound they found Glover Johnson, his daughter Rika, and Ralf Åhman, as well as the new WARSEC director, Hira Dorjee-Sherpa and her husband, Temba. Aisha wondered if Rika realized how lucky she was to come as a tourist to Mars, as she was only seven and a half. Hira was wearing her earGlasses and she invited them all to sit around the little mess table.

Glover said: "It seems that summitting Mount Elysium has become one of the goals of this expedition."

"We believe," Hira said, "that by creating a new Martian attraction for private space companies, we may generate more income for WARSEC."

Glover turned to Sanne and her friends and asked: "How would you organize the summitting of Mount Elysium so that any rich millionaire could safely climb on it?"

"We thought about it," Sanne replied. "Mount Elysium is more than 1,300 km (810 miles) from here. We would need to deploy a minor Ascent Camp at its base, perhaps using one of the Space Hounds."

"From the base of the Elysium volcano, you still have 200 kilometers [120 miles] to go and 12,000 meters [40,000 ft] to climb," Glover commented.

"Yes," Thierry noted. "Though we can use some track-vehicles to drive from there. A thousand meters [3,300 ft] below the top of the volcano, we can build a level platform with some insect robots, where a landing would be possible. From there, we could build a safety camp every three hundred meters [990 ft] all the way to the summit. That way, millionaires could be flown to the platform and safely ascend the last 1,000 meters to the summit."

Though Glover was not particularly enthusiastic about the idea, it was a request from the new WARSEC director, and the goal of the remaining exercise was to kept astronauts busy on Mars. He appointed Antoine Léger as the lead of a twenty-man expedition to Mount Elysium.

First, they used one of the Space Hounds to shuttle all the necessary equipment to build an Ascent Camp at the base of Mount Elysium. It took them two days and two dozen rotations to fly habitable compounds and Martian tents, robots, and solar panels as well as three MX3- Crawlers.

They took another two days to assemble the Ascent Camp. Finally, the next day, Antoine, Samir, Torbjørn, Thierry, Temba, and other safety specialists departed onboard two MX3-Crawlers to build a road toward the summit with the help of six-legged universal robots.

After a four-day-long progression, they finally arrived at a spot a thousand meters below the summit. There, they had the robots level a landing platform, while they built up a lesser housing compound with solar energy supply. It took them another two days to complete the task, but then, Camp 0 was ready.

The following day, Temba, Samir, and Torbjørn climbed up 350 meters (1,150 ft) together with the robots helping them carrying the gears, and they installed Camp 1, which consisted of only two Martian tents.

Martian tents were small domes equipped with an air lock. They filled the waterproof space between the two layers of the dome with water retrieved from the ambient permafrost and let it freeze. The resulting ice layer was fifty centimeters thick and offered a rudimentary protection against solar protection. Around the tents, they deployed solar panels to power the tent generators.

When there were done, they climbed down again to Camp 0. Sanne, Aisha, and Amina had arrived with the last MX3-Crawler.

The following day, Antoine, Thierry, and two other engineers walked 700 m (2,300 ft) above Camp 0, taking with them a few robots, and install Camp 2, similar to Camp 1.

"The route is now completely safe," Antoine said when they were back at Camp 0. "We can summit tomorrow and build camp 3 at the same time, only 50 meters (164 ft) below the top."

The following day, they all started ascending again. 1,000 meters in altitude difference was easy to climb on Mars, where one was three times lighter than on Earth.

Samir, Temba, Torbjørn, and Antoine raced to the position of Camp 3, which they reached in only one hour and twenty minutes. They had installed the tents, but still had to fill their dome layers with water when they were joined by the rest of the ascending group.

"You go ahead," Antoine said to the arriving climbers as he was starting the generator meant to capture the ice from the ground permafrost. "We are almost done."

Aisha and Amina let Sanne and Thierry be the first to summit, and joined them a minute later.

"We did it!" Sanne exclaimed. "Not that there is any purpose to it, but we climbed the highest mountain of the solar system!"

Amina had to help Aisha, who had trouble hiking up with her artificial leg. When they finally got to the top, she gazed at the crater: "What a huge volcano. 14 km [8.7 miles] in diameter. We are lucky there is no more tectonic activity on Mars."

Aisha, who was standing beside her, turned around and said: "Look at the view behind us."

The others turned around, and they could see as far as the horizon could reach. The Martian Base Camp was too far ahead for them to see, but they could easily make out the Ascent Camp 200 km (124 miles) away. Mount Elysium was like a lonely mountain in the middle of a huge plain, and they now realized how much smaller Mars was than Earth, as they could easily distinguish the curvature of the horizon.

"We made it," Antoine said as he and the others were finally at the top. "Let's pitch the WARSEC flag and take some pictures."

"Antoine," Amina told him. "You want to admire the view first."

It was Thursday 7 May 2105.

23: A FINNISH MIDSUMMER (JUNE 2105)

The participants of the full-scale exercise were back on Earth on May 22nd. Back down in Vaasa, most went on holiday to visit their families or elsewhere, for those like Thierry and Sanne who had no relatives left.

Samir remained in Vaasa, though, partly because he was not interested in visiting his father and mostly because he was finalizing the sale of his restaurant, which he finally succeeded in. Anatoli was not happy with the outcome, but who cared? They would not be on the same starship anyway.

He spent a weekend in Umeå at his sister's, where his other siblings had come to visit. It was quite enjoyable to have a family reunion without their asshole father.

When he was back in Vaasa on the morning of Friday 19 June, most WARSEC personnel were back on the large campus. There was a party-like atmosphere. He was told that it was not a farewell party, simply a regular celebration occurring every year, the weekend of the summer solstice.

It was called midsummer. Samir was not at all familiar with the celebration, but it seemed that there was a lot of drinking, singing, and dancing. If it could be called dancing at all.

Amina, who had just arrived back from Switzerland, gave him a glass of vodka.

"Shall we go back to our previous arrangements onboard the *Eleonore Roosevelt*?" she asked.

"As you ask so nicely, I'm available," Samir replied.

"OK. Deal," said Amina.

Further away, Torbjørn was making fun of what he called a Swedish-Finnish bad taste party. He was proud of being Norwegian and coming from a more civilized country. However, when people started dancing around a pole pretending to be frogs, he insisted Aisha, Samir, and Amina did the same.

Aisha could not do it because of her artificial legs, and complained it was reminding her too much of the so-called '*Marche en canard*' they had to do in the Legion. They decided to go somewhere else, and they came upon Thierry, Sanne, and Tintin talking with Alice and Glover. Glover's daughter Rika was with them, and Samir wondered if it was a good idea to let so young a child watch such drunk people.

"I'm sorry," Alice was saying, "but my friend in China was certain. The IT department has been informed."

"That's very unfortunate," Glover said. "It is intriguing that only your computers and tablets were targeted. As if the hackers knew where to look."

"What has happened?" Samir whispered to Sanne.

"It seems Thierry's and Tintin's computers were hacked, and some data were stolen," Sanne whispered back.

"Do we know where it comes from?" Glover asked.

"Impossible to trace," Alice replied. "The worm they found was very sophisticated, though. My hacker friend says it must have come from a major power."

Glover was thoughtful. "Why would any of the major powers want to hack into your computers and steal data about warp technology?"

"It could also be a major space corporation," Thierry suggested. "To my knowledge, V-Space is the only one aiming to launch their own starships. National space agencies will receive starships from us free of charge."

"I will ask Hira to be extra careful," Glover said. "Everybody here. Keep this information for yourself. We won't press charges. If we do, we admit the vulnerabilities of our IT system, and this would impact our image negatively."

Amina and Samir found the conversation boring anyway and decided to go further away, where one could taste some kind of herring called *surströmming*. It was disgusting, but they enjoyed the punch.

They saw Aisha talking with another lady, seemingly of Indian origins.

"Preshti," she said, "let me introduce you to Amina and Samir. She is a geologist, he's an engineer. Guys. Preshti Ahma is a safety specialist on board the *Trygve Lie.* She was in the Legion, in the Parachute Regiment. We went to Legionnaire School together."

Samir considered briefly the short, thin ex-legionnaire. How could someone like her make it to the paratroopers? However, his eyes were attracted by something else.

On the ground, someone had drawn a giant clitoris.

"Samir, Amina," Torbjørn said gladly. "Let me introduce you to Jean-Claude Rheinfeldt, ex-legionnaire, and safety specialist onboard the *Trygve Lie.*"

Jean-Claude was a tall, bald, athletic man. He was too drunk to answer.

"Talking about clitoris," Amina told Samir, "I know one that needs stimulating. Let's go to my room and do some grown-up things."

24: THE FREEDOM CLASS
(JULY 2105)

There was a ring on the door of the large New York loft apartment, and Michael Vahlroos, who was watching TV from his sofa, spoke aloud in his living room:

"Who is at the door?" he asked.

"*Sophie Couillard,*" the computer voice of his home electronic butler replied.

"Let her in," Michael commanded.

A moment later Sophie showed up in the living room with a trolley bag.

"How was Burkina Faso?" he asked her.

"Excellent," Sophie replied. "We are on track. Let me come in, and I will tell you more. You were watching TV?"

"The UN broadcast," Michael replied, still sitting on the couch. "They are showing the boarding of the colonization starships of the first wave."

"Who the hell is that lady carrying skis?" Sophie wondered.

On the screen, a person from the UN press department was interviewing a young lady dragging with her several pairs of skis in the 0-G corridor pipe leading to the rear hatch of the *Eleonore Roosevelt*.

"The caption reads *Dr. Amina Dörflinger, geologist*," Michael said and he raised the volume.

"*Why are you bringing all these skis?*" the press officer asked the geologist on the broadcast. "Is *there any snow on Lawa?*"

"*Not at all*," the geologist replied. "*But we are gonna force an oxygenation event. It will decrease formidably the concentration of carbon dioxide, thus causing a global cooling. When it happened on Earth, 600 million years ago last time, it caused the Earth to turn into a big snowball. The goal is not to go that far, but in eight to nine years, we may have some awesome skiing to do over there.*"

Michael switched off the sound.

"Stupid geologists," he said. "They failed to predict the Big One, they failed to predict the Big Two, none of them believes in God, and they think that the purpose of interstellar travel is to do, I quote, some awesome skiing. Geologists should not be permitted to live."

"If we listened to you, Mike, no one would be permitted to live." Sophie retorted as she sat down on the smaller sofa perpendicular to the one Michael sat on.

"True. How was Burkina?"

"Outstanding," Sophie replied. "The Church of Quantology

really provided us with good information. We now have a much better blueprint for the V-craft. Let me show you on the TV."

She grabbed her laptop from her trolley bag, switched it on, and synchronized it with Michael's TV.

"That's our new project. The Freedom class. It will warp at 130 times the speed of light."

"130 times?" Michael repeated.

"Yes," Sophie confirmed. "Thierry had indeed hidden from us the true potential of the purple matter. We could even reach warp 250 if we did not have the constraint for an atmosphere entry."

"Warp 130 is still pretty good," Michael replied.

"It means that it would take only a month to reach Lawa from Earth. It will give us quite an advantage when this interstellar route is open for commercial traffic."

"Good," said Michael. "Tell me more about the ship."

"It's 80 m [262 ft] long and 20 m [66 ft] in diameter. There is only one gravitational deck, with room for maximum a hundred passengers and crew, since its primary purpose will be transportation around the Earth. In the non-interstellar configuration, without a gravitational ring, it can take up to 400 passengers."

"You mean that the Freedom class will be able to transport 400 people to anywhere on Earth in fifteen minutes?"

"Almost," Sophie replied. "With a payload of 500 tons, it has a take-off weight of only 900 tons. As you see in this animation, it deploys two wings at the front and two at the rear, together with eight CUBIC-R engines and a battery of electric powered ducted fans. It can either take off vertically or from a runway, using its thirty-two wheels. Runway take-off is more energy efficient, though."

"Of course," said Michael.

"It climbs to an altitude of 10,000 meters [33,000 ft] in only five minutes, from where it can safely warp into the higher orbit. Then, it can warp to different locations to find itself in the proper position to warp back into the atmosphere. With horizontal atmosphere entry, we can have it come out of warp at only 8,000 meters [26,000 ft] of altitude. From there, it takes only ten to fifteen minutes to land."

"Excellent," Michael said. "So, you mean the Freedom class ship can go from any position on Earth to any other location, on Earth, on the Moon, or on Mars, in less than twenty-five minutes?"

"Indeed," Sophie replied. "It's not as good as the V-craft promised, but it's still good."

"When will it be ready?" Michael asked.

"The first prototype should be ready in two to three years. But it will take another one to two years to obtain the necessary certifications. We have also started to work on the development of a new and larger class, more adapted to interstellar travel, but using the same principles. It will be a starship about 140 m long and able to transport 270 passenger and crew for an interstellar journey. It will also be able to travel at warp 130."

"Also with atmosphere entry?" Michael asked.

"Indeed," Sophie replied.

"We should call that class the *John Galt*."

"Who is John Galt?" Sophie wondered.

Michael shrugged.

"Never mind," he said. "Hopefully, we can use it as payment for the Church of Quantology. They can colonize a planet if they wish, as long as they do not involve us. We will only pay them with a few starships free of charge. That was our final deal."

25: Interstellar Departure (July 2105)

"Orbit control to UNSS Eleonore Roosevelt, *you are clear to warp."*

It was Sunday 7 July 2105. Ralf Åhman sat with Hira Dorjee-Sherpa in the WARSEC cafeteria at the orbital station. A few representatives of the UN member states were also present, including the EU Ambassador, Esko Punainen, sitting at the table behind.

On the large flat screen hanging on the wall, they saw a green flash, and only one of the two starships remained. Esko raised his glass.

"Go, Eleonore! Lead the way!" he said.

A moment later they heard the next call on the warp departure frequency.

"Orbit control to UNSS Trygve Lie, *you are now clear to warp."*

"Copy that, Orbit control," Anatoli Govorov's voice replied.

"We are now clear to warp. Over and out."

On the screen, they saw a second green flash, and there were no starships left to see.

Esko looked behind him and tapped Ralf on the shoulder.

"Well," he said. "Interstellar departures are becoming less and less melodramatic. Hardly any journalists to cover it."

Ralf adjusted his chair slightly so as to face the EU diplomat and said:

"Most people on Earth don't realize what is happening. In ten years, if we succeed, there will be another planet for mankind to live on. That may be the beginning of a large interstellar emigration."

"It certainly will," Esko admitted. "However, as long as what is happening over there cannot be followed live on Earth, nobody will really care."

"This may improve with time," Ralf suggested. "With the current warpedoes, it takes two months to send a message from Lawa to Earth. One of our lead physicists, Tintin Mutombo, assures me that, in four years, we will have warpedoes able to cover the distance in seven days. In ten years, we may even have warpedoes covering the distance in less than three days."

"Three days?" Esko wondered. "That's almost live. When that's possible, you could even organize the next Olympic Games over there."

"Are you being sarcastic?"

"I'm very serious," Esko replied. "In any way, I envy you."

"Why?" Ralf asked.

"My mission as EU Ambassador to WARSEC expires in four months," Esko replied. "I'm fifty-five. I'm looking for softer assignments. I have seriously considered converting to Catholicism to be appointed as the EU Ambassador to the city of Vatican."

"Is that a softer assignment?" Ralf wondered.

"As far as I am concerned, yes," Esko answered. "It seems I have a good chance of being sent to Brazil and, given the current border issues between the EU and that Amazonian country over Guyana, it will not be a piece of cake. But you, in Lawa, you will just represent the UN and do absolutely nothing. You are only forty-nine and will enjoy a relaxing career end."

"Really, Esko? Is that how you see it?"

"Well, Ralf… What do you know about deploying a Moon Base, or a space elevator? What do you know about a forced oxygenation event?"

"I admit I will not be of great use the first two or three years," Ralf acknowledged. "However, the Lawa settlement will rapidly grow to four or even five thousand people. It will require quite some administration. People living there will not want to live in a strictly hierarchic organization forever. It will develop into a local democracy. There will be a need for real economic development, and the society growing up there should not cut themselves from Earth. They should not isolate themselves, culturally, politically, or ideologically, or it may harm any plan for future interstellar emigration. Trust me, I believe a political scientist such as myself will not be completely useless over there. Besides, no other diplomat at the UN volunteered for the job."

"I would have applied for it if my beloved EU president had let me."

Later that afternoon, Ralf met the WARSEC director, Hira Dorjee-Sherpa. She told him that she had discussed with the new UN secretary-general the idea of a space patrol fleet, to control commercial space flight and ensure quarantine procedures were duly followed. The Vienna Treaties allowed for this possibility. However, the approval of three-quarters of all the member states was needed.

The secretary-general did not feel the time was appropriate for such a proposition. They were not in a hurry, though. UN space patrols to control commercial ships would not be really needed before interstellar trade and migration were a fact.

Ralf understood, but really hoped that UN space patrols would be authorized within a maximum of five years, or the Vienna Treaties' content would be emptied of their substance should space regulations not be properly enforced.

Ralf Åhman was back on Earth on Thursday 9 July. From Vaasa, he flew to Trondheim to pick up his kids for a two-week holiday in Scotland, with their grandmother.

Dag was now fifteen and was quite happy that his father would be away for almost six years. They barely saw each other anyway, and he considered that spending time with his father was a waste of time he could instead spend with his friends, and most importantly with girlfriends. He knew how to use condoms, that was the most important thing. Besides, Scotland sucked. Norway was better, and Scottish girls were not even good looking.

Eleonore, who had turned thirteen, thought that Dag was just an asshole. She was happy to be in Scotland and meet her grandmother, though she also said that it would be a relief for her to know that her father was away for five or six years. It had been too much traveling back and forth, and she wanted to have more time for her video log.

Ralf noted that only his own mother was unhappy to see him go on this colonization program. Her mother was now turning eighty-two, and though she was still in relatively good shape, she was at that age when everything could decline rapidly.

Ralf promised her she would be able to see her grandchildren, even though he would be away. He would make the necessary arrangements. He also took advantage of his trip to Scotland to store most of his private belongings at his mother's.

He was back in Vaasa on Sunday 2 August, and he spent the following week clearing his flat. The new director of the Exploration fleet, Synøve Solberg, would take it over. Most of the participants of the second wave were also clearing their flats or houses, and there was a kind of sad ambience on the Vaasa campus, despite the Finnish summer.

"Don't complain," Glover told him. "It was even more depressing in July. Now at least there are some barbecue parties."

Glover had barely any family left in the States, as both his parents had died during the Big Two in 2081. He had been there for one week at the beginning of July with Rika, but he did not like it. There was some tension with his ex-parents-in-law, who accused him of kidnapping their granddaughter to take her into space. On the other hand, his ex-wife Laura barely made any effort to see her daughter, and spent all her time with her new Finnish family.

On Friday 7 August, Antoine Léger, from the safety team, organized a barbecue party close to his building.

This was an occasion to mingle with the ex-legionnaire as well as with Sanne van der Maas and Thierry Diakité one last time before they all met again on *Lawa*. They would make the journey on the *Dag Hammarskjöld*, rather than the *Ralf Bunche*.

If something happened to the *Ralf Bunche*, Thierry Diakité would become the acting director of the Colonization Coordination Center, while Sanne van der Maas would become the acting colony administrator instead of Ralf. She was young, but they had not found any more senior economist or political scientist willing to embark on a five to ten-year interstellar mission. Anyway, he trusted her completely.

On that evening, they were joined by Tintin Mutombo and

Tatjana Aydemir, who would remain on Earth. Tintin called the participants of wave 2 'losers' again. Had they waited five more years, they would have been able to make the journey in one month instead of eleven. He would meet them on Lawa in five to six years, he promised.

On Saturday 8 August, most of the leavers of the second wave boarded some Space Bears and Space Hounds to the orbital station. Since Ralf's role on board the *Ralph Bunche* was unessential – he was just a regular passenger – he had to wait until Monday 10 August to board a shuttle flight to the orbital station.

He hated the wait, but Tintin cheered him up by giving him a homemade comic album he had drawn: *Tintin and the Interstellar Journey.*

"You will like it," he said. "Keep it for the journey."

Finally, it was time for Ralf to board an aerospace shuttle for the orbital station. He had with him little luggage but had brought the two small cactus plants he had had since he was a student in Uppsala. They were both, surprisingly, still alive, despite the fact that Ralf had not been the best plant caretaker. He had therefore decided to give them a chance to live a bit longer in space.

At the orbital station, he briefly greeted WARSEC director Hira Dorjee-Sherpa and boarded the *Ralf Bunche* directly. He felt better once he was inside.

Thanks to his seniority and rank, he had a room of his own, but most of the crew were two to four per room.

"It was better traveling on the *Shackleton,*" Rebecka told him. "We are too many people on this starship. I have not had any roommate since my civil service in Aleppo. Bedmates, yes, but roommates, no."

Rebecka Levi and most of the scientists of the oxygenation program were to arrive already with the second wave to prepare the work of the fourth wave.

"Believe me," Ralf replied, "It's still much more comfortable than the nuclear submarines I did my military service in."

On Tuesday 11 August, the *UNSS Ralf Bunche* and the *UNSS Dag Hammarskjöld* undocked from the orbital station and navigated to the far side of the Moon.

On Wednesday 12 August 2105, around 13:00 UTC, Orbit Control gave warping clearance first to the *Dag Hammarskjöld* and then to the *Ralf Bunche.*

At 13:06 UTC, the *Ralf Bunche* was warping spacetime toward Epsilon Eridani.

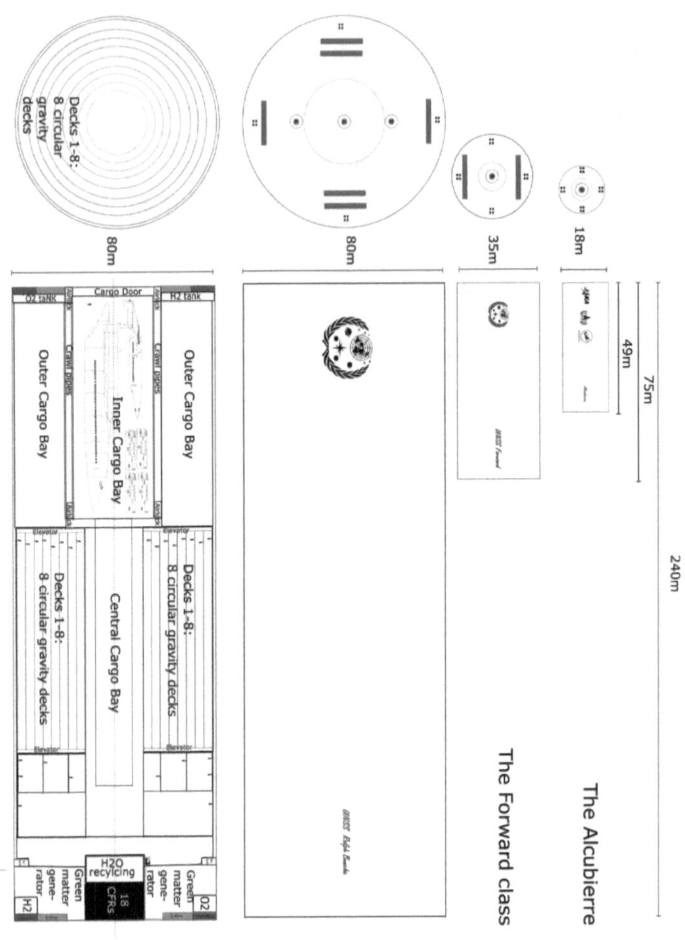

The Ambassador class

Figure 16: drawing of the Ambassador class ship UNSS Ralph Bunche with its eight gravity decks and large cargo bay, together with a starship of the Forward-class and the Alcubierre.

26: Interstellar Cruise
(Aug 2105 – Sept 2106)

Ralf Åhman had been nervous and anxious until the Alcubierre-drive was activated. Once the *UNSS Ralph Bunch* was at warp speed, the tension decreased onboard. Ralf had never been on a boat cruise on Earth, but he soon realized that their interstellar journey was a lot like a thirteen-month cruise.

They were 672 souls onboard the *Ralf Bunche*, 60 crew and 612 passengers. Among the crew, there was the pilot team wearing pink, the engineering team in orange, the safety team in green, and the medical team in blue. The passengers were mostly safety specialists, engineers, medics, and pilots for the landing party and to man the orbital station that would be deployed by the first wave. There were also a large scientific team in light blue, an R&D team in red, and a construction and mining team in dark green, as well as the administration team in purple, to which Ralf belonged.

Besides, there were thirty-eight civilians, including twelve children, one of them being Rika Johnson, Glover's daughter.

The starship's community had organized the provision of a kind of education to the children, and Ralf had accepted being in charge of the geography and history lessons. It kept him busy three afternoons a week.

Even if the passengers still had to clean their rooms and do their own laundry, life onboard the *Ralf Bunche* quickly turned into a pleasant routine. Wednesday was fire-drill day, with a three-hour-long fire exercise every afternoon, which the children loved, as they got an opportunity to miss school. Tuesday night was quiz night, and it was quite entertaining, except when the geologists were in charge of the questions.

There were many qualified and educated passengers onboard the starship, and it quickly turned into a cultural cruise. Nuclear scientists would arrange seminars about the future of compact fusion reactors, astrophysicists would talk about the unified gravity theory in terms one would understand, geologists would discuss the risk of super-volcanic eruptions on Earth. On that last topic, there seemed to be quite some divergent opinions among the geologists onboard.

Ralf had been asked to arrange conferences about historical and political topics every Friday afternoon, and he gladly accepted. The little conference room where he held his exposés was always full, despite the fact that his conferences were just before the so-called 'Friday gathering'.

Alcohol consumption was, in theory, prohibited, with the

notable exception of Friday evening when passengers would take over the cafeteria and most of the briefing rooms and drink more than was initially thought to be acceptable. Ralf soon discovered that the farming engineers and botanists were actively involved in producing wine, vodka, and whiskey, using homegrown ingredients.

"We are only limited by the amount of available water," Rebecka Levi explained. "When we urinate and defecate, our body fluids are indeed recycled into drinkable water. However, we cannot transform all the available water in the tanks into wine, so it's a good thing that we only drink alcohol on Fridays."

One Friday afternoon in November, Ralf gave an exposé on the origins of the United Nations Organization. After explaining how the term had been coined one night during the Second World War by US president Franklin Roosevelt and British prime minister Winston Churchill, he went through the drafting of the United Nation Charter at the San Francisco conference in the spring of 1945.

"You have to understand," he said, "In May 1945, the focus is on why the League of Nations, created in the aftermath of the Great War, has failed to ensure peace and security. As a result, mechanisms are devised to prevent a new conflict to occur. However, all these mechanisms are conceived in a pre-nuclear world. Indeed, in May 1945, none of the delegates of the fifty member-states present at San Francisco knows what a nuclear bomb is. Perhaps a few US delegates knew, but they never mentioned it to the other delegates. Anyway, the first use of the atomic bomb on Hiroshima on 6 August 1945 changes everything. The UN Charter becomes inadequate to the new world situation, even before it is enforced. Let me remind you that the United Nations was officially created on 24 October 1945, when two thirds of the signatories of the San Francisco charter had ratified it. This is the great tragedy of the birth of the United Nations. It was outdated even before it was created. And yet, it has survived so far."

Ralf then expanded on the early history of the United Nations, when it was a 'homeless organization', as he called it. The first General Assembly session, in January 1946, occurred in London, in the Methodist central hall. The second session, in 1947, took place in New York, and they were back in Europe, in Paris, for the third session, in 1948, when the Universal Declaration of Human Rights was adopted. In the beginning, the United Nations Organization was really homeless and the Secretariat moved from one location to another, between New York and Washington.

The current United Nation building in New York had been completed in 1952, on the location of a former slaughterhouse, after a donation by Rockefeller in 1948.

"This is one of the main successes of the first UN secretary-general, Mr. Trygve Lie," Ralf concluded. "To have managed to establish the UN headquarters in New York, which was then considered to be at the heart of the exchanges between an old and a new continent. Of course, Trygve Lie had been greatly criticized, but he should be given credit for this. Also, I shall remind you that Trygve Lie, who had been Foreign Minister of the Norwegian government in exile during World War Two, never wanted to become secretary-general. He initially wanted to be the President of the General Assembly. He became SG by default, when the five permanent members of the Security Council, the USA, the UK, the Soviet Union, China and France, could not agree on any other name. Of course, he has been known for going to nightclubs under various pseudonyms, and many have made fun of him, but in his defense, it must not have been easy to be secretary-general when Stalin was the Soviet Premier. Trygve Lie finally resigned in November 1952, but was succeeded by the Swede Dag Hammarskjöld in April 1953 only, after Stalin's death had made it possible. Stalin would indeed refuse to appoint any new secretary-general."

Ralf's first seminar on the United Nations was soon interrupted by the 'Friday gathering' which invited itself into the briefing's rooms. He soon found himself chatting with some botanists and geologists explaining how these two sciences could be combined to obtain the most perfect whiskey. A moment later, Rebecka Levi had him taste the first whiskey produced onboard. It was disgusting.

"Oh, mister the representative of the Trusteeship Council," she said and laughed. "That was an ugly whiskey face you gave me."

A second later, she was kissing him, and half an hour later she was dragging him to his room.

"I'd rather have a bedmate than a roommate," she said.

It was how Ralf started a relationship with Rebecka. He did not quite understand how it was possible. She was only forty-two, while he was seven years older. She was athletic, while he was not in outstanding shape, to say the least, though he was not overweight either.

She pushed him to go more often to the gym, though, and he could only welcome this extra motivation.

Time flies by when one is having fun, and the crew of the *Ralph Bunche* barely saw the first half of 2106 pass. In a way, it was quite comfortable to be in one's bubble and to be completely ignorant of what was happening in the real world.

Had New York City been destroyed by a tsunami, they would not have known it. Had a terrible famine hit Africa, they would not have heard of it. Had a war started between nations, they would not have been informed. They were in space, with only healthy and well-built passengers onboard, and earthling trouble seemed so remote.

When August came, and as they were closer to their warp-out in the Epsilon Eridani system, tensions rose again onboard. There was always the risk they would come out of warp too close to a comet and it could end up in a space disaster.

They spent the last couple of weeks of August going through

more and more safety briefings and procedures. Ralf felt more and more nervous.

Glover Johnson was more confident, though:

"We cannot cheat the random functions of the universe," he said. "In terms of probability, though, we would really need to be on the wrong side of the statistics to crash with a comet on warp-out."

That did not reassure Ralf.

27: SPACE DISASTER (SEPT 2106)

The *UNSS Ralf Bunche* was to come out of warp on Tuesday 31st August 2106 at 16:07 UTC. The warp-out location was about 150 Astronomical Units from the Epsilon Eridani star. For the occasion, Rebecka and Ralf had followed Glover to the control room, where Valeriya Limonov was sitting in the commander's seat.

On one of the large screens, a clock was counting down the remaining seconds: 5, 4, 3, 2, 1.

Immediately, all the alarms went off.

"Warning Terrain! Warning Terrain! Fifty kilometers… forty kilometers… thirty kilometers."

"Shit," Rebecka said, watching the screen. "A comet right in front of us."

Ralf anxiously looked at Valeriya Limonov, the commander, and her two pilots. They looked incredibly calm, given the circumstances.

"Collision in ten kilometers... Warning Terrain... 2 kilometers..."

"Warping in," another computer voice said.

"What happened?" Ralf asked.

"We went into warp again," Rebecka explained.

A moment later, Valeriya gave some extra information on the intercom: "This is the commander speaking. A moment ago, we came out of warp dangerously close to a drifting comet. The normal procedure would have been to warp-in again immediately, but we happened to spot a clear satellite signal to the *Lawa* location. We, therefore, took some extra time to adjust our course. We will arrive safely in *Lawa's* orbit in about twenty hours, one day ahead of schedule."

Ralf understood later that Glover had been quite unhappy with that maneuver and had given feedback to Valeriya accordingly. She had promised to be compliant with safety procedures next time. She, however, did not believe she had jeopardized the crew or the passengers at any moment.

Ralf decided it was not his problem to interfere with safety discussions, as he was unknowledgeable on the matter, and tried to relax as well as he could. Tuesday night was quiz night, but the questions drafted by the astrophysicists about asteroids were considered to be of poor taste by the participants.

That night, Ralf slept poorly, despite several attempts by Rebecka to relax him. She had been to the Epsilon Eridani star system before, with the *Shackleton*. They were now warping beyond the inner asteroid belt. When they came out of warp close to *Lawa*'s orbit, it would be totally safe. Yes, some asteroids were flying around, but it was easy to avoid their courses. It did not reassure Ralf at all.

The next morning, they were informed that they would come out of warp at 12:29 UTC. Ralf tried to relax by reading one more time the comic strip drawn by Tintin Mutumbo. *Tintin and the Interstellar Journey* was indeed funny, but it was mostly about incompetent people and a dog in space.

He decided to have an early lunch at 11:30 with Rebecka and Glover, who had his daughter with him. September 1st was Wednesday and there was no school that day, even though the fire drill had been cancelled. Rika would turn nine in October, and she had now spent about ten percent of her young life in a spaceship at warp, Ralf reflected.

At 12:15, they all went to the control room. Valeriya Limonov was sitting in the commander's seat.

"We will warp out at 700,000 km [435,000 miles] from Lawa," she said, smiling. "It will be completely safe. The probability of jumping right into an asteroid is close to zero."

"But not null," Glover said. "What the hell! That's the risk of an interstellar journey."

At 12:25, Valeriya informed the passengers on the intercom that they would come out of warp in four minutes. For Ralf, these were very long minutes, but when they finally warped out at 12:29, nothing happened. There was no alarm, and the radars informed them they were clear of any celestial body.

"Excellent," Valeriya commented. "Let's navigate toward Lawa with our EM-drives. We should soon make contact with the *UNSS Eleonore Roosevelt*".

One of the radio operators tried to make some calls, but there was no answer.

"Weird," Valeriya commented. "They may be on the other side of the planet, I can see the communication satellites on the radar. They should broadcast our radio signal to them."

"Strange," Glover admitted.

"Glover," Valeriya said, "This is not Earth, and there are no warping regulations. If you agree, I could warp us right into a 2,000 km [1,200 miles]-high orbit above the planet. Otherwise, it will take us another twelve hours to get there."

"You're the starship commander, Valeriya," Glover said. "Your proposal is in accordance with current safety procedures. Your call."

A moment later, the *UNSS Ralf Bunche* was warping out on a low orbit above Lawa. Once again, the radio operator tried to make contact, but they got no answer. The *UNSS Eleonore Roosevelt* was obviously missing.

Valeriya decided to have the *Ralf Bunche* orbit several times around the planet. They spotted some communication satellites deployed by the *UNSS Eleonore Roosevelt*, but there was no orbital station.

"Their orbital station should be here," Valeriya pointed out.

"Try to call the *Trygve Lie* on orbit around *Kusha,*" Glover suggested.

"We can try," said Valeriya. "However, *Kusha* is currently on the other side of the star. The communication satellites orbiting in the asteroid belts are not always reliable. That was my experience on 61 Cygni."

The radio operator tried to make some calls to *Kusha* and the *Trygve Lie*, but they received no answer.

"You see?" Valeriya commented. "That does not mean that they are not there. It's probably only the relay satellites not working."

"Hmm," Glover said. "We know that the *Eleonore Roosevelt* has deployed some satellites. We should check the status of the Moon Base."

"On the radar, it seems that the Moon Base Elevator has been deployed."

"Then why don't they answer?" Glover aske. "Let's go and check that out."

"Shall we warp there?" Valeriya wondered.

"If you can do it safely, please do," Glover answered.

Five minutes later, they were orbiting Lawa's largest moon. On the screens, they could see that the Moon Space Elevator had been deployed and that a Moon Base at been installed close to the moon's north pole, as was planned.

"Why aren't they answering, and where is the *Eleonore Roosevelt*?" Glover asked. "Can you fly low over the Moon Base?"

"We can come safely as close as 25 km (82,000 ft) to the Moon's surface," Valeriya said. "But I can ask a White Parrot to get ready and land on the Moon Base."

"Let's try to make radio contact first," Glover replied.

While Valeriya and her pilots were navigating the starship to a low altitude over the moon's north pole, the radio operator kept calling the Moon Base. Suddenly, they got a reply:

"*UNSS Ralph Bunche, this is Lawa's Moon Base, it's nice to hear you,*" answered a voice which Ralf identified as Samir Benyamina's.

"What happened?" Glover asked on the wireless. "Why weren't you answering our previous calls?"

"*Apologies, Glover,*" Samir replied on the radio. "*We are a bit short on personnel down here, and we were not expecting your arrival before tomorrow. The radio station was not manned.*"

"True, we are one day early," Glover admitted. "But why are you short on personnel? Where is the *UNSS Eleonore Roosevelt*? Where is the orbital station?"

They waited a short moment for Samir's reply on the wireless:

"*The orbital station crashed in the atmosphere after its deployment. No casualties. All pilots and engineers are safely onboard the* Eleonore Roosevelt."

Glover acknowledged: "Copy that, Samir. Too bad for the station, but good there were no casualties. Where is the *Eleonore Roosevelt*?"

"*In Kusha,*" Samir replied. "*We received a warpedo with a distress call thirty-two hours ago. The* Trygve Lie *needed assistance. The* Eleonore Roosevelt *warped to the rescue.*"

Published Books in the WARSEC Series

Book 1: Regulation
Book 2: Oscillation
Book 3: Exhibition
Book 4: Exploration

Available now for paperback and Kindle on Amazon!

ABOUT THE AUTHOR

Ash Gawain is an EU citizen living in Northern Europe. When not working, writing, nor drinking, Ash is being kept in adequate physical shape by an ex-Swedish military, in order not to die of heart failure before the WARSEC series is complete.

About the WARSEC series:

When I went to the cinema and watched Christopher Nolan's INTERSTELLAR, in January 2015, I first thought I had got into the wrong theatre room. The film opened like a kind of documentary about farmers. After overcoming the first moment of surprise, I admitted the concept was brilliant, though I was willing to challenge everything else about the film.

At that time, I was studying political science, while spending a lot of my time with earth and ice scientists. This, added to a good dose of Finnish Vodka, led to the WARSEC interstellar series.

More on: **www.ashgawain.com**

ACKNOWLEDGEMENTS

The first four books of the WARSEC Interstellar Series could not have reached their final stage without the help of Deborah Murrell, whose thorough edits and comments in the margin have been critical. Any error or mistake is my sole responsibility. I am also forever grateful for Lisa Robbins's valuable feedback and advice, and most of all for her patience with a non-native English-speaker.

Of course, the book could never have been without a book cover. I would like to thank Mark Thomas, not only for his wonderful cover design but also the beautiful paperback edition.

Finally, I would like to thank my family and friends for their support and encouragement, especially Eliah, for reading so many of drafts, and Lumi for forcing me to spend less time in front of my screen and more time exercising.

www.ingramcontent.com/pod-product-compliance
Lightning Source LLC
LaVergne TN
LVHW041451170726
843492LV00005B/1182